99 NIGHTS IN LOGAR

Jamil Jan Kochai

BLOOMSBURY CIRCUS
LONDON • OXFORD • NEW YORK • NEW DELHI • SYDNEY

BLOOMSBURY CIRCUS
Bloomsbury Publishing Plc
50 Bedford Square, London, WC1B 3DP, UK

First published in Great Britain 2019

A portion of this book appeared in slightly different form as 'Nights in Logar' in *A Public Space*

A catalogue record for this book is available from the British Library

ISBN: HB: 978-1-4088-9842-0; TPB: 978-1-4088-9843-7;
eBook: 978-1-4088-9840-6

2 4 6 8 10 9 7 5 3 1

Designed by Amanda Dewey
Printed and bound in Great Britain by CPI Group (UK) Ltd, Croydon CR0 4YY

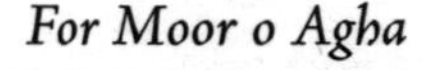
For Moor o Agha

Parler une langue, c'est assumer un monde, une culture.

—FRANTZ FANON

Herein he is as unaccountable as the gray wolf,
who is his blood-brother.

—RUDYARD KIPLING

1

لوگر

On the Thirty-Second Morning

Budabash got free sometime in the night.

We didn't know how. Just that he did and that we needed to go and find him. Me and Gul and Zia and Dawood heading out onto the roads of Logar, together, for the first time, hoping to get Budabash back home before nightfall.

This all happened only a few weeks into my trip, my family's homecoming in the summer of '05, back when it cost only a G to fly across the ocean, from Sac to SF to Taipei to Karachi to Peshawar all the way up to Logar, where, at the time, though it wasn't dead, the American war was sort of dozing, like in a coma, or as if it were still reeling off a contact high from that recently booming Afghan H, leaving the soldiers and the bandits and the robots almost harmless. So that all that mattered then for a musafir from America was how he was going to go about killing another hot summer day.

Gulbuddin said it'd be a four-man operation.

He said it in Pakhto because my Farsi was shit.

"You see," he told me, Zia, and Dawood as we huddled in the orchard before our chase, "more than four and we'll look like a mob, but any less and we might get jumped."

Gul sat at the head of our circle, twirling one end of the thick black mustache his older sisters were always trying to tear from his lip because it made him look too much like the beautiful Turkish gangsters from their soap operas. From where he was sitting—up against the mud wall that ran between the courtyard and the orchard—he could spy on all the apple trees and the cow's pen and the big blue gate and even the very corner of the orchard where Budabash once sat and slept and ate my goddamn finger.

Gul was my little uncle. About fourteen. The oldest of our bunch.

"What about four and a half?" I said, thinking about my little brother.

"What did I *just* say, Marwand?"

"More than four is a mob," Dawood answered.

"But an extra half might come in useful," I said.

"Not the half you're talking about," Dawood said, squatting at the farthest edge of our circle, taking up too much space.

Dawood was my other little uncle. Around twelve years old. Same as me.

"Listen, fellahs," I went on. "Five is a good number. Five pillars. Five prayers. Five players on a basketball team."

"Only five?" Zia asked.

"Well, is it four and a half or five?" Dawood asked.

"Futball is better," Zia said. "In futball everyone gets to play."

"What do you think?" I looked to Zia. He was my cousin. Rahmutallah Maamaa's oldest kid. Probably thirteen—though you could never be too sure with the kids in Logar. But Zia just shrugged his skinny shoulders and aimed the barrels of his fingers at Gulbuddin. "Chik, chik," Zia said, "pow, pow," and pulled his triggers twice.

Gulbuddin nodded at Zia and pressed down on the air with his hands. His eyes, green like duck shit, shifted from us, to the gate, to the courtyard, where the rest of the family still slept.

We quieted down.

"We'll put it to a vote," he said. "Raise your hand if you want Gwora to come along."

Dawood rubbed his skinned head as if he were going to vote for Gwora but couldn't make up his mind.

Zia's scrawny fingers stayed nestled in his lap, counting out the ninety-nine names of Allah.

Gul didn't even move.

Only my busted hand went up into that morning chill.

"Well, fuck," I muttered in English, and relented to the will of the jirga.

With my little brother rejected, I didn't say much else for the rest of the meeting as they shifted, almost rapid fire, from one topic to the next: how to start, where to look, where to stop, where Dawood would sniff, when Zia would pray, what Gul would chance if we met a marine or a djinn or a bandit or one of our other uncles who'd already gone ahead of us on the chase.

"We go out. We find Budabash. We bring him home," Gul

said. "Simple as that. Dawood does some sniffing. I ask a few questions. Zia says a few prayers. And if we run into Rahmutallah, Marwand makes sure we don't get whupped. Right, Marwand?"

Rahmutallah Maamaa—my oldest uncle—was already out on the road looking for Budabash. Had he caught us that day, I was supposed to tell him that our mission was my idea.

"Okay," I said. "I'll lie."

"You swear to God you'll lie?" Dawood said.

"Don't say it unless you mean it," Gul said.

"You'll be bound by Allah," Zia added.

Gul and Dawood made pistols with their fingers and pointed them at my chest. I made a pistol too but put it to the temple of my head.

"Wallah," I said, cocking my finger. "I won't snitch."

Gul laughed and reached for my hands and put them between his own. "All right," he said, being careful with the gauze wrapped around my torn finger. "We were just joking, you see, a joke for the road. You understand?"

I said that I did.

After we gathered our supplies—biscuits and apples, four small knives wrapped in butcher paper, eight water bottles, the first siparah of the Quran, a packet of matches, two notebooks me and Gwora filled up with our observations on Budabash, four bundles of rope, duct tape, and my Coolpix—we headed out toward the big blue gate, and it was there, at the threshold of the gate and the road, the compound and the village, that Gwora, my little brother, caught me slipping.

He stumbled into the orchard, his arms filled with a jumble of papers and notebooks, howling about our work, our agreement, and pleading for me to take him along. I explained to Gwora in English, real calm, that he couldn't come, that it wasn't up to me; but he wouldn't listen, wouldn't understand, and all that time the fellahs were watching me from the gate, whispering to one another in Farsi, until I told him one last time, in Pakhto, why he had to stay home, and when that also didn't work, I *showed* him why.

It didn't take long.

After the whupping, I left Gwora in the orchard all crumpled up, trying again and again not to cry, while me and the rest of the fellahs headed out onto the roads of Logar to search all day long for the wolf-dog who, just a few weeks ago, had bitten the tip off my index finger.

لوگر

On the First Day

Wallah, on the morning of my homecoming in the summer of '05, I arrived at Moor's house: carsick, pockmarked, jet-lagged, and barbecued raw by the Pakistani sun after an eight-hour trek through the White Mountains (Kabul's airport belonged to NATO then, so we had to fly into Pakistan and drive up from there), while sweating floods in a black kameez and partug, two sizes too small, which Moor made me wear just before we crossed the border.

And although I was already confused by the earlier events of the morning—we first stopped briefly at Watak's marker, which was just this tattered red flag nestled in between some stones, in between a stream and a mulberry tree, whose story no one was willing to tell me—my mind fell into a deeper frenzy when we entered Moor's compound for the first time in six years.

About fifty of Moor's relatives had jammed themselves into the garden of the courtyard, up against the big green gate, and a flood of sparkling dresses and scarves swallowed me as I stepped in. Rahmutallah Maamaa locked me up in a bear hug as Baba stroked my hair and wetted me with old-man smooches, before Abo tore me out of my uncle's arms and enveloped me into her chest. She stroked my dirty hair with her calloused hands and kept cursing America for stealing her children.

A short while later, I found myself sitting in a big room of clay, not knowing how I got there, wondering where my parents were, and trying to avoid eye contact with forty or so relatives. I had so much Farsi hurled at me all at once; I didn't know what to do with it. When I told my khalas and maamaas and cousins that I couldn't speak Farsi, that I spoke only English and a little Pakhto, most of them murmured and tsked and smiled at me sadly—but not to be outdone, they started to speak, as best they could, in a butchered mixture of English, Pakhto, Farsi, and sign language.

They asked me if I was hungry, if I was sad, if I was tired, if I was thirsty, if I was happy, if I was scared, constipated, lonely, sick, confused, nauseated, stupid, smart, always this dark, always this cute, always this chubby, always this hairy, this tall, this quiet, nervous, shy, lost.

I said yes to every single question.

So they asked me what I wanted more than anything.

"I want to see the old dog," I said in English.

None of them knew what I was talking about.

"Sag," I said in Farsi.

They blew up with laughter, cursed me and my moor, and dragged me out to the orchard.

Wallah, when I first saw big Budabash standing three-legged

beneath his apple tree, pissing on the bark he was chained to, I still thought he was the same old mutt I met and tortured the first summer I came to Logar in '99. And though I don't remember much of that first trip, my memory of this dog haunted me all throughout grade school, leaving me sleepless most school nights, so when Agha announced, in the spring of '05, that he'd scrimped together enough cash for us to visit Logar again, all I could think about was how I was going to get the old dog to forgive me.

In the orchard, as soon as I saw Budabash, I broke off from my family and rushed his tree with nothing but sabr in my heart and love leaking out my fingertips (Wallah!), and it was only after he crouched and lunged and swallowed forever the very tip of my index finger, that I saw in his blue-moon's eye, in the heart of the eyeball, what no one else was willing to see up until that point: that Budabash was not a dog at all but something more like a mutant or a demon.

Wallah.

So seeing what I did, and with nothing much else to do in the country while my cousins were off at school, for the next few weeks I called a jihad against Budabash. Until, of course, about thirty-one days later, when he got free.

لوگر

On the Thirty-Second Morning

Just outside the big blue gate of Moor's compound, I rubbed my brother's snot off my knuckles and followed the fellahs toward the path. The road we walked curved upward into a bend that would lead into a sort of maze of interconnected clay compounds, which would then open out onto the main trail cutting through Naw'e Kaleh, Mohammad Agha District, Logar Province. If we walked this trail for long enough (a few miles or so), it would take us all the way to Agha's compound.

When we entered the first alley of the maze, I started counting the iron doors that appeared on either side of me, but because the walls of the compound all blended into one another, I soon got dizzy from all the twists and turns and lost track of where one compound ended and the next began. Luckily, we had Gul guiding us. We followed him, hopping back and forth along both sides of a drain or a little canal that was supposed to collect runoff from the neighboring rows of compounds.

If you didn't know your way, Gul explained, or if you didn't have a guide, it was easy to get lost in the alleys. That's part of the reason why the Russians had such a hard time taking Naw'e Kaleh in the early '80s. No space for the tanks, you understand, or larger artillery, but plenty of room for mujahideen ambushes. Some twenty years later, the American troops would have the same problem.

But that day no one seemed *too* worried about getting caught up in any Afghan-American crossfire. While places like Kandahar and Helmand, I heard, were getting fucked up with drone strikes and night raids, the US Army in Logar mostly carried out their secret operations in the surrounding black mountains, bombing the shit out of the burrows where the Ts and the other rebels (Pakistani double agents? Arab mercenaries? illiterate goat-men?) were supposed to be hiding with Baba Bin Laden and Mullah Omar and Carmen Sandiego, so that those of us down in the river valleys only ever heard the softest hum of gunfire, the gentlest tremble of stone.

Really, if we had anything to be worried about that day, heading out onto those roads, it was running into Rahmutallah Maamaa.

Earlier that morning he'd gathered the four of us together in the den and told us not to follow him. "I need some men to stay home in case Budabash comes back," he said. "You understand?"

He stood in the doorway with Budabash's chain slung over his shoulder. His kufi on his head. His black beard dripping sweat or morning dew. Whether Rahmutallah Maamaa was praising your crop or threatening your life, he always spoke in a calm, soft tone like he was just reading his thoughts aloud to no one in particular.

We all nodded our heads wildly even though we knew he was talking only to Gul.

Gul didn't argue, but after Rahmutallah Maamaa left, he scoffed at him and started talking shit. "Men?" he said, spitting on the carpet. "He's treating us like kids."

"We are kids," Zia told him.

"You stay a fucking kid," Gul said, and walked out of the den, leaving me and Zia and Dawood behind. The three of us stood in the doorway, not saying a thing but communing among ourselves with gestures and worried looks and groans. Zia seemed the most hesitant. He'd be risking more than the rest of us since Rahmutallah Maamaa was his father. Disobeying an uncle, like I was about to do, or disobeying an older brother, like Gul and Dawood were about to do, was nothing compared with deceiving your own pops. And if it was anyone else calling us out, we probably would've obeyed our natural instincts to avoid, at all costs, an ass whupping. But it wasn't anyone else. It was Gul.

So we followed him.

After Gul got us out of the maze, we found ourselves on the main road for the first time. It was made of a hard, dark clay and it sloped down in between some fields and another series of compounds. Rows of chinar and a thin stream ran along its edges. In the fields near the road, farmers and their laborers tended to their crop. The sun (acting ahjez) barely showed its face. I watched all this as a rush of wind rolled down somewhere from the black mountains and hit me square in the mouth. It stank of smoke, and I started coughing.

Dawood took a deep sniff, sighed, and nodded at Gulbuddin.

"That's where Budabash went," Gul said, pointing at nothing in particular, pointing, it seemed, at the whole country. Then he started down the road.

We hurried after him.

While Dawood paced ahead, sniffing for Budabash's scent of apples and gasoline, Gul stopped from time to time to ask a farmer or a day laborer if they'd seen a big black dog with a white scar running down its back.

Zia hung back with me. He held my good hand and pointed out the sights.

"That's Haji Ahmad's," he said, pointing to an orchard, "and those fields belong to Mullah Imran. And that trench there is where little Zabi stepped on an old mine. Lost his foot."

"In the name of God, Zia," Gul called back, and slowed down and wrapped his fingers around my right wrist, just above the gauze. "You got everything wrong. The orchard belongs to Mullah Imran's dad, who's still living, so Imran owns nothing yet, and the fields are Haji Ahmad's, and little *Nabi* got his foot run over by an army truck, not little Zabi. Little Zabi is fine. We played stickball with him a month ago."

"We did?" Zia said.

"Yes, bachem, go ask Dawood."

Dawood walked ahead by himself, sniffing at the wind, big black bag over his shoulder. He was fat for his age but also, I had to admit, pretty strong. No one liked to hold his hands because of his warts, so he always had them busy. Carrying or throwing or breaking anything that came near him. I tried to keep the fellahs from holding my hand too, but they were persistent. "This is what friends do here," Gul kept trying to explain.

"Zabi still got both feet," Dawood shouted back.

"See," Gul said, and pointed to Zia, "all this guy knows are hadiths."

"And surahs," Dawood added.

"What more do you need?" Zia said, squeezing my hand.

Gul shook his head. "You listen to me, Marwand. I'll tell you what's what."

And he did.

He told me where we were and where we were going. He told me the names of the roads and where they would lead. He told me who died where and whose grave and flag and stick and stone belonged to who, and he told me the names of the trees and the fields and the plots of land. And as he held my hand, he pointed me one way and could tell me what way that way was and he could point the other and tell me what way that way was too.

But, still, he couldn't tell me—for sure, at least—where Budabash went or why he ran away in the first place, though I had an idea.

Ah, but before I forget, here are a few more things I saw that day:

1. A cobra
2. Six kids, ages ranging from four to eleven, walking toward that cobra
3. A cobra, its skin stripped, its flesh bared, pelted to death by six kids

4. Laborers in the fields covered in mud
5. Laborers in the orchards covered in mud
6. Laborers, covered in mud, building a wall out of the mud that covered them
7. A little girl, about nine, walking with her donkey
8. The fields
9. My cousin or uncle (both?) Malang, who stank of hash and couldn't recall my name
10. Two strays that looked like what Budabash would've if he'd actually been a dog
11. Two American helicopters
12. Four kids playing cards in the corner of a field, betting walnuts and marbles
13. Four kids running from the stones we threw
14. Fifty-two cards left behind in the corner of a field
15. A man with a gun that might have been a T
16. A drone (I think?)
17. 1,226 white lilies
18. One true God
19. No Budabash

لوگر

On the Fourth Day

Three days after Budabash took the tip off my index finger, Ruhollah Maamaa (Moor's little bro) came back from whatever base he worked at, welcomed my parents home, and, as soon as he saw my bandaged hand, swept me into his Corolla and drove me and my brothers out to the black markets in Kabul, where he told me to pick out any prize I wanted. No joke. No limits.

"But no women!" He laughed too loud.

I didn't see many.

Me and my brothers stuck close to Ruhollah as he led us through the crowds and the bazaars, past checkpoints, potholes, and open sewers, away from the armored bases where the Americans hid, and toward the inner valves of the city. He dismissed the beggars and sweet-talked the cops, and he roamed about the streets in his blue jeans and his Shah Rukh Khan haircut, pointing out the bombed-out buildings (this one by the Ts, this one

Massoud, this one Sayyaf, this one Hekmatyar), and the whole time he was talking too fast, walking too slow, practicing his English, and asking us about America.

Ruhollah Maamaa had big plans. He was studying part-time at a Kabuli technical school (when he wasn't working at the base), and his dream was to get an American visa. Problem was he needed a sponsor to qualify. An upstanding American citizen willing to go to bat for him. So he asked me about Agha, fishing to see if my pops might help him. To be honest, I was pretty sure Agha didn't like Ruhollah very much, especially since he started translating with the US Army, but I realized that the more I could make him feel that Agha might help him, the more fluid Ruhollah got with the cash flow—and I wasn't above being bribed. Neither were my brothers.

Mirwais, my youngest brother, just wanted a Big Mac. Out of the three of us, the food in Logar (shorwa and tomatoes almost every night) was messing him up the worst. Days and nights of diarrhea. Almost shit his pants a few times, the poor guy. I mean, me and Gwora had the runs too, but not as bad as Mirwais. He was aching hard for some factory-processed beef, and we figured that if there was any place in Afghanistan with a Mickey D's, Kabul was going to be it. Sadly, though, we came to find that McDonald's hadn't infiltrated Kabul with the marines, so we had to settle for Ruhollah Maamaa's favorite kabob shop, where they grilled the lamb out on the street and used fans to attract customers. Ruhollah told us the shop had been open for more than seventy years, that they'd served slaves and servants and hippies and Commies and spetsnaz and jihadists and marines and now three little Logarian from America.

Gwora kept accidentally walking into bookshops. Never buying anything. Just looking around and sniffing the pages. Eventually, at some random stall near the Kabul River, Gwora picked out what he thought was a golden pocket watch that turned out to be a brass compass, which Ruhollah wanted to return, but which Gwora liked better than his original gift.

I had a whole list prepared. First, me and Ruhollah and my brothers went out to the garment district, and he fitted us in a few Afghan outfits: kameez and partug and waskat. Then we went from shop to shop, finding my desired items: a silver Allah, a pocketknife, and a basketball, and the whole time I blended into the crowds so nicely that if I kept my mouth shut, it seemed nobody even took me for a foreigner.

That was until near Asr, when we ran into this small pack of strays, nearly hairless and starving, and all of a sudden, I started breathing funny and my head got woozy and the stump of my lost finger started tingling. As the dogs got closer, the tingling got worse. To the point where a pain shot through me as though my finger were getting eaten all over again, and I let out a scream like I did in the orchard, which scared the strays and my brothers and Ruhollah and all the Kabulian surrounding us.

For a while, my breathing didn't steady and Ruhollah began to panic, offering me whatever came near us—juices, sodas, cigarettes, and tesbihs—until we got to the section of the black markets with the DVD vendors. He offered me a few movies, and suddenly, my breathing calmed.

On our way back to Logar, I clutched my DVDs and watched the torn buildings fall off into mountains, into fields and trees and the occasional compound, until we got to the checkpoint near Wagh Jan that was run by a local militia. In Kabul, Ruhollah got waved past each checkpoint as soon as he flashed his military ID, but these militiamen claimed that the Ts were disguising themselves as soldiers and forging government paperwork. They ignored me and my brothers and commanded Ruhollah to get down for a search. Afterward, Ruhollah drove us through Wagh Jan—past the small shops and stalls—crossed the Logar River, avoided the road workers, and entered the alleys of Naw'e Kaleh.

When we got back to Moor's compound that night, all my cousins rushed our Corolla as we crossed the big blue gate. There were maybe twenty of them—from toddlers to teenagers, dark faced and pale skinned, coming from as far as Jalalabad to as close as the Tangee. They crowded our car, fogged up the glass, and wrote our names on the windows.

مروند

متین

میر ویس

I hardly knew any of theirs.

Ruhollah Maamaa hopped out of the car first and almost smacked a few of them before Mirwais waddled in front of him, grabbed his hands, and asked him to give him a horseback ride, which he did, because no one said no to Mirwais. Meanwhile, me and Gwora and my cousins and my little uncles snuck back toward the den—a little room of clay, hidden in the corner of the living quarters closest to the orchard.

Inside the den, all of my cousins and half-cousins and little uncles surrounded me and my brothers, talking to us in Farsi and

Pakhto and a little English: being friendly in a way they weren't allowed the first few days of my arrival because immediately after Budabash bit my index finger, Abo and Baba and Rahmutallah Maamaa hauled me into a guest room and made me spend almost two days in there with just them and my parents.

They wrapped and rewrapped my bandages, ran an IV, fed me home remedies (sarsar and kappa and osh) until they deemed me fit enough for visitors. Gul was the first of the guys to approach me, sneaking into my room with a request.

"Listen," he said, "my big brother is going to come today and he is going to offer you Budabash's head. But listen, Marwand; you have to have mercy on him because God would want that and because we *need* Budabash. You understand? I mean he's the best guard dog in the village. Maybe the country. He's fearless and ruthless. His teeth are like razors. I mean you know that firsthand, but listen, Marwand; he only bit you because he doesn't know you, because . . . he was protecting us. Wallah, Marwand, he's a good dog, a little rough, but good, and we need him. You understand, Marwand?"

I told him I did, but my wound ached so bad, and it looked like such a mess of rot and pus, and I was so worried that losing the tip of my finger might have irreparably ruined my jump shot, that I stewed in my heart for vengeance. And yet I also didn't want to get off on the wrong foot with the guys, especially Gul, who seemed to love Budabash more than anyone.

As Gul predicted, later in the day, Rahmutallah Maamaa came into my chamber, by himself, and offered me a juice box, a slice of watermelon, and Budabash's life.

I declined all three.

After that, Gul introduced me to Dawood and Zia and the rest of the guys. Zia kissed me on both cheeks and sputtered a dua directly into my mouth. Dawood pinched my sides in a terrible crab hug until I pushed him away. The rest of my cousins took turns holding my hand or my pinkie. For a few minutes, I didn't have the heart to stop them.

When the guys weren't at school or doing farm chores, we played futball or stickball or rockwar or we waded through the canal in front of our house (I couldn't actually swim) or we just talked. Most of the time, they asked me questions about America, about the schools, and especially about the kids.

I explained to them that kids in America were mostly all right, except when they couldn't pronounce your name, and so they changed it for you, calling you Moe instead of Marwand, Joe instead of Jawed, Bell instead of Belqeesa, and when they mixed up your race with other races and ignored it when you tried to correct them, or when they thought Bin Laden was your grandpa.

That last one threw them for a loop.

"Wallah," I said, "they'll ask me where my grandpa's hiding so that they can go and kill him, thinking that's supposed to make me mad that they want to kill Bin Laden, and sometimes they'll act like they're joking, or like I'm in on the joke with them, but, sometimes, after they're done laughing, it's like they're standing there, looking at me, not saying anything, like they're actually waiting for me to tell them where Bin Laden is. So that they can go and kill him."

My cousins and little uncles burst out laughing.

They loved to hear stories like that. All of them gathered around me, some of them shouting, some of them quiet, but all of them, I knew, listening and waiting. And when I got back from Kabul that night and snuck into the den, every single one of them was waiting then too, ready to see what I got from the shops.

At first, I showed them only the silver Allah, the basketball (which they dribbled with their feet), and the pocketknife I bought at the bazaars, but as soon as the generator came on, I laid out the real goods.

"Bootleg DVDs!" I shouted.

Five films to a disc. Sometimes six. Sometimes the movies still in theaters or unreleased.

"Bootleg DVDs!" I shouted again because they didn't seem to understand.

"Yeah," Dawood said, "we understand, but what the hell movies are these?"

"Aww," I said, "these are werewolf films."

First, we watched *Van Helsing*. The next night: *An American Werewolf in London*. And by the third night, when we watched *Dog Soldiers,* I had my cousins seeing werewolves everywhere they went: in the trees and in the shrubs, in the kamoot at night and in the shadows of the chinar, in the fields where they cut wheat, and, of course, in Budabash's cold dead eyes.

Except for Gulbuddin, of course. While everyone else in the compound felt at least a little bit uneasy about the fact that their loyal guard dog, who'd never bitten any other human in his life, had so viciously torn at my finger, Gul loved Budabash so much, he didn't think much of it.

"He's just a dog," he used to say, "and dogs got teeth."

Well, I thought to myself, I got teeth too. And that was true. I did.

لوگر

On the Thirteenth Day

When the guys went to school those first few weeks, me and my brothers spent the day reading or writing. The last time I came to Logar in '99, my Pakhto got so good I ended up forgetting most of my English, went into second grade not knowing my alphabet—almost flunked that year. So on this trip Agha had us on a strict schedule: at least one page of writing and one chapter of reading every day. The three of us brothers groaned about it, though me and Mirwais knew Gwora was secretly thrilled. Kid was only in the fifth grade but reading at a high school level. Came to Logar prepared too. Backpack full of stolen library books and composite notepads. I ended up having to settle for some of Zia's old UNICEF notebooks and a Tom Clancy novel I found in a cupboard, one morning, in Ruhollah's room.

We read lying on red toshaks in opposite corners of the den. I read Clancy and Gwora read Twain. Mirwais napped in between us, with a beginner's Quran on his face. By the time I got through two chapters of my Tom Clancy novel, Gwora was already halfway done with *Huckleberry Finn* and well into his journal.

At some point while he was writing, Gwora asked me about Budabash.

"Marwand," he said, "why do you think he hates us?"

When we were alone, me and my brothers spoke in English. We were most comfortable that way. In fact, since our last trip to Logar, we hardly spoke any Pakhto at all. Our speech got so bad, we started to forget simple things. Like how a maamaa is your mom's brother and a kaakaa is your dad's. Once, during a dua, I asked Allah to have mercy on my Watak *Maamaa* instead of Kaakaa. Agha almost smacked me in the mosque. With Moor, it wasn't so bad. She'd correct me if I used the wrong word or ruined the structure of a sentence (the object went before the subject or maybe the verb?). But when Agha bit his lip and stared me down, saying without saying that our tongue is our life is our soul is our blood, I'd forget that Pakhto even existed.

"Because he's a lunatic," I said, and went back to my novel: South American terrorists were trying to figure out Agent X's true allegiance (he's CIA). They shocked his balls with a car battery and dunked him in water till he couldn't breathe.

"You know what Dawood said?"

I didn't reply. I kept reading: the terrorists shocked Agent X again and beat him and pulled out some of his teeth and his fingernails, demanding to know who he was, but by that point, the spy had made up so many different aliases and his mind was so messed up from the torture, he couldn't even remember which alias was the one he should give up.

"He said it's because of our stink."

"Dawood?" I said, looking up. "Dawood is the shittiest-smelling kid I ever met. He makes Kabul smell like Paris."

"You've never been to Paris."

"Listen," I said, closing my book and switching to Pakhto like Agha might've done, "we don't stink any worse than anyone else. Budabash doesn't like us because we know what he is. That's all. He's got everyone else fooled. That's all it is. You understand?"

"I don't know," Gwora said.

I threw my book at his head but missed him by a foot. "Come on," I said.

"Where are we going?"

"We're going to go and talk to Budabash."

First, we threw dirt clods because they were so easy to find. Me and Gwora stripped them from the edges of the gardens and the patches of mint and collected them in little piles at the base of an apple tree. Before throwing them, though, we climbed up into the highest branch of the tallest tree, where we could almost see the whole orchard and the courtyard too, and made sure no one could sneak up on us. From time to time, one of my khalas would enter the orchard to chop some wood or get a few eggs from the chicken coop, or else Rahmutallah Maamaa came by to flip some clay or to take the cows out to graze.

We had adjusted quickly to the rhythms of their labor, predicting when they might start, waiting for them to finish, and tossing our clods only when they were gone. But after we actually started pitching the rocks, we realized that neither of us had very good aim. Targeting the long white mark that ran along his back, we hit Budabash only once or twice.

After about an hour or two of climbing up and down the tree, we got hungry, and seeing all the green apples just within reach, we picked a few and started munching. They tasted sour and chalky. We ate maybe five apiece.

"You think these are raw?" Gwora said.

"Who cares," I said, and took another bite. "They taste fine."

Thirty minutes later, with me and Gwora hunched over in the two connected kamoots, shitting our guts out, Gwora yelled through the wall: "I think they were raw."

"They were good, though," I yelled back.

"Hey," he shouted, "you think Budabash likes apples?"

"You know what," I said, "I bet he does."

Then we chucked apples.

For at least three hours every day, three days straight, me and Gwora tossed apples and rotten eggs and bread lathered in mud or shit or filled with shards of glass, and we waited and watched. Budabash ate almost everything that came in his path. He'd sniff it and look up at us and gobble it down. Mocking us. After a while, the assault just got boring. Motherfucker had a belly made of iron. Never saw him barf or shit blood or anything. Not once. Three days straight we watched him from up in the trees for hours and got nothing.

"Explain to me," I said, sitting up in a tree branch, watching Budabash lap up a bowl of gasoline, "how that is a normal dog."

"He can eat," Gwora said.

Budabash scratched his ear and yawned.

"Nothing like he used to be," I said.

"How did he used to be?"

"You don't remember in '99?"

"I was four in '99."

"Well, he was a good dog then. Quiet and peaceful. I mean no matter how much I used to beat on him, he'd never even bare his teeth or bark or anything. Sometimes, I'd hurt him so bad, he'd be shivering in pain. Wallah. I can see it even now."

Gwora took a bite out his apple. We watched Budabash sleep. "So you still feel guilty?"

"No, Doctor Sahib, I feel swell."

"What I'm trying to say is you regret it, right? And you learned your lesson?"

I thought about that for a while.

Gwora took another bite out his apple, chewed it, spit it out, and tossed the rest at Budabash—hitting him square in the face.

I almost fell out the tree laughing.

Later on that same night, Moor called me and Gwora in for dinner. She shouted in Farsi instead of Pakhto, and so we knew we were probably late.

In the dark of pre-Isha, we hurried into the courtyard through a pathway that cut through the middle of the living quarters. One ran from the beranda to the bedrooms, while the other path ran from Nabeela's workshop to the door of the orchard from which we were coming. Smack-dab in the middle of the paths was the family well. The two pathways of the courtyard cut through Baba's flower garden, slicing it into four equal parts. Each of these smaller gardens had beans or mint or a whole mess of flowers. In fact, there were so many flowers blooming that summer in Logar that after a particularly windy night, the beranda and the tandoor khana would be so choked with flower petals that at least four of Zia's six sisters would have to spend all morning sweeping them up into the cesspits of the kamoots—along with a few cans of ash—neatly covering up the almost impossible stench of shit.

The sun had set a while ago, but Rahmutallah Maamaa didn't like to start up the generator until after dinner. So we approached the beranda in the dim light of a few lanterns. Almost every single night since I got to Logar, Ruhollah Maamaa kept assuring me that his brother—my missing maamaa, Abdul-Abdul—was going to help us become the first home in Naw'e Kaleh to get power lines. But until then, we had only the generator, which needed gas, which came from Kabul, which cost heaps, which was why we had electricity for only three hours every night.

Inside the beranda, Moor's whole family was already eating and chatting among themselves. We slipped into our spot on the men's side without anyone really noticing us. Then we poured our own food into a shared platter and ate quietly.

"How about I make *you* eat *his* hand?" Abo said to Dawood and Ruhollah, who were sharing the same platter of rice, well into their second serving and already eyeing a third.

Ruhollah made an appeal to his father (my baba), claiming he worked so hard in the base that he deserved six servings. Dawood quietly agreed. Baba looked to Abo and offered her his hand, and so Abo poured Ruhollah another platter of rice.

Meanwhile Agha and Rahmutallah Maamaa discussed the whereabouts of a local bandit named Jawed. Word was that Jawed had been pretending to be a T in order to spy for the Americans. But, supposedly, the whole time Jawed was feeding them bullshit intel, convincing the Americans that his personal enemies were prominent insurgents, tricking the American forces into assassinating men who had nothing to do with the Ts. Eventually his little scheme (not as original, Agha claimed, as you'd think) got caught up in the meshes. Now the Ts and the soldiers and a few local drug runners were all out searching for Jawed.

"Same thing used to happen in the eighties," Agha said.

"It's getting bad, brother," Rahmutallah said. "These days any young khar with a rifle can claim they're with the Taliban or the Americans or whoever else. They stop you on the road and then they're cutting you up, robbing you of your insides, leaving you to die in a canal." He ate a big handful of rice and sucked his fingers. Out of respect for Agha, he spoke Pakhto.

Though Agha had his own compound two or three miles down the main road in Naw'e Kaleh, most of his family had fled or died during the war, so his house was filled with distant cousins he didn't completely trust. That's why he let us stay at Moor's so often. They were almost untouched by the war. I think he thought they were blessed.

On the other side of the beranda, the ladies talked business.

Apparently, a bunch of Kabuli buyers had come that morning to see Nabeela Khala's dresses and were impressed with her designs. My khalas and Moor argued about the price they should set. Nabeela wanted to bleed them dry. Moor advised caution. "You try to take too big a bite out of a Kabulay and you'll find yourself eating your own arm." She laughed.

Moor had left her little sisters at seventeen—when Agha came to marry her—and during the first few days of our visit, my khalas treated Moor so respectfully it was almost cruel. But now all four sisters were getting along so well it was like Moor had never gone.

Moor's youngest sisters, Sadaf and Shireen, sat on either side of her, parting her curls and whispering secrets into her ears. Sadaf, the older of the two, most resembled Moor. She was chubby cheeked, with a head of curls and a chipped-tooth smile she flashed all the time for any reason. Shireen, on the other hand, was real pale, real skinny, with hair so brown it was almost blond. She was known all across the village for the crispness of her parathas and for her secret singing voice.

Across from Moor and her sisters sat Zia's mom, Hawa Khala, who, noticing me and Gwora, proceeded to offer us every single dish at the distarkhan at least six times in a row before accepting our denial, which she took as a personal insult because she handled most of the work in the kitchen. Moor told me that when Hawa Khala first married Rahmutallah, she was actually thick for a village girl, almost hefty, but Abo and Nabeela worked her thin. Hawa Khala never seemed to complain. She was a dark woman. Quiet and reflective and incredibly shy.

Abo eyed me from her place at the distarkhan. She always sat next to Baba during dinner. They had been eating together like that, side by side, from the same platter, since they were newlyweds some forty years ago.

"Marwand," Abo said, "what were you and Gwora doing all day in the orchard?"

"And without Mirwais?" Agha added.

I had trouble scooping rice into my mouth with my left hand, and the double death gaze didn't help. Usually, we ate only soups and stews for dinner, but Zia's mom had slaughtered a chicken that day, so we were eating big platters of rice with korma on the side.

"Just playing," I said.

"Tell your son," Moor called out, "to stay away from that dog."

But Ruhollah told her not to worry about any dogs and started retelling the story of me and the strays in Kabul for the sixteenth time.

"So why have you been playing without Mirwais?" Agha asked again, interrupting Ruhollah.

Mirwais sat on the other side of the distarkhan with Moor, eating his rice with both hands. He stared straight at me when Agha asked about him—completely unashamed.

"Mirwais was in trouble with us," I said.

"For what?" Agha asked.

"For snitching," I said.

Agha bit down on his lower lip like he always did right before he smacked me, but I kept on eating, quickly shoveling small bites into my mouth with my left hand. He wouldn't hit me with food in my mouth. Especially in front of Baba and Abo. Things got quiet and awkward like they always did before a sudden ass whupping, and to ease the tension, or to teach me a lesson, Abo decided to break the silence with a story.

The Tale of the Three Kings

I heard, child of my child, that there once lived an auspicious prince named Shah Zaman, who was the son of Timur Shah and a grandson of the great Ahmad Shah Baba. This Prince Zaman, after the untimely death of his beloved father, and upon overcoming all of his rivals, including twenty-two of his brothers, came to take up the throne. During his reign, Shah Zaman attempted to replicate the glorious victories of his grandfather Ahmad Shah but was thwarted time and again by the conspiracies of the English and the Iranians. Eventually, these serpents from the West nestled themselves into the hearts and minds of Shah Zaman's own brothers Mahmoud and Shuja, convincing them to betray their king and brother for their own good. Mahmoud, with the backing of the Iranians and the English and his brother Shuja, took the throne, blinded Zaman, and exiled him to India. In this way, Mahmoud was able to ensure that Zaman could never retake the throne. Thus, the rightful king of Afghanistan lived out the rest of his life in exile, a musafir forever clouded in darkness.

But listen, children of my children, Allah (subhanahu wa ta'ala) is all-seeing, all-knowing, and forever just. For the victories of Mahmoud and Shuja were short-lived and beset, time and again, by calamity. Mahmoud, king for only a short time, was overtaken by his co-conspirator, Shuja, who thenceforth suffered defeat after shameful defeat: losing the throne not once but twice, and then, in the process of attempting to regain power, lost Peshawar to the Sikhs and Kabul to the English, so that Shuja himself was to be exiled, disgraced, and forever shamed for his sins. Therefore, children of my children, be just with your brothers, treat them fairly, for time and again our kings have led our lands into calamity only because they were unable to do right by their blood and by our Lord.

Whispers of "Ameen!" and "Mashallah!" poured out from every mouth in the courtyard. Even mine. After the story and after dinner and after cleaning and after gathering and after the movie (*Rambo III* for the tenth time)—after the shoot-out and the boss fight and after the resolution and after the credits (dedicated to the brave warriors of Afghanistan)—and after the lights and the lamps all blew out, and after Rahmutallah Maamaa unchained Budabash from his tree so he could roam about the orchard all night, searching for the shape-shifting thieves whose unlucky destiny it was to climb over the walls and be torn to shreds, I went looking for my brothers, Gwora and Mirwais, before they fell asleep.

"From now on," I said, whispering in the guest room where my parents and brothers slept, "Mirwais comes too."

Even in the dark I could feel him beaming. It was a rare moment of discretion for Mirwais. He knew not to ask us what we were up to, whatever it had been, since he was lucky just to be invited.

Gwora shrugged.

"So," I said to him, "how do we bring the hurt here?"

"We need a new strategy," he said.

"Apples didn't work."

"Neither did rocks."

"Yeah, the rocks were pretty stupid."

"Almost pointless."

"Waste of time."

"But what's next?"

لوگر

On the Thirty-Second Day

A few hours into the search and we still had no real lead. The noonday sun wouldn't let up as Zia prayed his Dhuhr Salah on a short wall cutting between two fields. Though he looked real holy praying in all that sunlight, he got no sign from God. Gul interrogated almost everyone he saw: farmers and shepherds and kids running little snack stalls out of their homes. But he heard nothing from a soul. And I was starting to doubt whether Dawood's nose was as strong as the others claimed.

"He can smell ashak boiling from Kabul," Gul said.

"He can smell a fart before it's farted," Zia added.

"In all the time I've known this khar, he's never failed at sniffing out a scent. He's part bloodhound or something," Gul swore.

Dawood walked ahead with his nose held high, black bag over

his shoulder, taking in his brother's praise. Suddenly, his nose latched on to the unmistakable scent of cheap hair gel, butchered meat, and unrequited love.

At Dawood's signal—and Gul's confirmation—we leapt behind a row of chinar, into the sloping path of a river bend. A guy with his mouth masked in a dusmal and his hair slicked back into a weapons-grade pompadour came strolling down the trail.

"Who's that?" I said.

"The butcher's son," Gul whispered, and then gently placed a stone in my hand.

The butcher's son was walking the trail slowly, carefully, and, luckily for us, unarmed. Dawood gathered stones from the stream and set them at our feet, and just before we chucked them, we lifted our own scarves over our mouths, at the same time, like bandits out of an old John Wayne flick. We rubbed the stones in our dirty little fingers, huffing quick breaths that shook the tatters of our masks, and then there came this moment between the holding of the stones and the ambush itself, when I was watching the butcher's son walk the road, watching and knowing what was coming for him, knowing what he didn't know, would know only when it was too late, and I felt so bad for him and for me too, Wallah, because although I knew that the stones were coming, I didn't know why, and in that way, me and the butcher's son were the same.

Later on, I asked the fellahs why we did what we did, and they looked really surprised that I didn't know, that I was that much out of the loop over in America. But having taken part in the ambush, I thought it was my right, you know, to be informed.

Luckily, they seemed to agree.

The Tale of the Butcher's Son

Really, the story of the butcher's son was the story of Nabeela Khala. She was Moor's younger sister and, as the oldest of the unwed girls, she was also the next in line to be married. Problem was Nabeela wasn't the prettiest girl in the family, the slimmest, or the most polite. Word was she could slaughter a steer, chop down trees, whup on her nephews, dig ditches, toss bricks, and handle an AK as well as any soldier. When she wore her burqa in the city and the perverts tried to fuck with her, she'd beat on them before her brothers could. Agha even recalled a time in '99 when she threw a dude out of a moving bus because he was pinching her sides. Then this one time, at a wedding, Ruhollah Maamaa was having trouble with an AK during a machine-gun celebration, and Nabeela got so annoyed, she snatched the weapon and fired it up into the air herself. After unloading the whole clip, she handed the weapon to her little brother and went back to the ladies' side of the wedding to dance her ass off.

These sorts of incidents were becoming so common for Nabeela that no suitor wanted to come within a mile of her. That was until very recently, when her dress shop started getting more attention than her temper. She had her own little space in the lower half of the compound to sew clothes for the village girls.

There, Nabeela came up with a new design fusing Punjabi kali with the older fashion of the Kochian. It was a hit among the locals, but when the new design started getting popular with girls up in Kabul, it became clear that the dresses were turning into a hot commodity. Nabeela's little dress shop started netting a tidy profit. Baba and Abo were thrilled. They bought the family's first television with the extra cash.

Her little sisters, though?

Not so much.

While Nabeela was in the cool of the dress shop, sewing clothes and listening to Turkish dramas on the radio, Sadaf and Shireen had to take on the housework she left behind. She was also, at the ripe age of twenty-eight, holding up the marriage line, since her sisters couldn't marry the boys that were coming for them until Nabeela herself was finally wed.

But just as Nabeela was getting dangerously close to unmarriageable, the butcher's son came calling. He and his khala had been coming to the house intermittently for the past year, asking for Nabeela's dusmal. He was handsome, light skinned, with a head of hair like Ahmad Zahir. But also poor. Very poor. A butcher's kid, you see, and a failed butcher at that, so Baba, taking Abo's advice, proceeded to reject the kid's offer.

But the butcher's son came back.

Once.

Twice.

Again and again, until he'd been rejected some twenty times in a row.

Five months straight he came over every Friday in his only

pair of clean clothes, a dingy little waskat, his hair combed back, and his heart beating in his hands.

Meanwhile, Nabeela—to everyone's surprise—had fallen madly in love with him.

The last time he was rejected, she locked herself up in the dress shop and threatened to cut her wrists with her scissors, to hang herself with the dresses, to eat dirt until she vomited and died. Abo tried to explain to her daughter that the suitor only wanted her money, that the guy was six years younger than her, probably twenty pounds lighter, and, frankly, much prettier.

This, apparently, did not help.

With no other option, Rahmutallah Maamaa knocked the door down with an ax, dodged a few scissors to the chest, and took his sobbing sister up in his arms. After handing her over to Abo, Rahmutallah Maamaa began to shout, demanding she allow Nabeela to marry the boy and end the madness. Abo stood square to her much larger son and cursed him and his lack of honor. So Rahmutallah Maamaa, saying nothing to anybody, went and got his rifle, walked all the way to the butcher's house near Wagh Jan, in the middle of the night, with the Ts and the marines loose and everything, and he called on the butcher, warning him that though their families had enjoyed many years of peace, and though they'd had no issues in the past, if he could not control his son, the peace built up between them for so many years would very soon, and very suddenly, come to an end.

He said that to him and then he left.

The threat seemed to work for a while. Rahmutallah had a history, a reputation, and people didn't tend to fuck with him.

But about a week before my family arrived, the butcher's son came back again, ready, it seemed, to die for Nabeela.

"That," Gul explained, "is why we ambushed him."

Though jumping the butcher's son gave us a burst of adrenaline, it wore off about an hour later when the Logari sun hit its peak. I tried to stay in the shade of the compounds or the rows of chinar, but Gul made us search the roads and the edges of the fields. Even though all we found were clues that led to nowhere: patches of fur drifting in streams, paw prints that went up into trees, dog farts that led to flowers, and witness statements from kids or old villagers that ended up being bullshit. I mean it was getting so hot, I started to wonder if Gul wasn't chatting with a mirage or two.

Eventually, we made a pit stop at a stream that pooled sweetly into the bank of a dam underneath these long wellehs. Their branches hung limp toward the water. So we took a dip. Gul and Zia swam and Dawood floated. I stayed in the shallow end.

"Marwand," Zia shouted as he floated on his back like an otter. "Come swim!"

"He can't," Gul shouted back.

"But I heard Shagha is a great swimmer," Zia said.

"He is a great swimmer," I said. "One time he swam two miles with a bibi hajji on his back."

"I never heard that story," Zia said.

So I told it.

The Tale of the Bibi and the Flood

One morning, many summers ago, when Agha was young and his heart was still mast, all the rivers in Logar suddenly flooded with ice water from the black mountains. In a rush not to drown, Agha and his family gathered onto the roof of their compound and watched the waters fill the fields and the roads. Then, more out of boredom than courage, Agha snuck off from his family, built a makeshift raft out of an old aluminum gate, and used a shovel as a paddle to explore the flood.

With time, he came upon an old bibi hajji floating on a toshak in the middle of a drowning orchard. She didn't know where she was or how to get home and asked Agha for help, but because of the branches of the apple trees, he had to dive into the water, swim across the orchard, and watch his raft float softly away. As soon as he reached her, Agha put the old bibi on his back and swam for two miles until he came upon the citadel of a mosque made of mud. There he left the bibi, promised to return, and went on to search for more survivors. But by the time he got back, the bibi had disappeared. Agha swam home in great sadness and was very relieved when his mother greeted him with a switch.

Fifteen years later, one snowy morning, Agha arrived in a refugee camp in Pakistan—his land lost, his brother dead, and almost nothing to his name—to ask for the dusmal of a pretty little Logaray his aunts had told him about. Turned out the drowning bibi he had saved that day in Logar was actually Moor's grandma, Abo's mom, and at the time, the old bibi was dying of a fever that Baba's medicines couldn't cure. Still, she saw in Agha's eyes the young boy who had saved her from that flood so many years ago.

"My daughter," the bibi hajji told Abo, "by the will of Allah, give him your daughter."

They were married the next month.

A few minutes into our swim, four other boys, all of them wearing patus and pakols, approached our dam, knelt over its edge, and watched us in the water. One of them was particularly tall, another skinny, another fat, and the last one just looked lost.

We stopped swimming and stood.

Dawood's big belly glimmered in the sun, his teetees gleaming, while Zia rose up scrawny, not a hint of meat anywhere beneath his dark skin. I was a little chubby. Though my diet in Logar had eaten some of my baby fat, I was still soft in most spots. Gul, on the other hand, was all muscles: pecs and delts and lats and whatever else. He was paler than us too.

He stood in the front.

The tallest of the kids—his long limbs, raggedy hair, and too-small threads making him look like a scarecrow—spoke to us in Pakhto.

"You boys shouldn't be swimming here," he said.

"What's the problem?" Gul said in Farsi, signaling to us to reach for stones. Dawood and Zia were ready. I stood empty-handed.

"My kaakaa got his arm torn up by a wolf," he said, pointing toward the spot where we set our clothes and the big black bag.

"How terrible," Gul said, switching to Pakhto. "May Allah

preserve your kaakaa. Did he say, at all, what the wolf looked like?"

"Just that it was massive and dark, with a long white scar running down its back."

Gul thanked the kid for his warning and told us to get dressed.

Back out on the road, Zia kept holding my hand, which was slick with sweat, so after a few seconds, I offered to take the big black bag off of Dawood's shoulders and I only had to ask him twenty-seven times in a row before he finally relented.

I used both hands to carry it.

First, I threw it over my shoulder like Agha would've done, and then I balanced the big black bag on my head like the Kochi tribeswomen we passed on the road, and then—remembering the knives—I held it away from my body; but after a while, I just dragged the thing along the path, lifting it up only when Gul glanced back.

Zia and Gul stepped ahead, leading the squad, while Dawood, with his hands free, slowed down, put his arm around my neck, which I knew he knew I didn't like, and asked me to teach him a few more words for his English exam.

See, about a week into my trip, just as I was starting to get more comfortable with all the guys on the compound, Gul came up to me one morning in the den with a proposition. He tossed me a small packet of papers and asked me to read them.

"I can't read Pakhto," I said.

"I know," he said, and explained.

Turned out they were grade reports. Gul's marks were a little bit higher than Zia's, even though Zia was the one who studied the most often because his pops was always hounding him. Gul had free rein—more or less—with his schoolwork since his mom and pop were like sixty, and he was the fourth out of five sons, the eighth out of nine kids, and because (even though no one wanted to admit it) the lower you were on the birthing totem pole, the less attention you got. But Gul was bright. Got into trouble more than he should have: missed classes, ignored assignments, started fights. But he was doing well all things considered. Same as Zia.

Then there was Dawood.

By all accounts, he just couldn't hang in the classroom. Said that when he tried to sit down to study, he got plagued by horrible migraines, backaches, and finger stiffness. Gul argued that Dawood was a born laborer. Tremendously strong and fat, he had the pain tolerance of a donkey. But school just couldn't mold him. So while Gul and Zia mostly flew under Rahmutallah's ass-kicking radar, Dawood ate the brunt of his rage.

His plan, it seemed, was to beat Dawood into a doctor, an engineer, or a lawyer.

The holy trinity of all Afghan ambition.

Once upon a time, Gul explained, Rahmutallah Maamaa had his own dreams of being called Doctor Sahib, of opening up a clinic in Naw'e Kaleh, of being the first graduate in the family. But then came the war, the jihad, the flight, and while Rahmutallah's vision of stethoscopes and inoculations burned up with almost everything else in the country, he wasn't going to sit back and let the same thing happen with his son and his little brothers, who were also, in a way, though none of them admitted it, like his kids.

To Rahmutallah's ever increasing frustration, Dawood was

now on the brink of flunking. The one subject he could pass was English. Maybe because Ruhollah spoke it pretty well or maybe from overhearing military broadcasts and radio waves or maybe from watching *Rambo III* sixty times in a row. Whatever it was, Gul wanted me to work with it.

"When Dawood comes home from school," Gul said, "Zia will help him with his Arabic, you with his English, and me with everything else. You understand?"

"I just have to help him?" I asked. "I don't have to do his homework?"

"No, no, no, Marwand. Of course we don't want you to do his homework. He needs to actually learn. To pass the tests, you understand? We don't want him to cheat."

So for the next few days I did Dawood's homework. It was easier that way. We only pretended to study when Gul was around. Or we just randomly went over words like that day on the road when we were chasing Budabash.

"Meena," Dawood said, tearing a switch from the branch of a tree.

"Good," I said, big black bag on my shoulder. "What about 'hurt'?"

"Khog."

"Sad?"

"Khafa."

"Anger?"

"Qar."

"Rifle?"

"Toopac."

"Tank?"

"Tawnk."

"War?"

"Jang."

"No, jang is like a fight. War is bigger."

Dawood looked to Gul. "What's the word for 'war'?"

"I don't know if there is one," he said. "Zia, can you think of the Pakhto word for 'war'?"

"Woor? Like a fire."

"No," Dawood said, "war like . . ." And Dawood took up a stick and turned into a club, into an ax, into a sword, into an AK, and he picked off targets on the road—the steer in the fields and the kids in passageways and the sleeping donkey and the wasps in the mud and the dust on the road and the birds and the leaves and whatever else passed us by—and we were so impressed with his demonstration, we didn't think to stop him until he accidentally took a shot at someone Gul thought might've been a T.

We ducked down behind a short clay wall surrounding the field where the T slept. He lay underneath a tree, wearing all black, with a pakol over his face and a machine gun slung stupidly across his chest. We spied on him for a while. He seemed very small from where we hid. I took my Coolpix out of the big black bag and snapped a few photos, but Gul spotted me and demanded I delete them.

"But why?" I said.

"Because he's a T."

"How do you know he's a T?" Zia asked.

"His machine gun," Gul said.

"But we have a machine gun."

"We do?" I said.

"Oh yeah," Dawood said, "everyone in Logar got one. Rahmutallah moves it around so we never find it, and he thinks we don't know where it is, but we always know."

"So where is it?"

"Classified."

"You don't know."

"I've shot it too," Dawood said. "With Ruhollah. He took me out with some of his soldier buddies and we shot it at a mountain."

"Why did you shoot a mountain?" Zia said.

"Why not? It was fun. We shot a mountain and some trees and some birds. The gun goes chig chig chig in your hands and it hurts to hold it still because it wants to fly everywhere, but I held it still and I hit a rock right in the face. But man it hurts to hold because . . ."

I stopped listening to Dawood and started flipping through the pictures saved on my Coolpix. I was looking for the shots of the T but got hung up again with the pictures I didn't take of Budabash two weeks ago. The pictures that he wasn't in. The invisible ones.

Let me explain.

لوگر

On the Seventeenth Day

Me and my brothers started reconnaissance shortly after our preemptive assault on Budabash. We actually got the idea from the Tom Clancy novel I was reading. Spies always gathered intel before going in for a strike or an interrogation, so Gwora figured that since the rocks and the apples and the other poisons weren't hurting Budabash, we should lie back and watch him for a bit, study his habits and his character until we could find out how to put the hurt on him for real.

For the next few days, we kept detailed logs of Budabash's behavior: when he liked to eat (before dark), when he liked to sleep (during prayers), and when he was most ferocious (near me). We took measurements of his massive paw print, his dragon's teeth, his buffalo torso, and the long white scar (which I thought might be a chemical burn) that stretched all the way from the center of his torn ears to the beginning of his short tail. It was a burn that ran along his back like a white stream or a long trail, and here and there, along this stream or river, there were little pink sores, which from a distance looked like blossoms but when you got up close seemed to be on the brink of bursting.

We noted the color of his dark, discolored fur and his blue, almost human eyes, and argued about his scent. To me he smelled like burning leaves, to Gwora hot gasoline, and to Mirwais a dead pup's collar. Time and again, either Rahmutallah, who endlessly reinforced the walls, or one of my khalas would come into the orchard to watch us, but all they ever saw were three American kids studying and reading.

To keep up with the front, sometimes Gwora read to us.

We sat underneath the apple trees, in the dirt, with the stink of the cows and the chickens wafting one way and the scent of the flowers and the mint coming the other. And while I rubbed the gauze still wrapped around my wounded finger, I listened to Gwora read from his monster novels—*Frankenstein* and *Dracula* and *It*—focusing on the sections where the heroes killed their enemies.

Around the third morning of our surveillance, Gwora got the idea to snap some photos of Budabash for the sake of a visual record, but just as I started shooting, Agha came back from his compound and told us we were going to visit his saintly orphan nephew: Waseem.

See, Agha had an unwritten checklist of kaakaas and amas and cousins we needed to visit, and Waseem was at the very top. Me and my brothers (very quietly) groaned. Not only was Agha messing up our surveillance, but now we'd have to spend all night trying to stay awake at Waseem's house.

Though Agha was usually cool with us staying behind at Moor's compound—which had a TV, a DVD player, and a whole mess of kids to play with—he really wanted us to see Waseem. He was technically our cousin, but he always felt more like an uncle. His whole family (mother, father, three sisters, and a brother) died in the war. So Waseem's kaakaa, an OG named Masoom, took him in at the height of the famines in Logar and raised him as his own.

Abo and Nabeela Khala were coming along with us that night, and while it seemed like Nabeela didn't want to go (she kept mentioning how big Waseem's teeth were), Abo was being adamant about it. "He's a good boy from a good family with good prospects," she said, and dragged Nabeela to the car. Me and my brothers jammed ourselves into the front seat, while Moor and the ladies squished into the back. Agha drove.

Masoom and Waseem lived across the road from Agha's compound. It would be a short drive, but I brought my camera along just in case there was something to see on the road. On our way there, we stopped by Watak's marker and I snapped a few photos of the flag and the stones. They came out blurry in the dark.

We arrived at Masoom's compound in the late evening, after dinner, so that his family wouldn't feel an obligation to serve food. According to Agha, they might have went hungry the next two days just to make sure we were fed that night. Waseem met us at the entrance, where the men and the ladies split into different rooms.

Inside the men's chamber, we sat cross-legged on the same

pair of red toshaks every Afghan family on earth seemed to own. While Agha drank chai and chatted with Masoom, me and my brothers ate Afghan candies, had thumb wars and pinching contests, and whispered about all the things we would be doing back at Moor's house.

Maybe sensing our boredom, Waseem came and offered us cookies and cake, smiling wide, and just as Nabeela claimed, he had a huge mouth of teeth that jutted out from his face, smothering his little chin. Above these teeth grew a massive Turkish mustache. Though he wasn't the most handsome guy in Logar, Waseem was still a very eligible bachelor because old Masoom, who never even learned to read, went deep into debt paying for his university fees. He was a college graduate. Unemployed but searching. Poor but with potential. Not like the butcher's son, who according to Abo would only ever be a butcher.

The nighttime talks started with certain formalities: Agha informed his host about his time in America, about how it felt to finally be home, and after Masoom updated Agha with a brief summary of what was going on with his own family (certain things were always left out: the failing crops, the lost toe, the bruised face, and all the other secrets every family hid more out of habit than necessity), the conversation always seemed to circle back to the war.

Usually, it was some rumbling from the mountains, or the distant chatter of artillery, that triggered a memory or a dream from so long ago that the men couldn't even be sure how old they were when they first remembered it. And all of a sudden, Agha and his host were deep into the bad times. Every relative from the old generation—or what was soon becoming the old generation—had his own special story to tell: how he was imprisoned or beaten or shot or tortured, how or when he joined the resistance, and with which particular faction he aligned himself. Often, the names of lost ones were mentioned. Waseem said his mother's name at one point: Zarmina. I thought I heard Agha say Watak.

If there was a group of men, one of them sipped his chai and told his story, and when he got to a point where he couldn't continue, the point in the story I most wanted to hear, someone else took a sip of his chai and began his own story, and so on and so forth, until everyone was given a say and not a single story was actually finished. Eventually, it got to be Agha's turn, and though he didn't tell the story I wanted to hear, he told a good one.

The Tale of the Tale of Ghulam Ali

Once, very late in the night in '96, I woke up in Fremont to a call from Afghanistan.

Here come news of death, I thought, of dying, but instead I was greeted by the ghost of my old kaakaa Mahmoud come back to life. It'd been over twenty years since I last heard his Logari drawl, untarnished by his living in the north. I thought the civil war had eaten him.

"It didn't have the belly," my kaakaa said when I told him.

I asked him how he managed to get out of Badakhshan alive.

"That's what I'm trying to figure out. That's why I'm calling you. Tell me," he said, "the story of the Hazara."

I thought it odd at the time. Here was one ghost asking me about another. But curious to hear his story, I started mine.

The Tale of the Soldier from the Road

Though the snows were beginning to melt in Logar that winter of '81, it had become so cold and so quiet in Naw'e Kaleh that the stutter of machine-gun fire carried on for miles across the roads. One night just after Maghrib, my cousins and a few other mujahideen and I were coming home from our patrol, and we heard the drawn-out retort of an AK. We waited a few moments on the side of the road. When no enemies appeared, we thanked Allah for our fortune and continued home.

The next morning, my squadron and I were on our way toward Zarghun Shar, just past the black mountains, in order to meet with another coalition of mujahideen whom we planned to guide through the White Mountains into Peshawar. That night, it was a group of Tajik fighters, but a few nights earlier we'd assisted Hazara and Pashtun mujahideen too. At the time, the Afghan rebellion had not begun to eat itself.

It was on this road that I first spotted a Hazara soldier staggering toward us in a large winter coat: the garb of the Communists. He was covered in so much blood I thought for certain this man was dead but did not know it. Had he a weapon, any weapon, we would've laid him down immediately, but he was unarmed and alone, and he might have had information.

The first thing he did was he told us to kill him, we Pakhtuns, because he didn't care anymore. We'd killed everyone else already, all of his allies, and he was as good as dead anyway. I don't know what it was. Maybe because we were impressed with his bravado, or because he seemed certain to die, or because none of us wanted to live with another ghost in our dreams, we told him to calm down and to explain to us what he was doing on our road, in our village, with his blood leaking all over our land.

He lifted his shirt and showed us the wreckage of his belly torn up by machine-gun fire. When he saw that we weren't about to kill him on the spot, his bravado faded a bit. He asked us, as his Muslim brothers, to help him. I could tell he was going to live just long enough to suffer a great deal more before the end. At that point, I'd done things. Helped with the resistance. Brought in arms. Taken part in ambushes and firefights. But, to my knowledge, I had not killed a man.

I was terribly curious to hear how he got his wounds.

So while my cousins and the other mujahideen went on toward Zarghun Shar, I brought the wounded soldier back to my home. Put him up in the cow's shed, made him a bed out of hay, and called on my mother, who, during the course of the war, had learned to patch up bullet holes. She bandaged his belly as best she could and cursed me for bringing a Communist into the house. I couldn't fault her. Though my family and I were well respected by the mujahideen in the area, if the commanders got word that we were harboring a Communist, it wouldn't end well.

That night, I brought our guest his chai and asked him to tell me his story. Apparently, he'd been fighting alongside the Communists for only a few months. He was stationed in Kabul, where he and a few of his allies decided they were sick of the massacres and the bombings and the low pay and planned to make their way toward Peshawar.

Of course, the main route from Kabul to Pakistan then was through our little village in Logar, so one of his Pakhtun friends got in contact with a Pakhtun guide from my village and set up plans for their departure. But on the night they were supposed to flee for Pakistan, they never made it out of Logar. The guide had planned to meet up with them in an orchard just within Naw'e Kaleh. And it was there, beneath the apple trees, that they were ambushed.

The Hazara soldier and ten of his comrades—three Tajiks, two Pakhtuns, and five other Hazaras—were waiting in the dark of the orchard when machine guns lighted on all sides of them. His comrades were massacred, while he, who was in the very center of the bloodshed, survived. The carcasses of his allies shielded him. For a long time afterward, he pretended to be dead. When he was sure that the gunmen were gone, he climbed out of the carnage and staggered onto the road until he found my squadron.

The story of his desertion, whether a lie or not, lessened the weight of the guilt I felt about harboring a Communist. The next morning, I told my mother we would care for him just until his wounds healed.

She spat and said nothing.

Well, the months passed and his wounds healed, but instead of fleeing the first chance he got, he stayed on with us for another season, helping around the compound with the chores and the work, feeding animals and caring for the crops within our walls. He made chai with my mother, ate with us during supper, and kept his distance from our girls. Watak, especially, took a liking to him. They were always working together, you see, while I was fighting. At first, Watak claimed he was shadowing him just to make sure he didn't get near our little sisters, but they quickly became friends. Little by little, our guest was even learning Pakhto.

He lived with us for eight months, and who knows how much longer he would've remained, but after Watak was murdered, I decided it was time to leave Logar. I still remember how our guest wept when I told him we were heading for Pakistan. I pointed him toward Kabul and said he could rejoin the Communists, or he could continue his original journey toward Peshawar. Half of the country was fleeing. His path was his own.

We parted in the summer of '82.

After Agha finished the story of the soldier, he began the story of Kaakaa Mahmoud.

The Story of Kaakaa Mahmoud

My kaakaa's story begins in Badakhshan, when the wars reignited between the Taliban and the Northern Alliance. At the time, Massoud and his cronies were committing massacres against any Pakhtun they could find in the north, marking them as Taliban, torturing and imprisoning them, and redistributing their land and their goods among the northern soldiers. And even after Massoud and Sayyaf carried out the Afshar massacre, many Hazara soldiers still joined the Northern Alliance, and they too were committing massacres against the Pakhtun, who were being punished for massacres committed by the Taliban against the Hazara, who were being punished for massacres committed by the Communists against the Pakhtun, who were being punished for the Iron Amir's enslavement of the Hazara a hundred years ago, who were being punished for the Mongol invasion of Afghanistan almost a thousand years before that, and, to this day, Pakhtuns and Tajiks and Hazaras and Turkmen and Uzbeks, even in America, still argue about where exactly the violence all started, and none of us can really agree, and none of us can concede a point. And so it goes.

Eventually, one of these northern factions fell upon the village where my kaakaa was living at the time. They rounded up all the Pakhtun men, stripped them and beat them, locked them up in a small cell within a makeshift base, and tortured them routinely in response to atrocities committed by Pakhtun warlords. But my kaakaa wasn't a warlord. He'd lived for many years in

Badakhshan as peacefully as he could manage before that northern faction swept in and imprisoned him.

As the days went on, my old kaakaa rotted in his cell with the other Pakhtun. One by one the prisoners disappeared, and my kaakaa was just waiting for the day when they would come for him. Then, one morning, he was sitting in his cell, eating his own fingernails, when the commander of the entire faction decided to give him a visit.

He asked my kaakaa where he was from.

"Badakhshan," he said.

"Come now, Kaakaa," the commander said, "you're a Pakhtun and you speak the eastern dialect. Where are you from originally? Where is your father from?"

"Logar," he admitted.

"Mohammad Agha?"

"How do you know Mohammad Agha?"

The commander ordered all the guards and the prisoners out.

"And you have family in Naw'e Kaleh?" he said.

My kaakaa told him he did. He told him his brother lived in Naw'e Kaleh. He gave him his name and the names of his sons, and when he mentioned Watak and myself, the commander knelt down close to my kaakaa.

"You don't know what happened to Watak?" the commander said.

He didn't. We had not been able to reach him in Badakhshan. No phones, no mail, nothing. And so that night the Hazara commander told my Kaakaa Mahmoud what he knew of the sad story of Watak.

Afterward, the commander ordered that my kaakaa and the other men from his village be cleaned, fed, and released and that no other soldier or faction should touch them unless they wanted to be held accountable to Ghulam Ali. That was his name, you understand, Ghulam Ali, and as I spared him that night in '81 on the roads of Logar, so Commander Ghulam Ali spared my kaakaa on the morning of '94 in a prison cell in Badakhshan, almost two hundred miles away, because you see . . .

But Agha couldn't continue, and the men understood. Someone else took up the line and the tales wore on.

Near the end of the night, when Agha was listening or whispering so intently he didn't seem to see me anymore, I took my Coolpix out of my vest pocket and started searching for the pictures of Budabash. I found pictures of his tree, his chain, his shadow, his bowl, his bones, his food, his bed, everything, almost everything else, but no Budabash himself. He was absent from every picture. Not even a trace.

The next morning, when I got back to Moor's house, I took twenty more photos of Budabash, and I looked through them immediately, and at first, he was there in the image, but then maybe an hour or two later, I skimmed through the pictures again and he was gone.

I wanted to demonstrate this phenomenon for all of my cousins and uncles, especially for Gul, but Gwora thought better of it. He told me we should keep our work to ourselves until we really had a solid collection of evidence. More photos, he demanded, more notes, more data, more intel. More and more, until there could be no doubt left. Until the evil of Budabash was as certain as the good of God.

I agreed.

I wanted a solid case. I wanted him doomed for sure.

But about two weeks later—on that road that day—as I flipped through the invisible pictures of Budabash and ignored Dawood's story, I was starting to lose hope in our chase. That was until we came upon the carcass.

لوگر

On the Thirty-Second Day

Around Asr, the sun dipped into the late afternoon.

Gul was getting so desperate for some sign of a clue, he suggested that we pray on it, and although he was very clearly trying to bribe God with our salah, Zia was so ready to play the part of the imam, he didn't seem to mind.

We made wudhu, one by one, in a nearby stream and laid out our scarves on the rough clay. Zia made the call to prayer and Gul said the iqama and the three of us stood behind Zia and we prayed to Allah together, but by ourselves.

I had a list.

My list was in English, though it should have been in Arabic or at least Pakhto.

First, I prayed for Allah to forgive me and to save me from myself, and I prayed for Him to assist me and my buddies on our mission to capture Budabash or else to prove with his death that he was a fiend. Then I prayed for my parents, Moor and Agha, for her mind and his body. I prayed they wouldn't have to be so lonely all the time. I prayed that my brothers might become men, Mirwais especially, who I thought might become a snitch or a coward, though in many ways I couldn't admit, he was much braver than me.

Dawood was praying on one side of me, fidgeting and cracking his knuckles and scratching his elbows, but I went on with my list anyway.

I prayed for Baba and Abo, for Nikeh and Athai, for all my maamaas and khalas, and for my amas and my one dead kaakaa, Watak, and for all of my cousins, and I prayed for the health of the girl I might marry someday, and I prayed for the health of all the mothers on the earth, but in Afghanistan especially, and I prayed for the men in the village who took care of their families and prayed all their prayers and watched over their neighbors and worked all day in the sun and never beat their wives and never sold their daughters and never snitched on their people and never joined the Americans and never hurt anyone they didn't have to hurt, because I swear to God those sorts of men existed in Naw'e Kaleh, in Logar, in the country. I swear to God.

A few villagers joined our line—farmers from their fields, laborers from their homes, and shepherds from their trails—until there were maybe thirty men or so praying behind Zia as he was wrapping up his final rakah.

I went on.

I prayed for all of my family and all of my friends and for all of the innocents and the martyrs, and I prayed for so many people and so many things that, Wallah, just as Zia was turning his head to say salaam to the angel sitting on his right shoulder,

Raqib, the recorder of good, I prayed one more time for Allah to bring us home, safely, so that I had no time left to pray for my enemies.

When Zia finished greeting Atid, God's first snitch, and turned around to make his dua, he was flustered for only a second by the size of his congregation. He then recited a lovely little dua in what I assumed was perfect Arabic. Afterward, some of the men who had joined us in our prayer recognized Zia as Rahmutallah's son, and they asked him what we were doing out on the road.

But before Zia could answer, Gul spoke up, telling them that we were chasing after a dog. A young shepherd stepped forward and informed us that his flock had recently been attacked by something resembling a dog. He led us along a stream, back the way we had come, to a clearing in a pasture where his flock was allowed to graze and where he'd been briefly distracted by the erratic flight patterns of an American helicopter. By the time he brought his attention back to his flock, his sheep were gathered in a circle, baaing sadly, and so, pressing past one sheep after another, he came to the center of the circle and found the source of their mourning. At first, he thought his poor little lamb had exploded from the inside out. Then he saw the red paw prints leading away from the carcass.

We thanked the shepherd for his story, promised to capture the beast, and, following the red tracks, journeyed deeper and deeper into the valves of the country.

Unfortunately though, Budabash's tracks disappeared just as we got to Watak's marker.

So did his scent.

Dawood sniffed and sniffed as the sun dipped into the late afternoon but got nothing.

Watak's flag didn't look much different from the other flags littering the makeshift graveyards and the dirt roads all over Logar. It hung red and torn from a wooden rod. Stones gathered at the base of it. Ash too. It was the loneliest thing I had ever seen.

Near the flag there was a mulberry tree planted specifically in honor of Watak as a sadaqah. We gathered underneath it, catching our breath, rubbing our feet, and eating the toot from the branches, which belonged to Watak and so belonged to no one or else belonged to the whole village. To the left of the mulberry tree, there was a maze of compounds with these high mud walls that seemed to be on the verge of crumbling. Clay chipped. Thatch sprouting. First layer of mud giving way to a darker clay. It was quiet too. No kids screaming, dogs barking, cows mooing. Unlike the first maze just outside Moor's house, this one seemed almost deserted. To the right of the tree, there was the road, which, if you walked it for long enough, would eventually lead to Agha's compound.

Our search party stood at this fork in the chase, glancing from the maze to the road, from the road to the maze, and then back to the toot. We were so hungry and the toot was so sweet, we ate too much too quickly, and our mouths got sticky from the juice. Gul said he was going to wash his face and he gestured for me to follow him. We walked across the trail, past this hedge of chinar, and slid down a slope of clay into the bank of a canal, where I washed my whole face and where Gul mostly focused on his mustache.

All of Gul's sisters used to say that he had the most beautiful lips they'd ever seen on any man or woman and that it was a crime for him to cover them up with the monstrosity growing beneath his nose. But Gul wouldn't listen, and as he moved through his teenage years, the mustache grew thicker and thicker, and to the rest of the girls in his family, at least, Gul grew less and less beautiful. I mean, don't get me wrong, Gul was a good-looking kid even with his mustache, at least much better looking than me or Dawood, but we did wonder why he was so adamant about hiding his lips.

"You know what happened here?" Gul asked me.

I told Gul I didn't, which was true.

"You don't know what happened to your Watak Kaakaa?"

Watak was Agha's little brother. I heard that he was executed during the war by the Russians. Died really young, a kid practically. A shaheed of the highest purity.

That's all I knew.

"This is where it happened," Gul said, pointing to the earth beneath his feet as if that were the exact spot, as if we squatted right where he was standing when the Russians slit his throat or shot his face or filled his heart with lead.

The shade from the chinar fell slantwise against the bank of the water where we knelt.

He must have fallen in the water, I thought, it must have carried him.

"Shagha never told you that story?"

"Sometimes bits and pieces. But never the whole thing."

"No one hears the whole thing."

"Just bits?"

"Just pieces. Shagha'll tell you the story piece by piece. And you'll have to put it together yourself, and when you do, you have to come and tell me too. You understand?"

White lilies fell from the chinar, scattering on the water.

"Maybe we should go back," I said.

"We'll capture Budabash first. Then we'll go back."

"But how much farther you want to go?"

"Down that road," he said, "in about a kilometer or two, we'll get to your father's compound. I figure we can go at least that far. And if we don't find Budabash by then, we knock at the gate, and you tell them who you are, who your father is, and we spend the night there."

"Wallah?" I asked.

"Inshallah," he said.

Though I would've preferred a "Wallah," I took the "inshallah" with faith.

When we walked back out on the road, we found Zia and Dawood whispering to each other beneath the mulberry tree. The two of them had created a secret pact in order to gather the strength to call for a second jirga, demanding that we, as a clan, a tribe, a nation, reinitiate our former council and vote on whether we should abort our prolonged mission.

"It's getting dark," Zia said.

"I'm getting hungry," Dawood added.

Gul wasn't buying it. "We'll go a little farther," he said, "just until Shagha's house."

"Gul, you keep saying a little farther, just a little farther," Zia argued, "but you can't force us unless we vote on it. We all agreed to save Budabash, but now me and Dawood want to head back. You're the only one who wants to keep going."

"Marwand wants to keep going."

"Marwand wants to go back."

"Well, what do you say, Marwand? You want to go home?" Zia asked.

"Or you want to go on?" Gul added.

The three of them looked to me for an answer and, Wallah, I was trying to come up with one that might make everyone happy, but the toot juice in my belly wouldn't let me think.

"What's your vote?" Gul asked.

And just as my guts were about to give up and give in, I shouted: "Ghwul!" as loud as I could, and ran off through the chinar.

Hidden in between some bushes near the fields on the other side of the bank, I squatted and waited. Down the road the voice of a child called out the adhan from the megaphone of a mosque's citadel, and even with the static and the echo and the cracking of his pitch, it sounded so sweet in the fading light, with the fields darkening, and the crickets chirping their songs.

When the adhan finished, Zia stepped through the chinar and started to pray his Maghrib Salah near the stream. He recited his verses out loud, singing the surahs even though he prayed by himself. Funny thing was Zia didn't even know Arabic. Couldn't tell an Aboo from an Amoo from an Aloo. But he sang surahs like a little Oum Kalthoum. The way he stretched the Name. Just the Name by itself. God, it ached you to hear it.

Behind me, the fields rustled and the dark crept at my back.

"Asalamalaykum Rahmutallah wa Barakatu," Zia said to the angel sitting on his right shoulder, and just before he turned his head toward the angel on his left to say his final salaam, I too peeked past my left shoulder, through Atid, God's first informant, and clenched my guts and watched the dark fields at my back, whose every single stalk of grain trembled back and forth and side to side, while the whirlpool in my belly spun wildly into itself.

And all at once.

Zia finished his salaam.

I shat my flood.

Atid wrote this down.

The wind parted the wheat.

And a shadow leapt from the field, toppling me over like a pile of rocks.

لوگر

On the Thirty-Second Night

Gul came bursting through the chinar, shouting half phrases in Farsi and Pakhto: "Zia, goddamn it, Zia, Budabash, Zia, fuck, Zia, Budabash, Zia, quit praying, Dawood, sniff, get to sniffing, sniff the Budabash, Budabash, and where the fuck is Marwand?"

I was still hiding between the bushes and the fields, desperately trying to wipe the shit off my clothes. I worked quietly, without breathing, and as soon as Gul left with a curse and a huff, I hobbled over to the canal, took a deep breath, and jumped in. Gul must have heard the splashing.

"Marwand . . . ," he started saying before he spotted Zia a little ways up the canal, still facing toward the Kaaba, his hands before his face, his head bobbing to the tune of a song we couldn't hear.

Standing in the stream, I looked to Gul as Gul looked to Zia as Zia looked to God, and I could see that Gul was being torn at the moment between his uncle's inclination to beat the shit out of Zia for ignoring him and his long-held Afghan's esteem for the act of worship, whether faked or not.

Gul ordered me to stay and wait for Zia, but it took such a long time for him to finish his prayers. At first, I sat beside the stream, watching him, waiting for him to finish, trying to guess which head bob, which dua, which surah would be his last, but he just went on and on until I got tired of it and went back toward the road and sat beneath Watak's mulberry tree.

It was cold on the road by myself as wet as I was.

About two seconds later, Zia came crawling through the chinar, finally finished with his prayers, and sat right next to me. I gave him a suspicious look, like *I see you.* And he, in response, gave me an expression of innocence as if to say, *God sees all,* which was true, you know. I guess I could have pressured him, made him explain why he kept on praying his fake prayer when Gul needed him most. I wondered if he was making a stand, if he was tired of Gul's rule. Or if maybe he was just scared. But mostly, I think, I was so relieved we didn't enter that dark maze in the night, with some shadow of a creature roaming its walls, I didn't want to question why. Besides, Zia was all I had left, and I was all he had left, and so, even though I stank horribly of toot-shit and mud, Zia unfurled his patu and wrapped it around me and him both.

We sat there side by side and watched Watak's marker and waited for Gul and Dawood to come back with news of Budabash, still hopeful. To pass the time, Zia asked me for a story.

I told him I didn't have any.

Zia glanced at me. "You've said that before. When was it?"

"A few days ago."

"But someone told a story," he said.

"Yeah, someone did."

And so I began.

The Tale of the Tale of Marena and the Shit-Eating Djinn

Listen, my maamaazai, on one of those nights when the generator busted or there wasn't enough cash for the fuel, you and me and the guys snuck up onto the roof of the main compound, where we lay back on the rough clay and watched the stars mark the sky.

"When the Commies came," Gulbuddin started, "a man or a kid from every house would sleep on the roof—like we're doing now—in case the helicopters or the bombers came up over the mountains in the night, so that the kid on the roof would hear them first and could warn the rest of the family to run toward the shelter, even though he'd be the last one in. And you know who was the guy who always lay up on this roof here? Do you know?"

We knew. But we never said who.

When Gul's stories got too depressing, Dawood told Mullah Nasruddin jokes, like the one where Mullah Nasruddin carried his donkey on his back so that it wouldn't get tired, or this other one where Mullah Nasruddin tried to teach his donkey to read to impress an emperor, or the one where Mullah Nasruddin got mad at God for killing his donkey because he prayed for God to kill his cow. And even though they weren't really that funny, we always laughed, especially me and my brothers, who told so many stories during our first week, I said we had no more left. But you wouldn't listen.

"Tell us a werewolf story," you said.

"No, tell us an American story," Dawood said, "about American girls."

"What about Shagha's war stories?" Gul asked.

But before I could tell them I had no stories left, Gwora spoke up.

"I have a story," he said.

I shook my head at him.

"I heard it someplace," he said.

I bit my lip the way Agha did when he got angry.

"Well, how does it go?" Gul said.

"Once, before the war," Gwora started.

"Which war?" Dawood said.

"All of them," Gwora said. "Once, before the war, there was a wicked girl named Marena. Who one day was doing the bad thing in the kamoot and while doing the bad thing got distracted by a light she saw in her head and fell through the hole and drowned in a pile of her own shit." Gwora sucked in a deep breath and went on. "But before she could die she met a shit-eating djinn—dark green and hairy and smelling of rot—and with the permission of Shaytan, the shit-djinn made a deal with the girl. He would bring her back to life, re-created from the shit, but from then on she had to crawl from compound to compound and hide in the kamoots, where if a boy or a man came there to squat and do the bad thing, she got them by the balls and pulled them through the hole and drowned them in their own—"

"Astagfirullah," you said, looking more worried than the rest, "how does she die?"

"One day," he kept going, "after many years in the dark. After many men yanked and swallowed and drowned. After forgetting everything from when she was a girl. Even her own name. She pulls herself up through the hole of the kamoot where she first tried to die and seeing the sunlight and hearing the water and smelling the mulberries she used to pick when she was a girl. For the first time in a long time she walks out into the hottest day of the hottest summer of the decade, and the shit and the mud dripping from her skin hardens in the light and she freezes where she stands. Beneath a tree. Reaching out for a mulberry she would never eat."

Gwora took one last deep breath and closed his mouth.

"Is that the end?" Dawood said.

"Yeah," he said.

Gulbuddin clapped him on his shoulder. "Mashallah," he said. "Nice try. Really nice. But Gwora, the ending was no good. Next time you tell it," Gulbuddin advised, "change it up a little. Put in a hero or, even better, a bunch of heroes. And a love story. Because, Gwora, it's okay to change a story a little if you can make it better. And heroes and love, they always make things better. Otherwise, you know, what's the point?"

Later that same night, Gul wouldn't let us off the roof. He demanded that we sleep up there and keep an ear out for the copters, which roamed about the heads of the black mountains, dropping, every few minutes, some rumbling thing that barely touched us kids in the valley. It was odd, I thought, how a few miles could turn bombs into lullabies.

In between the quakes from the mountains and the snores from the guys, I listened to the shuffling from the orchard where Budabash roamed. The nights in Logar never got too quiet, but there was a rhythm to all the sounds: the howls and the rumbling and the crickets and the snores, which always put me to sleep so much quicker than the sound of America.

Eventually, I dreamed of my finger.

I dreamed it was mended and whole and that none of me was missing anywhere, and when I woke up to the howling of a wolf I couldn't see, the ghost of my finger started wriggling at the end of my hand and—

"Like Yaseen," Zia interrupted my story beneath Watak's mulberry tree.

"I don't know Yaseen," I said.

"Yaseen's my third best buddy. He's got no foot."

"I've got my foot."

"Yeah, but Yaseen's foot haunts his leg just like your finger haunts your hand. He stepped on a mine, lost his foot, and got a ghost in its place. Says he can feel it sometimes. The lost foot. Says that sometimes he forgets it's not there. Says he wakes up in the morning and feels it there and jumps out of bed and starts running without a foot and slips and falls flat on his face. Says the ghost of his foot tricks him, and makes him fall, and he doesn't know why." Zia laughed for some reason, nervously. "So you should be grateful it's just the ghost of the little bit of your finger and not a whole foot."

"It hurts, though," I said. "You feel it there wriggling and when it's gone again it hurts like the day Budabash took it."

"You shouldn't have got so close so fast. You thought he was like an American dog."

"I thought he was like the old dog."

"What old dog?"

I told him what I did to the dog in '99.

The Tale of the Old Dog

Six summers ago—I remember—me, Gwora, and Mirwais were out in the orchard in Moor's compound, searching, I think, for this nest of chicks we planned to feed with fresh worms and toot until they evolved into phoenixes or falcons.

The orchard was wet with flood because Baba and Rahmutallah Maamaa were rebuilding entire portions of the compound from scratch. Your whole family had just returned to Logar from Peshawar. That's why Agha brought us back that summer. It was the first time my moor had seen her home since she fled the Russians in the '80s.

So there we were, Agha and Moor helping Rahmutallah with the rebuild, while me, Gwora, and Mirwais helped some chicks with their lunch. As we walked deeper into the orchard, toward the corner of the northern wall where the little red chicks hid inside the puncture of an old rocket's blast, we didn't realize just how muddy the orchard had got that morning. In a rush to grow the chicks into woodpeckers, Gwora and Mirwais ran ahead of me, and before I knew it, the both of them were ankle deep in mud. Not only that, but every time they lifted their feet to try to slog out of the muck, they only sank deeper, as if the orchard were trying to swallow them and their new white clothes.

So I stood there on the edge of the mud pit, still as clean and as white as I would ever be, and with my brothers in the heart of the muck, being eaten, and with Moor's wrath waiting for us somewhere within the newly forged walls of the courtyard, I looked at my brothers, and they looked at me, and I knew we were all doomed no matter what.

I couldn't handle it any longer.

I leapt.

All three of us hopped and skipped and played in the mud until we found more worms, until we fed the birds, until we made mud angels, mud pies, and mud men, until we turned ourselves into *Scooby-Doo* swamp monsters, until Moor, maybe sensing we were gone for too long, called out our names from the courtyard.

When she saw us, she lost it. Whupped me and Gwora with whatever she could get her hands on: chaplacks and boots and branches and those old school Afghan brooms made of spindly sticks tied together.

A little while later, I went to visit the dog.

He was prettier then. No scar or mange or stink. Wallah, even his fur was blonder.

Listen, Zia, I could tell you that I was beating the dog because I was beaten, that I was six and stupid and knew no better. But here is the other thing I have to admit: the more I hurt him and the more he took it, as quiet as he did, without even a growl, the more I became attached to the dog. You see, I spent all day sitting on him, kicking him, punching him. I used to throw knives and drop huge stones on his back and watch his skin tremble and jerk. But no matter what I did, the dog just suffered it. His head down, his eyes in the mud, doing nothing to hurt me. He suffered so quietly. Day after day I went on torturing him until this one morning when Rahmutallah Maamaa caught me bashing the dog's back with a log. He took me aside and explained about Raqib and Atid, the recording angels, and he asked me why I did it.

"The dog never barks," I said. "It never tells me to stop."

"Then I tell you to stop," Rahmutallah Maamaa said with all the love he could muster in his little black beard.

But I didn't stop. I was just more careful. And it was only after I flew back to the States—where my American teachers taught me that dogs were supposed to be loved, hugged, cuddled, chained, and sometimes whacked, often neutered, but never tortured—that I realized how much I'd wronged the old mutt.

After I finished my story, Zia recalled for me a hadith recorded in the Sahih Muslim, which Abu Huraira once reported that the Prophet Muhammad, peace and blessings be upon him, once said, "A prostitute once saw a dog lolling around a well on a hot day, hanging its tongue, about to die of thirst. Upon seeing this, the prostitute took off her head scarf, tied it about her shoe, and drew some water for the dog, letting it drink to its content. And so, because of that, Allah forgave her."

Zia went on to emphasize that the Prophet (peace and blessings be upon him) loved all animals, even wolves, since in the days of the Prophet animals could sometimes speak like humans, expressing their desires and their rights. For example, Zia recited for me a hadith recorded in the Sahih Bukhari, wherein it was narrated by Abu Huraira that the Prophet (peace and blessings be upon him) once reported that a hungry wolf once caught a sheep, and when the shepherd chased it, the wolf said to the shepherd, "Who will be its guard on the day of wild beasts, when there will be no shepherd for it except me?" Upon hearing the wolf speak with such intelligence, the shepherd clapped his hands and declared: "What could be more miraculous than this?"

Then Zia recited that Abu Huraira narrated that the Prophet said that the wolf replied: "There is, indeed, something more curious and wonderful than this, and that is the message of Allah's chosen Apostle, Muhammad of Mecca, who is now inviting people to Islam." After which the shepherd, following the advice of the wolf, took his sheep to Al-Madinah in order to speak with the Prophet. There, the shepherd told the Prophet the story of the wolf. Upon hearing the story, the Prophet went out to the believers and asked the shepherd to tell his story again, which he did, and so the Prophet proclaimed that the shepherd had witnessed one of the signs of the Day of Judgment. By the One who controls my soul, the Prophet went on, the Day of Judgment will not occur until beasts speak to humans. And so it was.

Zia kept on like this for a long time, reciting hadith after hadith about spiders hiding the Prophet in a cave, about talking birds and helpful horses, and so on and so forth, until we both noticed that Gul had been gone for too long. We'd been telling stories underneath the mulberry tree for almost an hour. And though Gul was always a hardheaded guy, we figured he would've either caught Budabash by now or else returned to us before Isha fell.

The roads darkened. The crickets chirped. The donkeys brayed. And everywhere there was a smell of smoke and sadness. From time to time, a breeze would rush down through the roads, shaking the tatters of Watak's flag, and then a gust would blow forth from the maze, rustling the leaves of the mulberry tree, so that it almost seemed as if the flag and the tree were whispering to each other. Eventually, me and Zia decided to take up Gul's original plan and travel up the road a kilometer or two until we got to Agha's compound. But just as we rose and packed, ready to continue our journey, Dawood came stumbling out of the maze.

We ran to him in a jumble and hugged him very tightly as he hollered about going back home and getting his brothers and saving Gul, and we were so overjoyed just to see him and to hear him that when he stopped hollering and became heavy in our hands, we didn't even notice that our hug was all that held him up.

He passed out in our arms.

We tried for a long time to wake him up: slapping and punching and lifting his eyelids and smearing toot under his nose and splashing water in his face and rubbing his belly raw and pinching the skin at his wrists. But nothing woke him. We listened closely for his heart, the both of us, and made sure it was thumping.

Without any other option, me and Zia pulled Dawood underneath Watak's mulberry tree and stripped some bushes from the side of the road, and after wrapping ourselves up in Zia's patu, we watched the flag of Watak's marker and smelled the ash and listened for every footstep of every killer in Logar: the psychopathic white boys, the ravenous bandits, the Ts and the gunmen and the drug runners, the kidney kidnappers, the robots in the sky, the wolves from the mountains and the coyotes from the rivers, the witches in the cesspits, the djinn in the trees, the ghosts from the graveyards, and the monsters in the maze.

We lay on either side of Dawood. I held one hand and Zia held the other. A few moments in and I looked up over Dawood's belly and whispered to Zia, "It's so dark."

"You scared?" he asked.

"It's just that back in America it doesn't get so dark because we have lights going on all night in the streets."

"But who pays for the fuel?"

"I think taxes."

"You miss it over there?"

"No," I said, "fuck America. I rather be here."

"Wallah?" he said. "Don't lie in the night, Marwand. Snakes will hear."

"Well," I said, "maybe not right this moment. But in general."

"So you are scared."

"Maybe a little."

"Of dying?" he asked quietly.

I didn't say anything. I just breathed.

"If we die," Zia said, "God will be there."

"If we die," I said, "will you tell Him I was good?"

"All right," he said, and asked me to give him my right hand, which I did, and after carefully unwrapping the gauze still clinging to my skin, he traced for me—with a single finger—his evidence of God's existence.

The Tale of the Evidence of God's Existence

On the palm of your right hand, if you look at it, God has etched into your flesh the Arabic numeral ١٨, or 18.

And on the palm of your left hand, if you look at it, Allah has traced into your skin the Arabic numeral ٨١, or 81.

Now, if you add these numbers together, you get ٩٩.

Allah (swt) has ٩٩ names.

And if you take ١٨ and subtract it from ٨١, you get ٦٣, or 63.

The Prophet (peace and blessings be upon him) died at sixty-three.

"So, you see," Zia explained, "God has etched into the palms of your hands one reminder of His own glory and another reminder of his most beloved servant, and so . . ." But he didn't finish his point, and instead, after concluding his demonstration, he rewrapped my hand with the tattered strips of gauze and gave it back to me.

. . .

For a long time afterward, in some way or other, I knew we would be saved, either in the night or in the day or in the days to come, and that it was only a matter of when, not if. At some point, both me and Zia fell asleep, and for the first time in a long time, Zia forgot to pray.

لوگر

On the Thirty-Third Morning

Just before dawn I woke up to a pang in my belly, as though something were eating me from the inside out, and I lay there for a while beneath the mulberry tree, clawing at my stomach with the tip of the finger I didn't have, until the adhan for Fajr rang out from one of the nearby mosques, stirring Zia awake.

Dawood still slept in between us, dreaming, I imagined, of feasts and platters, of Kabuli palaus and Logari stews, of kormas and kabobs and curried chickens, of ashak and mantu, of quroot and maastay, of distarkhans so long and dishes such aplenty (and with so many different guests) that the feast would stretch from Kabul to Kandahar to Herat to Mazar all the way back to Logar, all the way back to the spot beneath the tree where he dreamed it, where me and Zia were waiting, where my belly grumbled miserably for the dreams I imagined Dawood still dreamed.

We tried to wake him, shouting and shaking and pinching and pulling. Then we whispered into his ears. Me into his left.

Zia into his right. So that my threats of violence and Zia's pleas for mercy would bang around in his brain. I told him bandits were coming and Zia whispered that dinner was ready. I said a knife was at his throat and Zia promised him that the knife was a gift. I told him he was being a lazy coward and Zia said he would become a courageous hero if only he'd wake up and help us home. None of it worked. We soon realized that Dawood was in a slumber so deep it was more like a coma—or a spell. He needed a doctor, an imam. He needed Baba or Abo. He needed real help. Not two famished kids on the road too weak to carry him, too stupid to wake him, and too scared to do anything else. Poor Dawood, I thought, he needed saviors, but all he had was us.

In the blue light of fajr, I examined him closely.

Stained from neck to ankle in smudges of ash and dust and what I thought might be blood but was probably just clay, he had scratches on his face and hands and his left sleeve was torn completely from his shirt.

I wondered what the maze had done to him, what it would do to Gul.

The wreckage of his outfit left me feeling as if I were inside of a dream, and neither Zia's sudden sadness (he hung his head and would not pray the Fajr Salah), nor the blue light of dawn, nor the jackal's howls, nor the child's adhan, nor the peace of the roads, nor the babbling stream, nor the return of the ghost of my finger, wriggling at the end of my bandaged stump like a grub, did anything to lessen the dreaminess of that morning.

Neither did our visitors.

With Dawood knocked out in between us and with no donkey or cart or wheelbarrow to move him and with Gul still lost somewhere in the maze and with us as stinking and tired and dirty and broken and hopeless as we were, we decided, without speaking on it, to just sit and wait by our tree until some kind Logari came by to assist us.

And, by the grace of Allah, we were sent more than a few.

First came Jawed the Thief.

Even though he strolled up to us with a mask on his face, a machine gun beneath his patu, a donkey at his side, and a pair of blue eyes—which, I learned from Abo, could almost always mark a man as having a predilection for theft—I didn't guess him for a thief until he knelt near us and calmly started rummaging through our big black bag. Only after the Thief found my Coolpix did he ask us what we were doing on the road. So we explained to him about how we lost Gul and found Dawood.

He knelt down near us, so close I could smell the hash on his breath, so close I could feel the warmth of the rifle throbbing beneath his patu, so close I could see that his eyes were more turquoise than blue, so close I suddenly knew he wasn't going to kill us, though I couldn't say why. He proceeded to take off his mask, unveiling a face much lighter and handsomer than I thought it was going to be—though his mutilated fingers and scarred scalp revealed old tortures—and he offered us a deal.

It went like this:

"How about I go into the maze, all right? And I find your Gul. And I bring him back. And I take you boys home. You understand?"

We said that we did.

"I do all of this on one condition. Well, two conditions. Actually, okay, three. Yeah, just the three conditions, you understand?

Real easy, boys. Three steps to salvation. One. You let me keep this camera, all right? Two. You show me how to work this camera. Three. You don't fuck with that boy while he's sleeping. Four. And this one is the most important. If anybody comes down this road and asks you if you've seen a thief named Jawed, you tell them you have and that he went off toward the black mountains. You understand?"

We accepted every condition of his offer and finalized our verbal agreement with an oath to Jawed's third mother, a literal saint and living ghost, and then he strolled off into the maze, flipping through the pictures of my camera. After he left, I realized how much Jawed the Thief reminded me of the T in the field whose pictures I took and never deleted.

Next, there came a small clan of Kochi nomads—all five of them fitted in those old school Kochi dresses that girls in Fremont wore at weddings or cultural banquets when they danced the attan. They led along a two-humped camel.

Before we could ask for help, they asked us about Jawed.

"Who's Jawed?" Zia said.

And all five of the girls answered at once: "Our dead fiancé."

But in Pakhto, of course.

Apparently, the five girls were all distant cousins from rivaling families whose men had been killing one another for decades over petty disputes regarding sheep or honor or God, and according to the leader of the clan, Zarghoona, who had an assortment of rusted blades strapped to her camel's hump, Jawed had proposed to each of the five cousins on the same night, going from one family's tent to the next, promising each family a two-humped camel as a dowry. But, by the will of God, only a few hours before Zarghoona was to be given to Jawed, she came upon one of her cousins in the market in Wagh Jan while shopping for the engagement. Feeling blessed by the recent events of her proposal, she decided to make amends with the girl she had no personal quarrel with and went to kiss her cheek and hold her hands. After which the both of them found out that the other was soon to be wed, and they were randomly met by another distant cousin, who also revealed she was soon to be wed, until each of the five cousins had, by the will of Allah, come together and shared the same story of approaching matrimony. Understanding that they'd been deceived, the five cousins united their rival families under the ever-encompassing banner of vengeance and decided to find Jawed for themselves.

"He has beautiful blue eyes, is probably armed, and should be wearing a mask," Zarghoona concluded. "Have you seen him?"

Even under the gaze of her rusted machete, me and Zia lied to her, partly out of fear of Jawed, partly to stay true to our word, and mostly because snitching just didn't come easy.

Zia told them that we had spotted a blue-eyed gunman a few minutes ago and that he had passed us by and gone off toward the black mountains. I pointed them in the direction they needed to go. But Zarghoona didn't buy it.

"Boys," she said, "serpents lie. Not men."

With that word, she led her tribe into the maze.

Just as they left, we were visited by a pair of Pakhtuns, not much older than us, who claimed allegiance to the Ts and were wearing these dirty black garbs and black pakols, strapped to the chest with old rifles that looked like they'd been forged 150 years ago to shoot at shitty Englishmen.

The mini-Ts led a steer, on whose hide was a pair of prisoners, tied up, sitting back to back, bloodied and beaten and wearing rice bags over their heads. The prisoners whispered to each other. Arguing, it seemed like. One of the mini-Ts, the uglier one, stopped, greeted us, and asked about a thief named Jawed.

We asked him what for.

The ugly T (who seemed so unaware of his ugliness—his mustache trimmed, his locks oiled, his wrists stinking of perfume—it made you feel prettier just looking at him) smiled big at us, his mouth a graveyard, and pointing to the prisoners on the steer, he said: "He's joining these guys."

"No, he's not," said the other T, the handsomer, dirtier, hairier (patches of beard sprouting out of his chin and cheeks like weeds), smellier, and sadder one.

"What did they do?" Zia asked.

"They're hash-heads," the ugly T said. "One of them is a seller and one of them is a smoker, but we can't figure out which is which. We caught them together near a madrassa, in the middle of an exchange, but when we busted down their door, there was so much smoke in their dirty little shack we couldn't tell which one was passing the hash and which one the paper. They dropped everything and begged for mercy."

"In the name of God," one prisoner called out in Farsi, "I'm the buyer. It all started when I traveled to Iran for work to feed my one-armed father. We built roads in Tehran for sixteen, eighteen hours a day and they'd give us coke to keep us awake and heroin to calm us down. After the drugs ate all our strength, our bosses tossed us on the streets and the police jailed us, beat us, and deported us back to Kabul. I'd lost all the money I made to the heroin and came back home a disgrace. My father wouldn't even touch me. I'm not a seller; I'm a fiend. I'm a fool. I smoke hash to stay off heroin. But I'd never put this affliction on another soul, for the love of Allah you must believe me."

"In the name of God," the other prisoner shouted in Pakhto, "I'm the buyer. It all started when a squadron of Americans came by our house because they thought a squadron of Taliban were hiding in our orchard. And although we would've been happy to help the Taliban, there weren't any Taliban, and so there was nothing to hide. Their translator misinterpreted my father's Pakhto into a confession. They were going to take him, and I confessed in his place, and the motherfucker misinterpreted my confession as denunciation, and it took ten minutes for him to understand that I was the confessed conspirator, not my father, who would've died under the tortures. They took me to the base and beat the shit out of me for three days and three nights for information I didn't have and couldn't make up. After they broke my rib, they let me out, but the rib keeps cutting me in the night, and so I came to buy this hash because it's the only way I can sleep. In the name of Allah, speak to my father, and he'll confirm my story."

"See," the ugly T said, "they've got different stories and we can't figure out which one to beat and which one to shoot, and so we'll shoot them both. Along with Jawed."

"What did Jawed do?" I asked.

"Jawed is with the Americans," the pretty T said, eyeing me. "Where are you from?"

But before I could answer, the whistle of a rocket rang out somewhere from the roads and the mini-Ts and their prisoners hurried off into the maze.

Up next was a squadron of American soldiers.

There were five of them. Four soldiers and the one translator, who asked Zia in Farsi if he knew the whereabouts of a blue-eyed bandit named Jawed. Apparently, Jawed had stolen armor, weapons, and an expensive coffee machine from a nearby base.

The translator was a scrawny, dark fellah, visibly sweating under his helmet and armor. If it weren't for his drooping eyes (he almost looked bored), I would have thought he was scared out of his mind. The four soldiers behind him were all wearing so much armor, with the goggles and the helmet and the chin strap and the mouthpiece, I couldn't tell one of them apart from the other. Most likely, each of them had his own rank and name and story. But at that moment, those four white boys—possibly the first white boys to have stood on that particular spot, on that particular road, since poor Watak Shaheed got executed almost twenty years ago—probably assumed that if they tried to speak the only tongue they knew, we wouldn't understand them.

As with our other visitors, Zia informed the translator that we had seen a blue-eyed gunman pass our way, but that he carried no special equipment, no mechanized armor, no night-vision goggles, no Teflon vest, no M4 carbine with the ACOG sight and the foregrip, and no coffee machine. Just a single AK, a patu, and a black pakol. Also, he seemed to be heading toward the black mountains.

The translator translated most of this in an English so broken he had to repeat himself six times in a row, explaining and reexplaining the location of the black mountains. One of the soldiers nodded his helmet, acting as though he understood, and told the translator to ask Zia what we were up to by ourselves, on this road, so early in the morning, without consent from them or their government.

The translator did as he was told, though he left out the part about consent.

Zia said something to him in Farsi I didn't understand. And the translator told the soldiers that Zia wasn't cooperating.

"These fucking village kids," the same soldier said (which, for a second, made me so happy), "you tell him that if he doesn't tell us what happened to the fat kid that all three of them are coming back with us to the base."

The translator translated this to Zia, leaving out the part about going back to the base.

But before Zia could tell him the truth, I spoke up, addressing the soldiers directly, in English, and I told them a long lie about how me and Zia and Dawood were all half-brothers, each of us having different mothers but the same father, a native of this village, who was forced to leave Zia and Dawood and their mothers behind in Afghanistan, so that me and him and my mother could go to America to learn to be good Americans, and that after me and my mother and father got our citizenships we came back to visit Logar, so that I could reacquaint myself with my half-brothers and become a good Afghan, and that's why he dropped us off here, where he used to go swimming in this stream with his own brothers, who were all killed by Communists and then warlords and then Ts, so we could play and get along and know one another, but the thing was while me and Zia were getting along fine since both of our mothers were Farsiwan, we didn't have much to say to Dawood since his mother was a Pakhtun, and so he got bored of our Farsi conversation and fell asleep, and although he's a Pakhtun, he's still our blood and so we couldn't just leave him here and we couldn't wake him either since our father taught us it was a sin to even wake up a snake, but that's okay since fortunately our father will be coming back to pick us up at any moment.

Then I took a deep breath and shut my mouth.

The same soldier from before stepped in front of the translator, sort of pushing him aside, and asked me where exactly I was from.

But before I could answer, the soldiers got a report over the radio about the possible location of a runaway squadron, and so they marched off into the maze without another word, translated or otherwise.

Finally, near Dhuhr, we were visited by a solitary laborer covered from head to toe in wet cement, who was pushing a wheelbarrow that was also completely stained in cement. He looked like he was in a rush, and at first it didn't seem that he would stop for us, but when Zia evoked the name of God, he halted. He came slopping up to us, big globs of cement trailing behind him. Zia explained our ordeal and pleaded for his help.

"How far?" he said in Pakhto, his face so thickly lathered with his labor, I couldn't tell if he was sixteen or sixty, if he was dark or light skinned, if he was handsome or ugly or anything in between. Hell, if it weren't for his clothes and his hair, I could hardly tell he was a man at all.

Zia told him.

"Listen," he said, spitting a hock of cement, "I've got to take this to a work site. My mule's stashed over there. How about I bring you boys that far in my barrow and I'll ask my boss for some time off to bring you the rest of the way home. You understand?"

We did and, Wallah, if it weren't for the cement, me and Zia would've kissed his hand as if he were our old father returned to us after a long journey. Instead, the three of us lifted Dawood into the wheelbarrow and began to travel down the road. Before we left sight of the maze, I asked Zia if we should head back to the marker and pray for Gul's safe return.

"The faster we get home," he said, "the faster we bring help."

"At least a dua."

"I'll whisper one as we go," he said.

But I never saw his lips move.

لوگر

On the Thirty-Third Afternoon

The new cement road contracted by the Kabuli government was to extend from the main highway in Logar, through the Wagh Jan market, past the bridge built above the Logar River, which connected Wagh Jan to the inner villages, deep into all the passages and clay mazes within the countryside.

"That way," the cement-man explained in a Pakhto so slow and simple it was like he knew I wasn't a native, "all the crops grown by the Logarian in the valley can be better transported to Kabul, and as the sale of food becomes more fluid, so too will the cash flow between the landowners and the merchants."

The cement-man had not stopped talking since we left Watak's marker. I didn't mind it so much because I appreciated how loud and comfortable he was on the road, and although I knew we couldn't truly trust him (me and Zia each pulled one of the kitchen knives out of the big black bag when he wasn't looking), it was still nice to feel like we had a guide again. Besides, I was the one who made the mistake of asking him about his work.

"Trouble is," the laborer went on, wiping the cement from his lips to make his pronunciation even clearer, "whenever we try to pave a new road from the bridge to the inner roads, the Taliban come in the night and set off explosions."

"But why?" I let slip.

"You see," the cement-man spat, "although the roads will make it easier for the trucks and the shipments to get around within the village, it will also make it easier for the Humvees and the tanks. Plus, these homes are built too close together. In order to make a proper road, there will be demolitions. Certain people in this village know that. They can see what is coming. A cement road is never just a cement road. It's the beginning of a whole new town. So while every morning the Kabuli government orders the road to be repaved, rebuilt, and reconstructed, every night the Taliban come back to blow it up again. As long as the Americans are footing the bill, the contractors just subcontract the project to a lesser contractor, pocketing millions, and that subcontractor does the same thing to another subcontractor. Until the roads are never actually built and I'm never out of work. Nobody really minds all the lost cement. Well, except for the Americans."

I thought he looked straight at me as he said that last word, though I couldn't be sure because of the cement on his face and eyes and clothes, dripping behind us on the road. Leaving a trail.

When we finally got to the work site, the cement-man unloaded Dawood and our big black bag near the donkeys' post (we sat him up against a tree, returned our knives, put the bag under his arm, and tucked a pakol over his eyes to make it seem like he was just resting), and he went over to talk to his boss.

Almost immediately, we lost our man in the bustle of the site.

And almost immediately after that, someone gave us a job to do.

We weren't the only kids at the site, and we weren't the youngest either. While me and Zia unloaded bags of cement from the trucks and pushed barrows of gray slush back and forth from the road and the mixing trench, little kids, some of them as young as nine or eight, carried buckets of water from the Logar River, just underneath the bridge, and hauled bags and pushed barrows.

On the other side of the bridge, closer to Wagh Jan, there were also men building up power lines. Rows of wooden poles ran from the start of the bridge up through Wagh Jan, all the way, it seemed, back to the highway toward Kabul. I wondered when those pole lines might reach Moor's compound. We could run the electricity all night. We could watch movies forever.

About an hour or two into the work, me and Zia slipped away to check on Dawood, who was still sleeping soundly with the donkeys, and there, by the side of the road, in the cover of the trees, we found the cement-man's mule, unhitched and licking Dawood's fingers.

It seemed like a sign. We had no idea where the cement-man was or when he might find us, and he already promised us the mule. Maybe, I thought, he left it unhitched on purpose, just for us to come and get it. Who could say otherwise? And just as I was coming up with my argument to borrow the donkey, Zia made it unnecessary.

"Marwand," he said, "let's take this thing."

"You sure?"

"We'll take it, ride home, and return it afterward."

But it wasn't that simple.

After lifting Dawood onto the mule's back, we realized that without a harness or a whip, it wouldn't move. Nothing to persuade it. That was until I shuffled through the big black bag and pulled out one of the kitchen knives.

Even through the thick layer of cement lathered on his face, I could see Zia's heart sink at the sight of it. For a second, I thought he might recite a hadith or a surah about cruelty. I thought he might guilt me with a suggestion of Allah's sadness or remind me of the sins I'd confessed to him. What I did to the dog.

But he didn't.

"It's for Gul," I said, offering a knife. "Allah will forgive us."

"No, it's not," he said, and took the knife anyway.

At first, Zia only gave the mule a little prod, barely a pinprick, but it wouldn't budge. Then, although I had no ill will toward the mule, I was just so sick and tired of being lost, I stepped up and cut sideways into its hide, a deep slit, and as soon as I drew blood, the mule started forward at a slow trot.

The whole ride home I kept cutting at the mule as gently as I could, pushing him along the trail, and, Wallah, anytime I stopped bleeding him for just a few seconds—because my hand was getting tired or because the twitching of its flesh left me breathless—he stopped moving, and Zia would have to cut him, and like that we made it all the way back toward the roads near our home. There, at the beginning or the end of the first maze we entered, I cut the mule a final time, deep and sure, sending him off one way, while me and Zia dragged Dawood home.

لوگر

On the Thirty-Third Evening

Before we knocked, we tried to clean ourselves up as best we could, especially Dawood, whose clothes we scraped of cement and whose face we washed in a nearby canal. We held him up between us like he wasn't knocked out at all but maybe tired, and just as Zia stepped forward, readying his fist, Abo opened the gate.

She stood there beneath the doorway in the biggest, bluest burqa I'd ever seen. With a log in one hand and a hatchet in the other, Abo looked like the punishment I'd been waiting for, but then she uttered the word "bachyan," dropped her weapons, and didn't even try to stop all the other ladies from flooding out onto the trail. They surrounded us, kissing and pinching and passing me along until I got back to Moor, who held me to her chest and smacked me and blessed me, just as Zia's mom did to him.

Down in the dirt, Abo held Dawood in her arms, crowded on all sides by his sisters, who were also trying to wake him up:

bringing their fingers to his mouth and his eyelids, shouting and pleading, before Abo pulled off her burqa and began to kiss him, little pecks on his forehead and his eyes and his hands.

Then she started counting.

She held Dawood in her arms and glanced from him to Zia to me, and she counted:

One two three.

One two three.

One two three.

And on the final number of the third count she asked the question I'd been dreading to answer ever since I realized, maybe a few minutes beforehand, that we were actually going to make it home.

"Where is our Gul?" she said.

About half an hour later, Rahmutallah Maamaa was asking me the same question.

I told him what I told Abo. "He's in the maze."

"Which maze?" he said. His hand on my shoulder, sinking.

"Watak's maze," I said, not knowing what else to call it.

All of the men (Baba, Rahmutallah, Agha, Ruhollah, plus a few more of my distant uncles and older cousins) and a few of the mothers (Moor, Zia's mom, and Abo) were interrogating me and Zia in Baba's chamber. They didn't seem to think it was necessary to give us the whupping I thought we were destined to receive. In fact, as soon as the men got home from their search and realized that only three of us had made it back, they didn't even take the time to yell at us. It was a huge letdown. By that point, seeing the family in the torment that we put them, I felt so guilty about leaving Gul behind, I hoped some punishment might relieve me of the pressure. Instead, it was all business: they just wanted to know as quickly and as accurately as possible where and when we last saw Gul.

After we told them what we knew, Rahmutallah gathered all the men from his side of the family and they called on all their cousins and distant relatives and close friends from all across the village, and Agha did the same thing with his side, and all of them got together somewhere near Watak's marker. They took Zia as a guide, leaving me behind with the kids and the ladies.

In the courtyard, as soon as she got me to herself, Moor inspected my butchered finger, which by that point was infused in so many layers of dirt and shit and toot and blood that it seemed like it was decomposing. When she peeled back the rotting gauze, even I could tell the thing was infected: pus leaking, meat turned mushy and white, stinking too.

At first, she just stared her Afghan's death glare.

Even though Moor was an especially small woman, I'd only recently gotten taller than her, and it was still odd to look down into her eyes instead of up at them. She dragged me into the washroom with the iodine and the rubbing alcohol. After disinfecting my wound, she inspected my face and my arms and my chest. Then, taking up a washcloth, she rubbed my skin so raw, I thought the flesh might tear free. But with Moor as tense as she was, I was not ready to deny her anything.

She put both her hands on my face and declared: "Gul is okay."

Moor had calloused fingers scarred rough by fire and dirt, and when she touched me like this I was always so ashamed of how much softer my skin was than hers. Even at that moment, with all the dirt and the blood and the cement just barely washed off, with all the suffering I thought I'd gone through, it was nothing.

"Marwand," she said, "is Gul okay?"

The washroom we knelt in was made of stone, hollowed out of the clay like a cave, and just like a cave, it echoed out and bounced back every drip and every word, so that it was not as if Moor, by herself, were asking me the question, but that the whole family or the whole village was asking it over and over.

"Inshallah," I whispered, because it was the quietest thing I could think to say.

Later on, when I searched for my brothers, I found that the both of them had shunned me. Gwora spent all his time in the den, writing and reading, ignoring my pleas, and forcing Mirwais to do the same. Nothing I did could make them hear me.

Meanwhile, all the ladies in the house just wanted me to retell the story of how I got lost, of how I led the boys out, of how Gul tried to stop me, and of how, after losing Gul, I did nothing to get him back. And every time they asked, no matter who it was, I told the story just the way Gul would've wanted. I mean, in a way, it *was* my fault Gul got lost. But there was no punishment for me, the American guest, who started all the trouble, acted a coward, left Gul behind, got back home, and didn't even get a whupping in the end.

What a shitty story, I thought. But that was the one good thing about my brothers' shunning me: they never came out to hear it.

For the rest of the day, the men were out searching the area near Watak's marker: the fields behind the canal, the roads leading up to and away from the flag, and, of course, the maze itself. The ladies, on the other hand, stayed home to look after Dawood.

We all sat in the den where Dawood slept. Abo cradled his head and stroked his cheeks. Nabeela and Sadaf Khala sat behind him, rubbing his belly and reciting surahs they memorized as children. Moor held his feet. Just held them. Hawa Khala and Shireen were running back and forth from the kitchen, cooking all his favorite meals (samosas, shorwa, landi, and halwa), placing them before his nose, and stealing them away when they failed to wake him.

I sat in the middle of the room and told my story, over and over, until I began to forget little facts I mentioned earlier, which Nabeela Khala (more than anyone else) would correct. But she wasn't even mean about it. "Wa Marwand," she would say, softly, almost as though she didn't want to wake Dawood, "didn't Gul say this?"

"Didn't you fail here?"

"Weren't there five soldiers?"

"Six Kochian?"

"Two interpreters?"

"Weren't you afraid of the maze more than the road?"

"Wasn't the second visitor the Thief?"

"And didn't you forget to ask the cement-man his name?"

I said yes, every time, to every question, late into the night, until Moor sent me away to sleep a sleep that wouldn't come. For hours afterward, I could hear the echo of a sad song I knew belonged to Shireen, but which I wished were coming from me.

"Marwand," Moor whispered to me in the room where I pretended to sleep.

Gwora and Mirwais lay on one side of her, and I was on the other.

Agha was still out on the roads.

"Marwand," Moor whispered again. And with her eyes closed, she felt for the gauze wrapped around my finger and held my hand like when I was little. "I wasn't here for Gul's birth," she said. "Or Dawood's. I blessed their lives from thousands of miles away, over the phone, while my sisters wept on the other end. Marwand, do you remember the last time we came? Gul almost died from a fever. An everyday fever. A few days after that, Dawood got kicked in his chest by a donkey. It should've caved his heart in. Do you remember?"

I said that I did.

"I don't know what it is. What it is that I do to them. I'm not there for their births. I'm away their whole lives, and as soon as I come back, all my duas become curses. Your father. He almost lost himself when his brother died. It's a terrible, terrible thing, my little bird. It's like waking up one morning without a limb or an organ. Without your lungs. Your skin."

She squeezed my hand and an ache shot through me.

"Marwand," she said, "once more."

I told it slow this time. Giving her every single detail. Every sigh and breath and beat. Every image from the road. Some real. Some not. Like this, I took as long as I could before getting to the part where I failed. Where all our sorrows began.

Moor fell asleep sometime between the carcass and the marker.

In the morning, when the men returned without Gul, the

news of his loss got all the way back to my missing maamaa, Abdul-Abdul, who finally decided to come home from the base.

The Tale of Our Ghost Maamaa Abdul-Abdul

According to Agha (and a few other sources to be left unnamed), Abdul-Abdul was secretly a distant cousin adopted by Moor's family after his parents were killed in a Soviet bombing. But Baba raised him like a son, and Moor loved him like a brother, and even though I'd never actually met him or seen him in real life, she always made sure I considered him a maamaa.

"He just has a bad habit of disappearing," she used to say.

Started young too. As a kid in Pakistan, he'd vanish for hours among the tents in the camp. Rahmutallah Maamaa would search for him all day, only to find him in bed the next morning, stinking of naswar.

Moor said that in Baba's youth, he would beat Abdul-Abdul to the brink of exhaustion, and after he got too old for it, Rahmutallah Maamaa inherited the switch and the belt, but, sadly, Abdul-Abdul never accepted the punishments or the life of the farm. When Moor's family returned to Logar in '98, Abdul-Abdul didn't follow them, knowing that there was no place for him in a T-run state.

For a while, Moor's family thought they'd lost Abdul-Abdul to the cityscape. Until the American invasion in '01, which, in a way, sort of saved Abdul-Abdul. Our ghost maamaa found himself an occupation as a translator, which didn't require too much education or experience, immediately put him in a position of power, allowed him to spend most of his time at a fortified base, and, best of all, paid him pretty well. Soon afterward, he returned to his family in Logar, wearing some crisp fatigues, an air of authority, and an envelope of cash. Although the source of his income was an issue for Rahmutallah Maamaa (especially since the Ts still had a presence in Naw'e Kaleh), Baba was cool with the new cash flow and welcomed his son back into the family.

Around the time that Gul got lost in the maze, Abdul-Abdul had been caught up in a six-month stint in Kandahar, assisting the marines or the special forces with a top secret operation. But on the second day of Gul's absence, when word got back to Abdul-Abdul's base, he decided to come home with a foolproof plan to save his little brother.

لوگر

On the Thirty-Fifth Day

Abdul-Abdul announced his plan before the entire family.

Well, except for the kids.

Me and Zia had to sneak up to the corner of the roof right above Baba's room, where we inched as close as possible to an open window and eavesdropped on the proposal. In a voice as sweet as it was brittle, Abdul-Abdul claimed that during his time with the American military, he'd accrued himself quite a few favors. So much so, he went on to say, that if Baba and Abo let him call in the Americans—with their radar and their night vision and their robot's eyes—he could find Gul within a few hours.

Honestly, it seemed like a good idea. Or, at least, the best idea we had. Though there were a few pressing issues. Abo, who was quite familiar with her son's propensity for bullshit, wanted to know how/why the Americans would help Abdul-Abdul look for Gul, when they still hadn't found that Saudi they'd been trying to get at for the past four years.

"Sweet Mother," Abdul-Abdul said, "if I could reveal such information, I would, but it is precisely because the Americans trust me with their secrets that they will be willing to return all the favors I've done for them."

"The Taliban will give us trouble," Rahmutallah said.

"Your neighbors too," Agha added.

"The Taliban are finished," Ruhollah spoke up, defending his older brother.

Abdul-Abdul agreed, arguing that in a matter of months the Ts wouldn't even be an issue in Logar, that from their base in Kabul, the Americans were coming to fully secure all the bordering provinces, that the Ts hadn't pulled off a successful bombing or an ambush in months, that they were fighting the most technologically advanced military force on the planet with rusted Kalashnikovs and cheap IEDs, and that it was only blind will, fear, Pakistani brainwashing, and suicidal tendencies that kept them fighting.

Wallah, it was a convincing speech. Started in Farsi, switched to English, and then ended with Pakhto. According to Agha, Abdul-Abdul was known all over Logar for how smoothly and quickly he could weave a parchment of bullshit (in four different languages!), but it was still impressive to hear it up close. His argument was so damning and so fast. I wondered if he needed to rehearse.

In the end, Baba and Rahmutallah Maamaa decided to go along with Abdul-Abdul's plan. The men had lost their confidence in themselves and were willing to try anything. The whole meeting, Agha was pretty quiet and didn't object to anything in front of the family. Immediately afterward, he sought out

Rahmutallah Maamaa and spoke to him, one on one, in the guest room.

Me and Zia shadowed them along the roof.

Agha started in Pakhto.

"For the sake of God," he said, "don't let your brother do this."

"It's been two days, Shagha. If Gul is not already dead, then someone has got him."

"There are other ways. We'll get more men. Weapons. We'll spread word to every house in the province that if someone's holding the boy for ransom—"

"If they're still holding him, it's not for ransom."

"God forbid."

"Such things happen."

"But the village knows him. You. Your father."

"And where is the village? Why hasn't it spoken? Two days and we've heard only silence from our neighbors. You've been gone a long time, Shagha. The village has changed. The people are not like they used to be."

"Who changed the village? The people?"

"Boys don't just vanish from the earth. Bodies turn up. Ransom notes. Fingers or ears. Something always turns up. Except when . . ."

"God forbid."

"He thinks he's a man, you know, but he's just a boy."

Agha said something in Pakhto, real quiet, and then the both of them switched to Farsi, going back and forth like that for a few rounds.

I asked Zia to translate, but he said it was the same. "Your father doesn't want my father to allow it, but my father has to."

"No, he doesn't," I said.

Zia looked at me, but before he could reply, Agha hollered my name at the top of his lungs. He called for my brothers and Moor, and he was in such a rage, I slipped off the roof with my muscles twitching.

The whole family gathered in the orchard, surrounding the two Corollas parked underneath the apple trees. Abdul-Abdul and Ruhollah were in one car, heading out to the nearest base to ask for their big favor, while me, my brothers, and Moor were in the other car with Agha, who was driving us back to his own compound.

After some hasty goodbyes, our car started up the path toward the big blue gate, with Abdul-Abdul following close behind. Moor sat in the back seat with my brothers, and I rode shotgun. Far as I knew, Agha didn't tell her why we were leaving, and she didn't ask. None of us wanted to go, Moor especially, and everyone knew, but no one argued either. We just went along with what was being done by our father, without a word, even if it might not be undone.

We fast approached the big blue gate. Someone had to open it for us. Zia was the one. And, Wallah, before anyone else noticed, before anyone else saw them waiting just beyond the gate (about to knock), I saw the butcher and his son, and there, sitting sleepy upon a beautiful black donkey, was our Gul.

2

لوگر

On the Thirty-Fifth Day

Gul's return broke something in me, in the whole family.

As he got off his donkey and limped in through the gate with the help of the butcher and his son, me and Agha ran to him. We were the first ones to touch him, and that was when everyone else caught sight of him. His skull was wrapped in bandages, his face a mess of cuts and scratches, even his big black mustache had the line of a wound running through it. He hugged me and held my hand as I let loose, sobbing away like on the day Budabash first bit me.

"Gul," I said, wiping snot with my gauze, "I thought you died."

"Did you really?" he said, still sort of dazed.

"I did, Gul. Wallah, I did."

"I promise—" he started just before Moor snatched him away, and for a quarter of a second I almost resented her for it. She clutched him to her, the white of his kameez rippling against the blue of her burqa. Next, Ruhollah and Abdul-Abdul snuck forward and took up their share of Gul's grace, at which point the whole family began to move in and through and over the top of the Corollas, toward the boy who had returned. Almost everyone in the family started circling toward him, to hold him and kiss him or at least to touch him, and when their turn quickly passed, they went up to the butcher and his son to thank them.

Only Zia hung back near the gate. He had probably been the first one with a shot at welcoming Gul, but he didn't. When I went up to him later on, and he saw me coming, he slipped away down the side trail of the compound, toward the main gate.

Everyone else continued to cry big sloppy tears, without shame, without tissues, wiping their snot and their dribble on their skirts and their hijabs and their beards. Even Agha cried a little. There was so much tenderness in that orchard, it got to be too much—condensing and collecting—but before it had a chance to reach its peak, Gul sobered everyone up.

"Where is Dawood?" he asked.

We went to show him.

As soon as Gul entered the room where Dawood slept, he smiled and seemed to see something in his brother the rest of us didn't. Dawood's nose started twitching and sniffing, and by the time Gul sat next to him, his hand above Dawood's mouth, about to touch his lips, Dawood's eyes shot open. He sat up too quick, groggy and confused, seeing the whole of his family trying to squeeze into his chamber, and he glanced to Gul and reached for his fingers, and they both held hands for a bit. The first and the last time I saw them do it.

"How you feeling?" Gul asked.

"Hungry," Dawood replied.

We went from tears to laughter to tears again and eventually settled on soft smiles. Soon afterward, Agha and Rahmutallah heeded Dawood's desire and went out to buy a few kilos of meat while Zia's mom and Moor and her sisters and even Abo rushed out to the tandoor to start up the fires. And just like that, the family decided it was time for a feast.

That night we laid out a distarkhan in the orchard, hung lamps in the apple trees, ran two lines of mosquito netting from one wall to the other, which draped down to the dirt, shimmering in the lamplight like spiderwebs, and we invited the butcher's family to eat and drink with us.

During the feast, I sat near the butcher's son. His name was Hameed, and even with the bruises Gul gave him a few days ago, he still held pretty. Abo sat him as far away from Nabeela as she could. He spoke Farsi in an accent Moor had a little trouble translating. A northern dialect, she told me, maybe from his mother. Everyone's eyes (except Nabeela's) were fixed on him. We were all eager to hear the story of how he saved Gul, and he knew it. So he waited awhile, eating dainty bites of rice, and about halfway through dinner, he finally obliged us.

Supposedly, on his way toward Wagh Jan, Hameed stopped by a canal near his home to wash his pretty face, but when he saw a scattering of flower petals and blood drops running with the water, he stopped and followed the petals up the canal, almost a mile, until he got to a small makeshift bridge of branches and mud. He spotted Gul caught up in the bridge, his mouth barely above the water, his head gashed and leaking. A mess of dust and dried blood. The butcher's son said he tried to stir Gul awake, but seeing he was knocked out deep, he picked him up out of the water and threw him over his shoulder without even wringing him dry. Then he carried Gul all the way back to his house, almost a mile or so. There, his mother and father fed him and clothed him until Gul was well enough to head home.

The family nearly applauded, thanking Hameed over and over, in three different languages. To repay him for his kindness, Abo offered him food and money and blessings. She offered him Dawood and Gul as assistants in his father's shop. She offered him her home as a sanctuary and her husband as a source of guidance. And she offered him almost everything and everyone she loved or controlled except for the one person he truly desired.

Nabeela was oddly quiet throughout dinner.

When the butcher's family finally left in the night, thanking us for our hospitality but knowing we were obligated to offer more in the coming days, the rest of us, I mean the rest of Moor's family, all the ladies and the men, all the kids and even the babies, gathered in the beranda so that Dawood, while still munching on the bone of a spent chicken, could start the story of the maze.

The Tale of the Two Mazes

"Marwand was taking a ghwul," Dawood started. "Zia was having a prayer, and Gul was losing his mind because for the first time in forever no one was listening to him. Meanwhile, I was sitting under the mulberry tree, dying of hunger, when some big black shadow of a thing jumped up out the chinar and flew off into the maze."

"It wasn't a shadow," Gul interrupted. "It was Budabash."

"So then Gul comes up to me, and he's jabbering about Budabash, losing his mind even worse than before, and he is saying we need to run off into the maze after that shadow, except he didn't say shadow, he said—" Dawood sucked loudly from one bone, tossed it aside into a little pile in the corner of the beranda, and picked up another.

"And he goes off past the chinar and he can't find Marwand or Zia or he did find one of them. I don't know. But anyways he's mad as hell and he sprints off into the maze after the shadow he thought was Budabash."

"It *was* Budabash," Gul repeated.

"And me, being the sweetie I am, I go and run after him to make sure he don't get eaten."

"But you couldn't keep up?" I asked.

"No, I could keep up," he said, sucking another bone. "I did keep up. But I hadn't eaten and my leg was cramping and Gul had a head start. The whole time I was right behind him. I was keeping up. Wallah, I wasn't going to lose him. I wasn't going to lose my brother. But as I was running, the walls of the maze started closing in real slow. And right when I thought to myself that a man might get stuck in such a tight alley, this rush of wind hit me with all of these white flowers and this sand and the walls closed in so tight that—"

"You got stuck?" Ruhollah Maamaa laughed.

"Just for a few minutes," Dawood said. "I got unstuck. Eventually. But my clothes tore up and I'd lost Gul's scent and I had no other way to go. So that's why I headed back toward Marwand and Zia, but at some point, I think, I fell asleep."

"Did you have any dreams?" someone asked.

"I did," he said. "I dreamt of a long distarkhan, stretching for miles, where we laughed and ate and never got hungry or lost again."

There were no more bones to gnaw. Dawood's story was over.

Gul picked up the thread.

"First of all," Gul said, "I saw Budabash. Our Budabash. Four legs, two eyes, one scar, and a bunch of teeth. Not a shadow. Not a demon. Not anything else but—"

"We understand, Gul. On with the rest of it," Rahmutallah Maamaa said.

"All right, well, Budabash leaps out of the trees and flies into the maze, but he leaves a path of black tracks behind him—"

"Never saw any tracks," Dawood said.

"And noticing the black tracks, I try to get Zia and Marwand to get going, but Marwand was wet in his shit and Zia was pretending to pray. So I let them both be and called for Dawood, and we ran off after Budabash, but Dawood, being as slow as he is, started falling behind, and I tried to slow down too, but the black tracks of tar were getting smaller as we were running deeper, and I was afraid I was going to lose Budabash again, and so I started running faster, and Dawood's yelping and wheezing fell behind, until I couldn't hear him at all anymore and it was just me and the tracks and the maze and—"

"But the walls didn't close in?" I asked, and a few of us glanced quickly at Dawood.

"A little bit they did," Gul continued, "but I think I went a different route because the walls opened up wide too, and then they closed in a little, and then they got even wider, the space between the walls, but also the space between each door, because in the beginning there were so many doors and gates, you know, at least one or two gates or doorways for each compound, but they stopped appearing, and the other odd thing was that all the walls were changing color. Nothing crazy, like green or blue, but just different shades of red and brown, which got darker as I ran deeper, until the trail and the walls and the maze itself turned into a mud so black I couldn't make out Budabash's tracks anymore, and by the time I stopped running, about to die of breath, I couldn't see a thing in that black maze in that black night. Almost blind, I wandered about for a few minutes and decided to knock on one of the doors and ask some kind neighbor for their protection, but I couldn't find me a single door. I felt along the walls for hours, looking for some touch of steel or iron, but it was just mud. And the whole time I had this odd feeling that something was near me, and sometimes I felt as if the thing that was near me was watching me, maybe protecting me, maybe hunting me, and sometimes I got this feeling in my heart that I wanted to find that thing just to know what it was, and then other times I got the feeling that I didn't want anything less, that I would've run straight across Afghanistan, Iran, Africa, Europe, the ocean, the Americas, all the way to Shagha's house—"

We laughed at that part. Especially Agha.

"—to get away from that thing in that maze that I felt was with me."

"So what did you do?" someone whispered.

"I walked and walked, about to die of walking, until I heard the sounds of water, running water, and I knew I was getting near some sort of an end, and I started sprinting with the last bit of strength I had, and I shot into that dark, toward that water, running, until my legs buckled and stumbled forward and I lost myself. The next thing I know: I'm waking up."

"In the butcher's house?" Abo asked.

"No, Ma, I woke up on the road."

"With the butcher's son?" Nabeela asked, and immediately regretted it as she was struck with big grins on all sides.

"No," Gul said, "it wasn't with the butcher's son."

"Well then, who was it?"

The Tale of the Butcher's Daughters

Turned out it wasn't actually the butcher's son who pulled Gul out of the water and carried him all the way home. It was his daughters. His twins, to be exact. Gul explained that he passed out, as tired and as thirsty as he'd ever been, and when he woke up floating on the road, staring up into the prettiest blue sky he ever saw, not a copter or a jet in sight, he thought, for a second or two, he was dead.

A chorus of "God forbid" passed through the family.

Then Gul realized he wasn't floating off toward some heaven in the sky promised to him by his imams, but that he was in fact being carried, and when he made the mistake of looking up to see who was carrying him, both of his saviors yelped and dropped him headfirst on the floor. That's how he got the gash.

See, the girls were carrying Gul to safety so early in the morning that there was hardly a soul on the road to see them or help them or chastise them for not wearing their chadors, though they were right around that odd age (between twelve and thirteen) when girls, depending on how old they appeared—or how pretty—were sometimes expected to stay covered and sometimes not. At that particular moment, when Gul woke up floating, not only were the girls' faces uncovered, but even their tikrais were dangerously close to coming undone as they struggled with the weight of the stupid boy they had to pull out of a stream, all by themselves, or else let him be drowned.

After the girls dropped him, but just before he landed, Gul swore that he got a clear look at one of the girls' faces. That is, falling toward the clay, he saw the butcher's daughter's skin framed in the light of the sunrise, by the backdrop of the falling leaves, and he took in her eyes the color of chinar's bark, her skin like grain, her lips dry and bright, and the cleft of her chin, the tiny scar beneath her left nostril, her eyebrows barely touching in the middle, a birthmark or a slight burn on her right cheek, and the strands of her hair—not really red but more of an orange—falling about her face as he was falling toward the dirt, toward the road, and toward something else he couldn't quite name.

But then he did name it.

Gul, to the family's audible awe, declared that he had very clearly fallen in love and so intended, by any means possible (or impossible), to marry the butcher's daughter, to devote his time to her happiness, and to repay her for saving his life.

He sat there quietly before his whole family, bubbling with love, waiting, just waiting for someone to deny him.

So Abo denied him. "Absolutely not," she said.

The surety of her answer was almost as startling as Gul's declaration.

"Then I'll sit right here," Gul replied, "and I'll die."

"Marg!" Abo hollered, and all the men seemed so surprised by the sudden turn of events that only Rahmutallah Maamaa had the foresight to get in between Abo and Gul as she leapt at her just returned child.

The men surrounded Abo, trying to reason with her, and the ladies did the same with Gul, and after only a few minutes, the family was able to come back together so as to discuss the issue at hand.

Baba urged Abo to hear the boy out. But she wouldn't have it.

"If we go there," she said, "crawling on our knees after some girl who didn't even have the shame to cover herself up—"

"While saving my life," Gul said.

Abo went on: "That shameless shit of a mule coming over here like he was Eesa. You know he's not going to give us his daughter unless we give them Nabeela. He'll demand a badal. You want to sell Nabeela to a crooked meat hacker with a—"

But before Abo could finish her assault, Nabeela, as if on cue, glided over toward her brother's side and took his hand. The two of them, driven mad by love, sat squat in defiance of Abo, ready to take on whatever was coming.

Abo got very quiet.

Actually, everyone got very quiet.

Night birds sang in the orchard, not knowing how much danger they were in. Wolves like Budabash yelped from the mountains, and the crickets did not stop chirping. Abo burst into a barrage of curses so nasty, so complex, so intricate and personal and cruel, so creative and dirty, that I could not help but take offense as she marched off toward the washroom, shoved Ruhollah into a rosebush, made wudhu, prayed, and spent the rest of the night by herself in Baba's chamber, which Baba himself was then not allowed to enter.

Gul and Nabeela were beside themselves with joy.

The next morning, as almost everyone predicted, Abo donned her finest Kochi dress, a pair of her sturdiest shoes, and her biggest, bluest burqa, and without consulting anyone else, she demanded that Baba, Rahmutallah Maamaa, and Moor all accompany her to the butcher's house, where, inshallah, they would settle the negotiations for the badal.

And so it went.

لوگر

On the Forty-Second Day

For the next few days, all the talk in the house was about the negotiation. With the courting situation reversed, Abo and Baba offered up a fair and simple badal: your son marries our daughter and our son marries your daughter. No walwar. Split all the costs for the double wedding straight down the middle.

On the first visit, the butcher rejected it outright, but by the fourth or fifth visit, progress was being made: the butcher had more or less agreed with the badal in theory, but he hesitated to have his daughter wed at such a young age to a boy without any clear prospects. The butcher's counteroffer was as such: his son and Nabeela get married as soon as possible, while Gul and his daughter would be wed just as soon as she turned fifteen—the legal age for marriage according to the interim government of Kabul.

Most of the ladies in the compound thought it was a reasonable request and urged Abo to accept the conditions of the proposition, to settle the matter. But Abo wasn't having that. "If the girl has had her period," she argued, "and she agrees to marry the boy, she should be wed on the same day as Nabeela. Don't give me any shit about legal age."

And no one did.

Meanwhile, I had my own troubles.

See, the night Gul got home I dreamed about a girl in a burqa, sitting on a road, with all these flower petals falling down from some tree I couldn't spot because of the sails of the boat I was steering. So many flower petals collected at her feet, I was worried she might drown. When I woke up at about fajr, my busted finger was tingling with the ghost, and I felt seasick: my stomach tumbling and my head spinning. And to top everything else, I had an ooze running down my leg, which at first I thought was blood but which later on I realized was an ooze I couldn't name. The feeling of seasickness stuck with me, sometimes ebbing, sometimes flowing, but always, it seemed, on the verge of knocking me out.

It didn't help that I was by myself all the time either. Gul and Dawood were back at school, leaving me with just my brothers, who still hadn't forgiven me for abandoning them. When I felt really desperate, I popped my head into the den while they read or wrote and I just lay with them for a while, rubbing my gut, hoping they might say something; but they just went on blocking me out with a constancy I'd never seen before. Honestly, it was a little bit impressive. Back in the States, they used to crack by the second day of a silent treatment. Maybe the countryside had hardened them.

Anyway, with the guys at school and my brothers still mad

and Agha back at his own house to finish some repairs and Ruhollah at work and Abdul-Abdul back at the base and Rahmutallah patching up every crack in the compound and Moor and all the other ladies busy with the badal and with Budabash still lost somewhere out on those roads, I had pretty much nothing to do with anyone all day.

Until Zia's six sisters came out of hiding.

Their names were Bibi, Miriam, Susu, Sahar, Bahar, and Asma. Bulbul—or Bibi for short—was my age. The grown-ups called her Bulbul, which is a type of songbird, because of the way she whistled when she laughed, and whenever she laughed, which she did often out of nervousness, she held her hand over her mouth because of her buckteeth. All the kids called her Bibi because she was always playing the mother. She was not *as* tall or *as* dark or *as* thin as her own mother, but all of those things nonetheless. Hardly ever left her side. Helped with the cooking, the cleaning, the babysitting, and even when she played, she never seemed to sit down and relax. Her eyes were always glancing about, watching for Hawa Khala, who she knew was overworked and overkind and who she was determined to relieve any chance she got.

Miriam was a few years younger than me. Small for her age and prone to getting sick. A pale girl who, unlike her older sister, hardly laughed or smiled at all. Always living, it seemed, in anticipation of the next time she got sick. When healthy, though, Miriam spent almost all of her time with her baby sister: Asma. She carried her around everywhere she went. Fed her during dinner. Washed her, read her stories, played with her, and picked out her clothes.

Susu was only six at the time, but already brilliant. Twenty surahs memorized. Could read and write in Pakhto and Farsi. Multiplication, division, fractions. Daddy's little scholar.

Sahar and Bahar were twins. Four years apiece. Little balls of fire.

Asma was just a baby.

During my first few weeks in Logar, I never really noticed Zia's sisters except when they were doing their chores. But now, with no one else to play with, they seemed to keep popping up all over the compound, interrupting me in my lonely wandering. One day they needed an extra player for their card game, saw me moping about, and offered me a spot in the circle.

I acted like it wasn't a big deal.

We played teka in the orchard, and me and Susu would pair up against Miriam and Bibi and we always lost, but Susu never faulted me for it. We bet apples and berries and sometimes candy. Miriam always won because no one could read her face except Bibi. They had a secret series of unnoticeable facial tics that they used as signals. See, teka is all about outwitting your opponents, making them think you got one card but somehow letting your partner know you got the other. Susu tried her best to teach me to talk without talking, but I never really got it.

When we weren't playing cards, the girls tried to school me. In the tandoor khana, they showed me how to toss dough and bake fluffy ovals of dodi, but after I lost three breads in a row because the fires burned me quicker than it did the girls, Shireen and Sadaf Khala tossed me out. Then the girls let me in the chicken coop, but the little white rooster, George Bush, flew at my hands anytime I picked up an egg. I ran out of the coop with yolk staining my fingers. Later on, when I tried to milk the family cow the way Bibi showed me, I ended up drawing blood instead of milk. "Gently!" Bibi almost screamed.

I gave up after that. Stuck to teka.

But during one of these card games, Zia came up to us in an odd huff. He'd been acting weird ever since we got back from the road: praying seven, eight times a day, fasting in the hot sun and then breaking it with a single date and a glass of water, reading the Quran without being told to, and when he wasn't off trying to talk to God, he was in the pen or in the coop whispering to the cows or the chickens—instead of to me, his buddy.

Zia asked me to talk with him for a bit (the first time in a week), but Miriam told him to hold up until she took me of my bundle. Zia got himself into a rage, saying something about he didn't want to hear any back talk, and Bibi, who was barely eleven months younger than him, told him to calm down, which only got him more mad, until Zia and Miriam and Bibi were in a full-on shouting match, cursing in Farsi at the top of their lungs. I just watched them, but when Zia clenched his fists and his sisters clenched theirs, I got up and pulled Zia aside to see what he had to say.

He explained to me how I wasn't a mahram no more, and I was too old to be playing cards with his sisters, which itself was a sin, and he lectured me like that for a good five minutes, and I listened and nodded my head because he was quoting hadiths and verses, and by the time he was finished I told him I would do as he asked. I mean, he had the Prophet backing him up.

So I fell back into solitude, into boredom, into dizzy wandering, and the big thick walls of the compound—which Rahmutallah Maamaa was always patching or making thicker in preparation for some calamity he sensed in his gut but couldn't explain too well in words—didn't feel like they were protecting me anymore. They felt like they were closing in.

I sat up on those walls, looking out on the black mountains or on the canals between the fields or on the roads we roamed, and a few times I caught myself scanning the landscape for the shadow of the beast we never caught. Sometimes I felt tempted to just leap down onto the trail and start walking, but whenever I was by myself, and especially when I was near the wall, I knew Abo's eye of Sauron always followed me, watching my every movement, knowing, it seemed, my every intention.

"The fall is too high," she said to me one day after I came back in from the orchard. We sat in the beranda. Zia's mom and Bibi were mending a kameez on the other side. "You'll break your leg," she whispered. "I know it doesn't seem like it, but it's only because your boredom and your seasickness have driven you insane."

"I'm not sick, Abo."

"You think I don't see you rubbing your gut when you think no one's looking? You think I don't hear your machine-gun farts when you're squatting in the kamoot? You think I can't see the pain in your skin? It's been a month, child."

I kept quiet.

"The only thing I can't figure is how you got yourself seasick on dry land."

"It's not bad, Abo. I just get a little dizzy, my belly aches a bit. It's not bad."

"No, I know bad. You're weak, but you're not bad. You know

why? Because I cast a blessing on you when you were born. Because I was the one that pulled you out of your mother. You understand? I was the first one to see you, hold you, and to give you the word of Allah. Me and you are connected by something realer than blood. I'll make you good. A few more weeks and we'll flush the sickness right out of you. Bulbul," Abo called out in a boom, though Bibi was just a few feet away, "get me my mortar."

Abo crushed up spices and tea leaves and mint and tree bark and a chunk of brown sugar and the yolk of a hard-boiled egg and a pinch of what looked to be just plain old dirt, and she mixed in a teaspoon of well water, spat a surah, stirred the potion for about a minute, and poured it into seven unmarked plastic bottles. The little ones. She ordered me to drink one bottle every week after the Jumu'ah prayers for the next seven weeks.

"Remember that I'm watching," she said. "Always."

But that wasn't completely true.

Between the hours of one a.m. and five a.m., I knew for certain her gaze didn't reach the orchard because me, Dawood, and Gul snuck out there, almost every night since Gul got back, to sit up in the highest branches of the apple trees and watch the roads in the dark. The three of us hadn't slept a good night in over a week.

Actually, it was the four of us, since Zia was awake too, somewhere in the compound, praying all night long, reading Quran, memorizing surahs, hadiths, perfecting his tajweed, all the while counting out the ninety-nine names of Allah on his fingers.

The rest of us sat up in the trees, watching the little fires light up in the black mountains.

"What are they doing out there?" I asked. "What could they be killing?"

But neither of them answered me.

Gul because all he wanted to talk about, think about, dream about, was the butcher's daughter. All day and night with the descriptions and re-descriptions of every single detail of her face, her clothes, her manner.

"When her mom was patching me up in their house, sometimes I pretended to be asleep and she'd pass by my room and I could smell her, I swear to God, like wood smoke and wet leaves."

It was getting weird.

Dawood, on the other hand, just had his mouth full. Ever since he woke up he'd been gorging himself at an almost absurd pace, until this one dinner when he dipped into Ruhollah's side of the platter they were sharing and Ruhollah smacked him so hard that Rahmutallah got mad and cursed them both.

Again, a little light shone in the dark, then the rumble, and then the gentle stirring of the tree branch we were sitting on.

"Maybe they're looking for something," I said.

Dawood chomped at his apple.

"If I could paint," Gul said, "I'd paint her face. That's all I'd do all day. Wallah."

"You know," I said, "Gwora's a pretty good drawer."

"Yeah?" Gul said, responding to me for the first time all night.

"Yeah, he drew a few sketches of Budabash that looked just like the real thing."

"You think you could get him to draw me a picture?"

"Not right now. You didn't want him to come along with us."

"He wanted to get lost too?"

"Well, he's still mad. Won't even talk to me."

"That's nothing," Gul said. "I can fix that."

The next morning, I snuck into the room where Gwora and Mirwais slept, wearing Agha's waskat and pakol, and, making my voice as deep and as soft as I could, I woke my brothers up.

"Little birds," I whispered the way Agha sometimes did on the weekend mornings when he wasn't working, "you want to hear a story?"

Rubbing his eyes of their gunk, Gwora squinted up at me in the sunlight and said: "Agha?" And just like that the spell of his silence was broken. Even if it was a trick, he spoke to me, acknowledged me; he gave me his word, you know. And before either of them could say anything else, I retold the whole story of how I got lost on the roads, from start to finish, from the gate to the tree to the bridge all the way back to the gate again. By the end of it, they just couldn't stay mad at me. They needed the details.

So Gwora ran off toward the den to get himself a notebook, but when he got back, Gul was there sitting with me. We had to ask him a few times in a row, and in a few different languages, but eventually Gwora gave in and agreed to draw a pretty picture of Gul's love. But just as Gul was about to speak of his girl's beauty, Bibi burst into the room, smile so big she couldn't have covered it up with six hands. When she and Gul made eye contact, she burst into a giggling fit. "You owe me a present," she managed to say.

"You're lying," Gul said.

At which point, she sang: "Mubarak!"

Everyone wanted to know how the butcher bested Abo in the

negotiations, but the truth was the butcher's daughter had melted the old woman's iron will. At first, Abo had found the girl to be too meek, too pale, too sickly to produce the horde of grandchildren she so desired. But with time, visit after visit, Abo realized that the girl actually had some spice to her, that she wasn't all salt and white rice. It started off with a single high-pitched laugh that Abo thought she must have misheard. Then, during the next visit, the girl sat right next to Abo, looked her in the eyes, and asked: "Honorable Mother, have you heard the one about the Hazara, the Tajik, the Pashtun, and the prostitute going out for a swim?"

She hadn't.

And from that point forward, though Abo never actually laughed, whenever her father left the room, the butcher's daughter whispered joke after joke, puns upon puns, old silly stories a dead ama of hers used to share, until Abo couldn't hold back the tiniest crinkle of a smile.

"The girl is worth it," she concluded. "She will return a measure of the joy we will lose with our Nabeela."

The date was finally set. Hameed would marry Nabeela within the month, and Gul would get his chance just as soon as the butcher's daughter hit the legal age for marriage, which, coincidentally, would be right around the time that Gul might start working.

Immediately after we heard the news, Gul rushed out into the courtyard, where all the ladies in the house were waiting to pounce on the someday-to-be groom. Nabeela was the one who hugged him last and for the longest. His love made hers possible, you know. Abo was the only one chilling in the beranda, sitting in her favorite spot, on a toshak, drinking a hot cup of chai but feeling, I was sure, cool as hell.

Gul went up to her and kissed her hand and her forehead and apologized for fighting with her earlier, and for a while she didn't say anything, just looked him up and down. It was her and him in the beranda. As Gul waited for her response, Abo sipped her chai, poured another cup, and kept on sipping. Only after she finished her second cup did she rise up from her spot, real slow, and walk past Gul, out of the beranda, and up into her chamber.

Gul understood. He didn't pout or talk shit or anything. Instead, he snuck into the washroom. Everyone else was still waiting for him in the courtyard, not yet ready to stop the early festivities. When Gul poked his head back out, all of my khalas started cursing.

"This motherfucker," they all said in one way or another as Gul stepped out into the sun, the light of it shining his upper lip for the first time in almost a year. Honestly, I had to admit, without the mustache, Gul was the prettiest I'd ever seen him.

And then the wedding preparations truly began.

لوگر

On the Forty-Ninth Day

For the next week or so, families from all across the village came to congratulate Nabeela and Gul on their engagements, confirming, in the process, that when the weddings arrived, they'd have a spot on the guest list. They rolled up to our gate one after the other, hour after hour, almost as if they'd organized it ahead of time, which they hadn't, of course, because occasionally a few families did arrive at once, and so the men and the women would split up, all the ladies sitting in the beranda while the men drank chai in the orchard. During one of these visits, me, Mirwais, and Gwora snuck up to the roof above the beranda. We lay prone on our bellies like soldiers, and while me and Mirwais just listened and whispered, Gwora busied himself with his journal.

Apparently, that was all he'd been doing since I left for the road. After getting beat up and left behind, Gwora collected all of his papers and locked himself up in the den and just wrote in his notebooks for the next two days straight. While the whole family was losing its mind because we got lost, Gwora kept on writing everything he heard or saw. At least, that's what I thought he wrote. Even after we made up, and he asked me to tell my story and to remap the entire journey, detailing every single twist and turn, he still wouldn't show me what he was working on. He kept each notebook near his heart or his balls, and whenever he filled one up, he hid it somewhere secret in the compound.

We lay close to the edge of the roof, near the orchard, to listen in on the men, but when they started talking about the condition of their crops, arguing over the best technique for harvesting—which could keep a group of Afghans busy for a few hours—we decided to roll over near where the women were chatting in the beranda.

We listened as the ladies were saying goodbye to one of the guests, an older Pakhtana who'd showed up all by herself, without her husband or her children, and who left the compound just as lonely as she came. After she was gone, the remaining guests wanted to know who she was and why she left all alone.

"Not a single brother or a son or even a nephew?" one of the ladies asked.

"She has a son," Abo said.

"Just the one?"

"Just the one."

"Well, let's hear it."

But before she began, Abo made sure to emphasize that she was not gossiping and that she was actually sharing this story for the sake of Nabeela.

The Widow's Tale

"Her name is Khaista," Abo said, "which once suited her since she had been a great beauty in her day. And as it goes with great beauties, many lonely men sprang up from all over the village to wait at the door of her compound. But to get to her, they had to get through her mother and father, decent people, to be honest, and her six idiot brothers, none of whom had accomplished a single thing in their lives except having a pretty girl for a sister.

"Eventually, though, as it goes, the suitor with the best reputation and the biggest dowry was able to win her dusmal. A young, handsome fellah by the name of Atal. So things started off well for her. All in all. It was only after the nikkah that her life turned to ash.

"Although an imam had made the nikkah between Khaista and Atal official, giving them the holy right to fuck as much as they pleased, poor Khaista was beset by her six idiot brothers, whose ghairat revealed itself only in times of ease or during opportunities for cruelty. They had not wanted their sister to sleep with her husband until after the actual wedding, which was still a few months away. So when the six wicked wives of the six idiot brothers reported to them that their sister was pregnant, the six brothers fell upon her one morning, beating her savagely for many hours in an attempt to kill the child in her belly. But being the fuckups that they were, they couldn't kill the poor baby with the first beating or the second or the third.

"After the fourth or fifth beating, poor Khaista, who was

maybe fifteen at the time, was so afraid for her own life that she went and drank an entire canister of oil, hearing from some old whore that the oil would kill the child without ending her in the process. But, by the will of God, she and her baby both outlasted the poison. That was until . . ."

Here Abo's voice got so low, her whispers so quiet, I was halfway hanging off of the roof just to hear her story. Gwora scribbled away at his journal while Mirwais held my legs with his little arms.

"Eventually, she gave birth. . . ."

I scooted a bit closer.

"And about a month later, the Russians and the Khalqian started their killings. . . ."

Gwora tossed his journal, held on to one of my legs and Mirwais to the other.

"So at sixteen she was widowed and shunned and with a baby. . . ."

By that point I was so far over the ledge that one of the guests saw my head poking down from the roof and she let out a quick yelp, which startled Mirwais, which made him bump Gwora, who let go of my leg and I tumbled down into the courtyard in front of all of the ladies.

لوگر

On the Fiftieth Day

The fall wasn't so bad. Just a bump and a few cuts and my busted finger got dirtied a bit. The aftermath was much worse. All of a sudden, everyone thought I was a snoop of a kid, possibly a perv, and who knows what else. Word spread quickly and got back to Agha, who decided I had to spend a few days away from Moor's house. Gwora and Mirwais got dragged along with me, and though we'd be traveling only three or four miles down the road, we said our salaams with a sadness that overwhelmed Mirwais. He started to cry. The only one of us still allowed to.

On the way to his house, Agha stopped for a few minutes by Watak's marker. We parked near the entrance of the maze Gul got lost in, and I stood for too long beneath the mulberry tree, staring into the clay alley, listening for any sign of life: a shout or a curse or maybe even a growl. Not hearing a sound, I knelt above the spot where me and Zia once slept and whispered, where we became afraid for our lives, and where he showed me the evidence of Allah's existence sketched on my palms:

۹۹=۱۸+ ۸۱

When I lifted my hands to look at these numbers, the ghost of my finger rose up with them, wriggling at the end of my wound, moaning, I felt, for Budabash's life. That was when Agha shouted my name. Quick and clear, but without anger. And, alhamdulillah, by the time I joined him and my brothers in front of Watak's flag, the ghost had faded.

Me and Gwora made a quiet dua for Watak's soul, but Mirwais told Agha he didn't know what to say. Agha smiled. He had the too-dark face of a lifelong laborer: scarred and pockmarked, with the signs of charring still drawn across his neck, his forehead, and at the edges of his nearly grayed beard. "Ask Allah to bless your Watak Kaakaa," he said. "Ask Allah to forgive him his little sins, to accept him as he is, and to let him look upon us with joy and pride. And after that, you can just talk to him for a bit; tell him you love him and that you are thinking of him. Our prayers are like gems for the souls that have passed. When we remember them, when we pray for them, they can feel it and it brings them joy. Like this, they watch over us."

"How did our Watak Maamaa die?" Mirwais asked.

"Watak Kaakaa was killed."

"By the Russians?" I asked because I could not help myself.

But Agha didn't answer. He picked at the ash near the base of the marker. Rubbing it between his fingers. He seemed a little lost, as if, for a moment or two, he forgot where he was and when.

Mirwais tugged at his sleeve and Agha looked down and said we could pick some berries if we wanted. He kept on praying by the marker as me and Gwora and Mirwais went over to the mulberry tree. I showed them where exactly I slept, and Gwora pulled out his notebook and he recorded my thoughts. It almost made me not want to tell the story, his writing everything. Just as I was about to take them to the canal hidden behind the chinar, to show them where the shadow leapt out from the field, Agha called for us to head on home.

As we rolled up toward the front of his compound, the first thing Agha pointed out was the crater indented into the middle of the big red doors, which, he explained, was left behind by a Russian rocket launcher.

"Your grandfather built these doors almost eighty years ago," he said, "and they took on all the bullets and the bombs, but look at them, boys, there they are."

Inside the compound, we walked past the sections of the house that belonged to Agha's half-brothers, who lived in Alabama and couldn't come back to Logar for reasons I didn't completely understand. In the meantime, they let cousins live on their portions of the land.

Agha's section of the house was in the very back.

During the first few weeks of our trip, he spent quite a bit of his time and his landscaper's income repairing these rooms, which led to a few hushed arguments between him and Moor. All the walls were built back up with fresh layers of clay, the roofs were patched, the bases reinforced, and, best of all, many of the craters filled in. It was nothing compared with Moor's house, but it was now the one part of the compound that wasn't rotting.

Malang met us at the door of Agha's section. He was a distant cousin who watched over the place. His own pops had sold his rightful land out from under him to a pair of Kabuli developers shortly after the US invasion, and if Agha hadn't helped him out, Malang probably would have been strung out under a bridge someplace. Although he was supposedly a hash-head and a bum, he was also a decent enough guy. The type that is too lazy to cheat anyone out of his share in a deal. "These days," Agha said, "that's really the best you can ask for."

"Salamoonaa," Malang drawled. His folks came from the mountains and he spoke Pakhto with the distinct accent of the hills. It was lovely to listen to. My father took his hand and gave him a hug and the three of us kids did the same.

"The boys are spending the night?" Malang asked.

"A few nights," Agha said. "They've been causing trouble at their mother's place."

"Not these boys."

"Her family is soft. They let the boys do whatever they want. So we're going to work them for a few days. You boys understand?"

We didn't, but we would.

The next morning, Agha had us up at dawn washing our balls, praying our prayers, making dua for Watak, and then we were out on the land. We planted seeds in the fields behind his compound. I flipped the earth with Agha, Gwora dug out little holes with his hands, and Mirwais sprinkled the seeds into the ground. From time to time, my belly started to swash, and when Agha wasn't looking, I had to stop and take huge huffs of the mountain's breeze. It calmed the waves.

Though we worked hard for Agha, he always worked harder. In his youth, he had developed a freakish capacity for labor. His father was almost sixty when he was born, his older half-brothers were always gone, and so at about twelve years old he took over most of the work on the farm. Started as a kid and never really let up.

This was why we didn't see him too often back in the States. It wasn't that he was a deadbeat like some of my buddies' dads, who just got drunk or high all day and then cashed in their mothers' disability checks. My father worked. From six in the morning till seven at night, he hauled barrels of pesticide, drove trucks, and landscaped the lawns in white neighborhoods. Weekdays, weekends, and holidays too. Sometimes when he got home, he'd be so tired, he just sat in his chair and drank his chai and whispered to Moor. He looked like he was trying very hard not to hurt any of us. I could see it in him even then. How hard he tried not to be broken, not to break us.

But that day with Agha out in those fields, that was a good one. The whole time he sang. Wallah, he sank his shovel into the rough clay and lifted massive slabs of the earth and flipped them back down and then I'd get at these slabs, cutting them up, and the whole time he was singing. Old Pakhto love songs or war chants or Sufi poems for God. He had the shrill voice of a mule, but me and my brothers still loved hearing him, smelling him, watching him in the sun. He was there with us in the work.

When we finished, Agha let us sit out in the shade of our nikeh's mulberry tree, at the edge of two intersecting fields, and he told us stories about his brother Watak, his half-sister Zarmina, his best friend Merzaghul, and all the other people he loved who died during the war. He told only the nice stories, though. We sat and listened and watched the fields, the black mountains, the reddening sky, until Mirwais fell asleep in Agha's lap. Then we all trudged back toward the house to eat gul-pee and chicken shorwa.

As soon as night fell, we started preparing for bed because Agha didn't have a TV at his compound. If one of us complained (usually Mirwais), Agha would tell us stories from his youth about how they never had any lights in Logar, and how he'd climb Seloo Mountain in the nighttime to watch the blinking bulbs from Kabul, and how he was almost sixteen years old the first time he saw a TV in Kabul.

"Back then," he'd say, "Watak and my cousins spent all night telling stories in the dark. We didn't need TV or movies."

When I argued that movies had stories too, he didn't even get mad.

"But not our stories," he said. "You understand?"

I said that I did.

Agha's house was only a few miles closer to the black mountains, but the sound of the bombs in the night rumbled much rougher than they did at Moor's compound. I couldn't sleep well regardless, what with my seasickness flowing and ebbing, but the bombs made it impossible to even try. Mirwais slept heavy, probably could've slept through the whole war if we let him, but Gwora was awake, jotting away in his notebook. When I left the room to go and explore the compound, he followed me.

On the edge of the rooftop, facing out toward the black mountains, we found Agha smoking. We thought he quit a few years ago, during Ramadan, so me and Gwora weren't eager to surprise him, but he sensed we were there and told us to come and sit with him.

From Agha's rooftop, the bombs didn't just rumble, they lit up the mountains, glowing out across the landscape in a red so pale it was almost orange, or pink, sending us first a sharp scream and then a thundering note, which over at Moor's house might've lulled us to sleep.

"Agha, what are they doing in those mountains?" I asked.

"I have a suspicion."

"What are they dropping?" Gwora asked.

"To be honest, I'm not sure."

Which was odd, you know, since most OG Afghans have been bombed on for so long, so consistently, by so many different nations, creeds, and organizations, by so many differing levels of technological advancement—IEDs to rocket launchers to high-tech jets to lonely grenades to mines shaped like butterflies to mortars to cluster bombs to motherfucking robot strikes—that they can tell you (with scary precision) the variation in pitch and destructive capability of a missile strike, a car bomb, a rocket, or a grenade. Agha knew bombs. He knew Russian bombs and Afghan bombs and recently he'd come to know American bombs too. Well, except for that thunder in the mountains. It was a mystery even to him.

"I've never heard those screams," Agha said, "but I do remember this story your nikeh once told me about the black mountains."

So we heard it.

The Tale of the Secret City in the Mountains

"You see," Agha began, "some seventy years ago, after the third time the English invaded Logar, your nikeh went off into the black mountains to ambush roving squadrons of the brightly dressed Brits like his father did forty years before him. But the

English quickly took control of a few of the villages in Logar, including Naw'e Kaleh, so many of the families fled through the black mountains. Your nikeh was guiding one of these groups of refugees when a British regiment—infamous for being donkey slow—caught up with the wanderers just as they were about to cross through the center of the mountains. A massacre ensued, during which the Englishmen picked off the fleeing, unarmed villagers, and only your nikeh himself escaped. He crawled so deep into a series of caves and underground tunnels that he became hopelessly lost within the heart of the black mountains.

"For several days, he wandered these tunnels, without food, without water, without knowing in which direction he should pray, without even being sure that God could hear him so deep within the black stone. Eventually, though, just as he was on the verge of collapsing from thirst, your nikeh came upon a secret city within the mountains. A city of gold and jewels, of statues and idols and other remnants of the kaffir fire lovers from which we descended. Best of all, your nikeh was able to locate a secret fountain. After drinking to his fill, he gathered up as much of the treasure as he could carry and started his journey out of the caves. But, again, he became so lost and weak that, one by one, he dropped every jewel he carried, giving them up to Allah in the hopes that He might free him in return. Your nikeh escaped the mountain with only a single golden nugget shoved so far up his colon that he supposed even Allah couldn't see it.

"By then, the war was over."

• • •

"So," Agha supposed, "maybe the Americans with their night vision and their radar were able to see something in the mountains worth finding or blowing out."

"What happened to our nikeh's golden nugget?" I asked.

"Your nikeh buried the gold beneath his mulberry tree and didn't touch it again for many years until we left Logar, and that's what we used to pay off the caseworker who got us into America. The funniest thing was that even after all those years in the earth, the nugget still smelled very distinctly of my father. He loved onions. Ate them raw his whole life. Right up until the end. That's how he lived to be a hundred and twenty."

"So there might be treasure in the mountains?" I said.

He took a long puff of his cigarette and gave me a look like *Don't even dream about it.*

And, Wallah, I tried not to, but whenever I closed my eyes I could see myself running through those tunnels, in those mountains, seeking out that cave of gold somewhere in the deepest bellies of Logar.

لوگر

On the Fifty-Seventh Morning

Over the next few days, whenever we weren't working, we were exploring the tombs of Agha's compound: excavating the bombed-out shelters, climbing over torn-up walls, and hiding in the craters to scare one another. We wondered which pile of rubble used to be Agha's room, Watak's room, or which torn-up shelter was the one where they hid the Communist, the children, the weapons, themselves. We had to stay inside the compound because Agha still didn't trust me out in the open with just my brothers. Then on Jumu'ah—the day I was supposed to take the first dose of Abo's potion—Agha went off with Waseem to visit some friends in Kabul about an old loan and left us with Malang, who disappeared almost as soon as Agha drove off.

Even without supervision, I was careful about escaping. First, me and my brothers waited around for a while, sitting up in Agha's room on the second floor of the compound. We pretended to read and write, occasionally peeking up through a big window to make sure Agha's Corolla wasn't turning down the main road. Once we were certain that Agha wasn't tricking us, me and Gwora and Mirwais snuck up onto the roof of the compound, crept along the walls for a bit, and at the very corner of the compound facing out toward the black mountains, we found a mulberry tree planted just close enough to the wall for a leap. I'd gotten so light by then—my baby fat melted through sickness and work—I didn't even need the head start I gave myself. Nearly floated to the tree. Next, I signaled for Gwora to toss me Mirwais. He'd gotten skinny too, so I caught him easy.

Before Gwora made his leap, he wrote in his notebook. The quality of his journals had been steadily declining since the beginning of the trip. On our first day in Logar, he had a green hard cover with a clasp and a lock and everything. Eventually, he went from hard cover to soft cover to torn cover. Now he was writing his notes into the same type of raggedy UNICEF booklet that I sometimes pretended to use for schoolwork.

"Your last will and testament?" I asked.

He rolled up his booklet, tucked it into his pants, and retightened his partug's knot.

"How about you toss me the notebook first," I said, "just in case it slips out your pants."

He declined.

"All right," I said, "but don't blame me when your notebook falls out your pant leg and the wind catches it and tears up all its pages, sending your secrets all across Logar, to the mosques and the mullahs, to all the houses and the hajis, to the pretty girls."

He went ahead and made the leap—his notebook still intact, tucked safely near his balls, where he knew no one could get at it. Up in the branches of the mulberry tree, we plopped toot into our mouths, picked at the old bullets stuck in the bark, and chatted about the fun we might be having at Moor's house. Even though the toot was bitter (from the bullets, Gwora suggested, which had been embedded in the bark since the early eighties), we ate just as many mulberries as we could before it got to be too much for our bellies. Ten berries for me. Fourteen or so for Gwora. And only five for Mirwais because his diarrhea wouldn't let up. To be honest, I shouldn't have let him eat any berries at all, but if he got sick again, Agha might feel obligated to bring us back to Moor's house. There was always a chance.

After we ate the berries, me and my brothers climbed down the trunk of the mulberry tree and landed on the free earth for the first time in what felt like a hundred years. To the left, I saw a thin dirt trail, which led out onto the main road in Logar and which, if we walked it for a bit, maybe asking for directions, might lead us all the way back to Moor's house. To the right, I knew, the trail wrapped around the house and eventually fell into the bank of this beautiful little stream. Acres and acres of fields rolled out in front of us, and in the distance loomed the black mountains. They stood lonely and proud. No planes. No bombs. No Americans.

I picked a single dirty toot off the ground and plopped it into my mouth, knowing that I was going to mess up my guts. Then I walked out onto those fields in the direction of the black mountains.

"Where are you going?" Gwora called out.

My brothers hadn't followed me. They stood near the trunk of the tree. No berries in their hands.

"Let's go," I said.

"Where?"

I looked back on the mountains. "We could go to Moor's house."

"Moor's house is that way," Gwora said, pointing to the left.

"This is the scenic route."

"You can't tell one route from the other."

I stood on this upraised trail, a little wall running in between these two fields of grain, and both of these fields, I knew, belonged to my father, which in a way also meant they belonged to me. That's how it went in Logar. Lands passed from father to son, father to son, from father to son to father again.

"Wallah," I said, getting a little desperate, "we won't get too far. We'll keep the compound in sight, and as soon as it gets small, we turn back. Or we'll head to Moor's house. Or I'll show you the way to Watak's marker. You just run along this stream. And across the stream is the maze. And between the stream and the maze is the marker. Do you see?"

Gwora and Mirwais stayed underneath the mulberry tree, just staring.

"Wallah," I went on, "we won't stray. And you can sketch a map as we go. I mean, how we going to get lost with a mapmaker in tow?"

But instead of an answer, I was met with the distinct chugging of a Corolla's engine, followed closely by the scraping of the big gate to Agha's compound. We scurried back up the tree as quickly as we could, leapt from branch to roof to the second floor to Agha's room, and by the time our visitors actually walked into Agha's section of the compound, we were already lying down on our toshaks, pretending to read and write. And that's how our visitors found us, strewn about the room, sweating and dusty, trying hard not to breathe heavy.

Our visitors stood around for a bit, immediately sensing, I thought, that something was off about the picture we laid out for them. From the corner of my eye, I could make out Rahmutallah Maamaa and two other ladies clad in burqas. I was sure one of them was Moor, but I couldn't say which one exactly.

"What were you boys doing?" Moor said, revealing herself.

I looked up, acting surprised to see her. "Just reading," I said.

"By yourselves?" She came up to Mirwais and wiped the dust from his forehead. "Where's your father?" she said.

"Business," Gwora said.

Moor looked to Rahmutallah. "He's left them with Malang."

"Then where's Malang?" he said.

"Probably high," Nabeela answered just as she was taking off her own burqa.

Moor whispered to Nabeela in Farsi and they went back and forth for a bit. Meanwhile, Rahmutallah stood up and looked out the window onto Agha's courtyard. He asked us what sort of work he'd been doing.

"Everything," I said. "He lays mud, bakes bricks, he's been repainting the rooms, replanting the flowers and the beans. He's been digging canals for the water too. And he's building up a new shelter for the grain."

"It's taking him a while."

"He doesn't have as many helpers," Gwora said.

"You boys haven't been helping your father?"

"We do when we can," I said.

"I bet the hash-head has done nothing," Nabeela said.

"Nabeela, for the love of God," Moor said in Pakhto, "can you keep anything in your mouth?"

"But Nabeela Khala is right. He doesn't do anything, and he's never here," I said, and just as I did, Nabeela spotted Malang through the window. She put her burqa back on, but Moor didn't because this house was, in a way, as much her own as it was Agha's.

When he walked into the room, Malang gave Moor and Nabeela one long stare before gradually looking away, down at the floor, and back up at me and Gwora and Mirwais, and then finally resting his eyes where they were supposed to be: on Rahmutallah's big hairy hands.

For the rest of the conversation, he didn't look at the ladies.

"Salamoonaa," he drawled.

Rahmutallah said Walaikum. Nabeela said nothing. And Moor skipped the greeting altogether, asking him straight up where he'd been and why he wasn't watching over her sons like he was supposed to. Malang ignored her question and asked Rahmutallah how he was doing and if he was thirsty or hungry. When Rahmutallah Maamaa repeated Moor's question, Malang claimed that he was gone for only a few minutes, helping an old shepherd slaughter a flock of his sheep.

"Just after Maamaa leaves," he began, "a shepherd comes knocking on our gate, weeping to me that a whole flock of his sheep have been crippled. So I go out and see what he's talking about, and the old man takes me to this clearing of grain, where he shows me a whole flock of his livestock, maybe twenty or so sheep, and each one of them has got one of its hooves torn off at the base, so that it can't trot no more. The same hoof for every single sheep too."

The adhan for Jumu'ah prayer rang out from the nearest mosque, and so Malang stopped and waited, looking annoyed that it had interrupted him or else just trying really hard to remember the rest of his story.

"Which hoof was it?" I said.

"The right one," he said, "the front right hoof on every sheep was cut away. So all these sheep are crippled in this field, bleeding and yelping, and the shepherd offers me a portion of the meat to help him halal them."

Malang went on to explain that just a little while after he helped out the shepherd, on his way back to the compound, he spotted a bricklayer crying over his own crippled donkey, whose right hoof was also stripped clean at the bone, and after that he came upon a farmer whose entire coop of chickens were missing their right talons, and then he came upon a hobbled steer and even a cow. All of them with the right leg torn up to shreds.

"With a knife?" Rahmutallah said.

"Looked like teeth to me."

Rahmutallah didn't say anything. Neither did anyone else. Malang seemed so content with the silence, his eyes drifting up toward the roof or toward the window, I became suspicious of his calm. After a while, Rahmutallah finally looked to Moor and asked her what she wanted to do with her boys.

"Let's bring them back," she said.

"What about Agha?" I said.

"We'll meet your father at the mosque for Jumu'ah prayer," Rahmutallah said.

"No, you won't," Malang said. "They pray early at Alo's mosque. You're going to be late."

"Why didn't you warn us?" Moor said.

Malang shrugged.

"We won't be late," Rahmutallah said, and stood up.

But we were.

Rahmutallah, Malang, Gwora, Mirwais, and me walked in during the second rakat of the Fard prayer, just as everyone was bending down to make sujud. The mosque was filled to the brim, so we had to slip to the very back, with our butts up against the mud wall. When I knelt in tashuhud I glanced up from my knees and tried to find the back of Agha's head in the rows of worshippers, but I couldn't remember what color kameez he wore that morning.

After the prayer, the imam stood up in the front of the mosque, asking for donations to repair the wiring in the minaret so that they could reinstall the loudspeaker.

"As it is, brothers," the imam called out, "the families near the river can hardly hear us."

Me and my brothers went around looking for Agha as Rahmutallah and Malang were busy saying their salaams to neighbors and friends. I went from one big-bearded Logari to the next, anticipating the face of my father, his beard, his smile, and just when I thought I wasn't going to find him, I heard what I thought was his voice and felt on my shoulder what I thought was his hand. But it was a stranger: a red-bearded, blue-eyed Sufi.

"Marwand," he said, noor shining out from his skin, "this is for you." And he handed me a Quran wrapped up in shimmery blue linen. "That's to be read," he continued. "Don't put it up on your shelf expecting it to protect you, to love you, without you loving it back, you understand?"

I said that I did, and he smiled at me with a mouth of perfectly white teeth, then he touched my face, my jaw, and walked away just as Rahmutallah Maamaa came up to me, asking if we found Shagha. When I told him we hadn't, Rahmutallah went to gather Malang, who was quietly arguing with a bunch of white-bearded hajis about the negative side effects of too much Coca-Cola. Then, just before we left, we heard one of the last announcements made by the imam. It was about a mysterious series of attacks that had left some of the local livestock maimed and wounded and without their hooves.

"Be wary, brothers," the imam concluded, "for the Signs are apparent. May you be in Allah's hands."

And so we left.

After we dropped off Malang and picked up Moor and Nabeela, we rode back to Moor's compound, and the whole drive there Moor whispered to Nabeela in the back seat. I got to sit up front with Rahmutallah Maamaa, and I wanted to ask him if he thought Budabash was the one eating those animals, but he was so focused on the road or on his thoughts, he didn't even think to ask me about the Quran I had in my lap.

I looked out the window of the Corolla and rubbed the gauze forever clinging to the stump of my torn finger, and it was as if all the trees and the grain and even the dust from the roads were drawing in toward me. Budabash was still out there.

He was still alive.

لوگر

On the Fifty-Seventh Day

When I got back to the compound that day, the first thing I noticed were the wooden poles installed just outside the big green gate. The laborers had only begun their work, so the poles stood naked on the path: no conductors or wires. Only wood and earth and a promise of things to come.

I rushed into the courtyard, searching for my little maamaas, and found them in the den.

First, I asked about the poles.

Turned out that Abdul-Abdul did have some sway with the local government, and according to Gul, by the end of the year Moor's house was going to be the first compound in Naw'e Kaleh with running electricity.

"Our brother came through," he said, as though he'd expected it all along.

Next, I told them the story of Malang's hooves and the imam's warning.

"Malang?" Dawood said. "Your hash-head cousin?"

If it weren't for the fact that Dawood had hulked up in the short few days I was gone, I might have defended my cousin's reputation, but Dawood had grown at least four inches and put on probably thirty pounds. His face was all bruised up too because Ruhollah had been kicking his ass every time he caught him sneaking food between meals. Apparently, he kept on sneaking and filling himself up whenever he got the chance. Beating or no beating. Stealing or screaming. Whatever it took. Wallah, he was getting kind of scary.

"No offense, Marwand," Gul said, "but I'm pretty sure Malang has seen much weirder sights than hobbled sheep on his adventures. We got bigger problems to deal with."

See, ever since Gul got officially engaged to the butcher's daughter, he'd been kicking ass in the classroom, studying between chores, acing all his exams, and staying out of trouble. No more fistfights. No more back talk. No more tardiness or absences or pranks or fun. Everyone was thrilled with Gul's sudden change of habit. Including Abdul-Abdul, who'd been visiting the compound more often to check on the power lines and for the sake, he claimed, of Nabeela's wedding. In fact, Abdul-Abdul was so happy with Gul's recent success, he went ahead and got him an early wedding present: a small Chinese motorcycle.

But Abo wasn't about to let her fourteen-year-old son—engaged or not, good grades or not, balls dropped or not—ride the roads of Logar, by himself, on a motorcycle like some sort of a bandit. She wanted it gone immediately. Abdul-Abdul refused to return it, and Baba and Rahmutallah Maamaa weren't willing to throw away good money. So they decided to keep it locked up in the tool room until they could find a buyer. Meanwhile, Abo refused to speak to her husband or any of her sons until the bike was gone. Gul said he was on the verge of getting her to forgive him for falling in love, but now the issue of the bike, which he never wanted in the first place, had brought him back to square one with his mom.

Dawood had his own problems: as Gul's grades got better, his plummeted. He failed his big English exam, swearing all the words were in his head, but just as soon as he sat down in front of that blank piece of paper, with his pencil and his brain, this *pop pop pop* started going off in his head, and he couldn't focus on anything except for the scent of white flowers.

"I can't smell anything else," Dawood said. "Even when I eat."

So from one side Ruhollah was kicking his ass for sneaking food and from the other Rahmutallah was kicking his ass for failing classes. To make matters worse, Abdul-Abdul came by one evening, cigarette in his teeth, an envelope of cash in the pocket of his army fatigues, and, maybe noticing how big Dawood had gotten, told him not to worry about school anymore because he'd hook his little brother up with a cushy job in the military just as soon as he turned sixteen.

When Rahmutallah found out about Dawood's new plan, he was about to kick Dawood's ass, but both Ruhollah and Abdul-Abdul got between the oldest and the youngest of the brothers, arguing that Dawood didn't have the brains for school and that there were worse things than being a soldier. Apparently, Rahmutallah had looked upon his three little brothers, all teamed up against him, his plans, his dreams, and he let it go. He hadn't kicked anyone's ass since. Dawood was all torn about it.

"It's like," Dawood said, almost about to sob, "he doesn't think I'm worth whupping anymore."

I made a comment about Abdul-Abdul always ruining things and Dawood calmly told me to shut the fuck up.

"Listen, Marwand," Gul said, "you're our buddy and our blood, but Abdul-Abdul is our brother, so you need to keep his name out of your mouth. You understand?"

I did, but I was still pissed, so I walked out of the den and into the courtyard, where all the ladies were still busy with the preparations for the wedding. Zia's six sisters were grooming the flower bushes, forever sweeping the petals and stringing them together into decorations for the walls and the doorways in the courtyard. Most of my khalas were in the beranda, sewing and resewing the three different wedding dresses Nabeela planned to wear for the ceremony. Nabeela led the charge in that department, instructing her sisters, including Moor and Hawa Khala, on what exact patterns and colors and floral decorations she wanted on each dress. Moor advised Nabeela to go subtler with the designs, more traditional, but Nabeela wasn't having that.

"This one day," she said. "This one day I'm going to shine out. After that, my sweet sisters, I'll fall back into line, I swear to God I will. Besides, think of all the guests waiting to see my new designs. They'll be customers soon enough."

So Moor let Nabeela have her way.

First dress was bright purple with these fluffy sleeves, a shimmering—nearly see-through—shawl, and a skirt as big and as billowing as a Kochi dress. Her second dress was the Kochi design she'd come up with on her own and was still all the rage up in Kabul. The final dress she wouldn't show anyone, especially Abo, because apparently it was going to be white.

As I stood by the well, pretending to draw water, Abo called me into the beranda. She sat in her corner, Moor right next to her, and they both made some room for me to sit in between them. After I took my seat, Abo held up my chin and examined my face.

"Your father been working you?" she said.

I nodded my chin in her palm while Moor took up my right hand, unfolded the gauze, and inspected my finger, which, she noted, wasn't healing very well.

"And look how dark your father has made you so soon before the wedding," she said.

Moor and all her sisters and even some of the younger girls were being real careful about staying in the sun too long. Nabeela, especially, had gotten into the habit of lathering her skin with this white paste she bought in Kabul.

"How is your seasickness?" Abo asked me.

"It comes and goes."

"Did you take the remedy I made you?"

"I'm sorry, Abo, I left all the bottles at Agha's house, so I don't think I can take it, but the seasickness is not so bad. I get a little dizzy, but I hardly notice it anymore."

"Don't worry," Moor said, "I remembered to grab the bottles. They're in my purse in the guest room. Why don't you go and grab one."

I went to the guest room and took up the bottle and sloshed the potion around, which had the same texture as soft mud. When I opened the cap and smelled the concoction itself, I gagged so hard I couldn't take another sniff. Instead of drinking my medicine, I snuck into the washroom and dumped it all into the drain. Back in the beranda, I handed the empty bottle to Abo, almost sure she was going to catch me in my lie.

Without smiling, she kissed my forehead. "Inshallah," she said, "you will be well."

After I tricked Abo, I went to look for Zia and found him in his parents' room, reading his Quran. He'd gotten so skinny in the past few days I almost didn't spot him where he sat in a corner of the room, with just enough light to read his surahs.

At first, he didn't want to hear about my time at Agha's house, about the mutilated sheep, but when I showed him my new Quran with the shimmery blue cover, telling him it was a gift, telling him I'd bought it just for him in the markets in Kabul, I caught his attention. He seemed to be touched by the gesture. But when he actually opened the Quran and saw what was inside, he closed his eyes, handed me back the holy book, and asked me, very quietly, to please please please please please please please leave the room.

So I did.

On my way out, I opened the Book and saw what Zia saw inside, what Jawed the Thief—dressed up as a Sufi in the mosque—had done to the word of God. In the center of the pages of the Quran was my Coolpix. The Thief had cut out the square of a hole to perfectly (secretly) fit the camera inside. It lay there, nestled within the tatters of the pages, with the lens facing up.

I stared at myself in the lens and wondered where else I might have been talking to the Thief without knowing it, and I became suspicious of all my memories, of all the people I met on the road, of all things I thought, and then I closed the Book, leaving the camera inside, and I went to hide it in one of my bags because I didn't know how you were supposed to dispose of a damaged Quran. I heard from Gul that the American soldiers at one of the nearby bases had gotten together and pissed on a whole stack of Qurans because one of their buddies got killed. They took pictures too. And while I wondered what they did with those Books, Moor called me in for dinner.

Abdul-Abdul arrived just before Maghrib and sat where Agha usually did, folding his long legs and filling the beranda to its max. We all got together to eat chicken shorwa, diced tomatoes, and onions, which I shared in a bowl with my brothers and barely touched because the smell of it made me nauseated.

I sat across from Dawood and Zia, who were sharing their own bowl. Zia broke his daily fast with a date and a glass of water and hardly touched his shorwa. Dawood devoured bowl after bowl. He ate with his mouth open, without hardly chewing, without even savoring the taste, but his eyes still seemed to glaze over with the joy of the meal. Shorwa was the one dish no one faulted Dawood for overeating since it was basically just bread and broth. Plus, he didn't have to fight for portions. Zia hardly ate.

Though (as far as I knew) Rahmutallah didn't tell Zia to stop fasting, his eyes were on him the whole dinner. Here was the boy he always wanted. His future qari, his soon-to-be sheikh, praying and fasting and becoming so holy it was eating him all up. Even Hawa Khala made saat to Zia only twice before moving on. I'm sure they were worried in secret, but no one could condemn Zia for his devotion to Allah. He was all that they had.

Throughout dinner, Zia didn't even glance my way.

On the men's side of the beranda, Abdul-Abdul and Ruhollah discussed the development of the concrete road sneaking into Naw'e Kaleh. Abdul-Abdul noted that for the first time in six months it was actually making progress. "At this pace," he claimed, "in a few years we'll have power lines running throughout the whole village. No more generators or lanterns, and when the insurgency is finally blotted, our land will be worth a fortune."

Rahmutallah and Baba chatted in Farsi about what I thought were the mutilations occurring across the village. But they also might have been discussing the migration of birds or the integration of harvesting techniques or Zia's hunger. I wasn't sure.

On the other side of the beranda, Nabeela and her sisters planned dance routines for the wedding. Apparently, Sadaf and Shireen had choreographed a whole number inspired by a Bollywood flick, but they still didn't know if Gul would be able to organize an attan with all of the younger guys in the family. Everyone expected me to take part in the attan since they assumed Shagha's son would know how to dance.

See, Agha had a reputation stretching from Naw'e Kaleh to Peshawar to Birmingham to Fremont to West Sac to LA for his skills as a dancer. He used to attan as a kid at all the local weddings, and because there was no war then, no occupation, no bombings, the weddings were aplenty and the funerals so few that Agha had the chance to practice whenever he wanted. He had small feet and light hands, a beautiful head of long hair, and, most important of all, the unrepentant swagger and mock bravado that all great attan men need. His spins were violent and quick, but the turning of his hands was graceful, and he kept his neck on a swivel, bobbing, twisting, cutting back and forth with the rhythm of the drums.

Agha arrived at Moor's compound a few minutes into dinner, but Moor and her family hadn't expected him—at least they claimed they hadn't—so when Agha walked up to the beranda and saw there wasn't anywhere for him to sit, he must have felt slighted.

Abdul-Abdul and Ruhollah both got up immediately to give him their spots, but Agha didn't even acknowledge them. He pulled up a chair just outside the beranda and was set on eating in the courtyard.

"I don't need to bother anyone," he said. "I'll eat right here."

Rahmutallah Maamaa had joined his brothers in their stand.

"If you don't sit down right now," Agha said, "Wallah, I will leave."

The men tried to plead with him, begging Agha not to shame them for eating without him, for not waiting.

"What shame?" Agha said. "Sit where you sit and I'll sit here and we'll all eat."

At this point, all of the ladies were also pleading with Agha. Well, all of the ladies except for Abo, who was oddly quiet throughout dinner, and Moor, who hadn't said a word since Agha arrived, even though it was probably her apology he wanted to hear the most. In the end, Agha sat down with us only after Abdul-Abdul and Ruhollah left.

Before dinner was through, I snuck out of the beranda and crept in the dark of the courtyard until I got to the guest room, where I supposed that Moor and Agha would be having their argument about me and my brothers. Hiding behind a stack of toshaks in a corner of the room, I waited for my parents.

Agha came first. He lit a lamp and smoked by the window, looking out onto the courtyard. He wore a white kameez on account of the Jumu'ah prayers, and the light of the lamp reflected off his clothes in a way that made him seem holy or ghostly. I tried not to breathe too much, worried that the stink of the smoke might make me cough.

When Moor arrived, she sat near Agha, by the window's sill, and didn't speak.

The lamp sat in between them. Its fire was long and thin and did not flicker.

To start, Agha asked Moor why she decided to bring the boys back to her father's compound without consulting him, and in response, Moor asked Agha why Malang was acting as our babysitter.

Neither of them yelled. In general, my parents didn't raise their voices or curse each other when they fought, especially not in the compound, where every word seemed to echo into every room. On occasion, Agha got mad and he broke a plate or he slammed his fist through a glass table, but never in his life—I mean as far as I knew—did Agha ever hit Moor. While all of my buddies' fathers used to beat on their moms (you'd hear about it over the great Afghan gossip line), I was the only one I knew who didn't have to hide that sin.

"You know Marwand has been acting up ever since he got here, leading the boys out on that chase," Moor said.

"Marwand didn't lead anyone."

"He said that he did."

"And he was lying. Boys that age are made to lie. It was either Gul or Dawood that led them out. Your brothers are the only ones with the balls."

"Again with my brothers."

"Right, again with your brothers. The spy keeps coming back every other day with his cash and his bullshit: buying a fourteen-year-old a motorcycle. Bragging about his military connections. Now he's going to get Dawood mixed up into it?"

"Rahmutallah won't let him."

"Like with Ruhollah? He was a good boy before he started helping the Americans."

"He's still good."

"You know what they do at those bases?"

"I know."

"With the booze and the heroin and the chai boys?"

"I know."

"So what then?"

"They have to eat."

"So they'll eat flesh?"

Moor didn't say anything. She looked out the window and

then back into the room, and, Wallah, for a good five seconds she stared right into the corner of the room where I hid. The lamp in between them brightened Moor's skin. While Gwora and Mirwais inherited Moor's light complexion, I became dark like my father.

"And we're innocent in all this?" Moor said. "We don't carry some of the weight?"

"For what? I work. I pray. I make sadaqah. I don't support the invaders."

"Adaam," she said, "we live with them. We work with them. Our boys study with them. They know their language better than ours. Their culture. Everything. And we don't support them?"

Agha bit his lip and got quiet.

"We don't," he started, taking a deep breath. He slipped down from the windowsill, knelt near Moor's legs, and took her hand. He blocked the lamp, but the light of it still shone from behind him.

"Listen," he said, "I've been thinking. Your family has been doing well. There's not too much trouble in Logar. I was thinking we could get a place in Kabul. Check out the schools. I've got a few things in the works. Just from the land and the trucks, we could make a living out here. You could stay near your parents. We could raise up the boys in their own country. What do you think?" he said.

Moor shook her head and touched Agha's cheek. Held her fingers there. Behind them, the long fire of the lamp seeped into the space between his skin and her hand. Their flesh seemed to burn in the dark. They didn't say anything for such a long time, I almost fell asleep. Then a knock sounded from the door.

It was Bibi.

She wept in Farsi.

"Abo" was all I could make out.

لوگر

On the Fifty-Seventh Night

Nabeela found Abo laid out flat in the washroom, barely conscious and mumbling a prayer just quiet enough that no one could make it out. After failing to wake her, Nabeela shouted for her father and was instead met by Bibi, who began to weep almost immediately, and it was the echo of her crying that alerted the rest of the family. Pretty soon almost everyone in the compound had surrounded the washroom. Nabeela, Rahmutallah, and Dawood were the ones who lifted Abo. Nabeela cradling her head. Rahmutallah holding up her spine. Dawood clinging to her feet. They carried her up into Baba's chamber and the rest of us followed after them. We sat listening to Abo mumble and moan and touch her face. Baba brought out his pharmaceutical equipment and was preparing an IV but couldn't seem to steady his fingers. Rahmutallah Maamaa had to do it.

Though it was already getting late when they started the IV, no one in the family—not even the littlest kids—went to sleep for the next few hours as Abo kept lapsing in and out of consciousness. At about four in the morning, Abo seemed to snap out of her spell just long enough for her to tell everyone to get out of the room immediately.

"You're going to catch it. You've probably already caught it. Doctor Sahib," she said, looking to Baba, "don't you know a case of land-induced seasickness when you see it? And you've let me contaminate the whole family."

"Wa, Abo," Baba said, "seasickness cannot be induced by land and is not infectious."

Abo sighed a deep sigh of the sick. "You'll see," she said.

And we did.

The next day, one by one, almost every single person in the family came down with a severe case of land-induced seasickness. The symptoms of which included the following:

1. A bout of dizziness so terrible it turned the earth beneath your feet into putty
2. A persistent sense of mild nausea that never actually amounted to vomiting
3. An occasional lapse into the in-between world of daydream, delusion, and mirage
4. Loneliness
5. Fatigue
6. Skull-piercing migraines
7. Burps the smell of burned saboo
8. An abnormality in the heartbeat causing an overflow of blood to the heart's ventricles, sometimes leading—though very rarely—to an explosion of one's chest

Baba was the first one to fall ill, either because of his weak immune system, or because he was in such proximity to Abo, or because he simply willed himself sick, seeing it as the surest sign of his love. Upon realizing that he had somehow been infected with Abo's case of land-induced seasickness, he resigned himself to his new condition, curled up next to Abo, and wrapped him and his wife in his patu, so that they might at least suffer in comfort. Rahmutallah Maamaa set up an IV for them.

Nabeela fell sick next. While hemming the skirt of her wedding dress—during a brief moment away from her mother—her head swirled and the earth turned to putty and she was so dizzy that if it were not for the fear she might vomit on her own wedding dress, she probably wouldn't have been able to hurl herself out of the dress shop. She lay in the dust for a bit, gripping her head as if trying to steady the sky, until Moor found her and carried her into the room where all the péeghla sisters slept.

Rahmutallah set up an IV for her too, banned everyone from visiting the sick, especially the kids, and then promptly fell ill himself. As he was gathering more medical supplies in his room, he got hit by the first surge of the seasickness, stumbled forward with his kit still in hand, and had to be caught by his wife, Hawa Khala, who somehow was able to take on all his weight, maintain her own balance, and then gently drop him on a toshak. After that, Hawa Khala took on her husband's medical duties but then very quickly fell ill as well. Just by chance, she happened to collapse beside her husband, where they both curled up in a thick patu.

Next, Sadaf and Shireen got sick. Gathering in Nabeela's room, in a big bundle of blankets and tissues, Shireen sang quiet songs for her sister's coming loss. They lay among themselves, as dizzy as lost birds, and seemed to forget all the lyrics to the love songs they grew up reciting.

Moor and Agha fell sick just before Dhuhr, while arguing in their room, where they curled up together in a thick patu.

The whole time Abo never told anyone that I was the source of the sickness.

So I didn't either.

By the end of the day, the only people still left standing were me and my brothers and Gul and Dawood and Zia.

We met up in the farthest corner of the orchard—as far away from the rooms as we could get without abandoning the compound—and gathered near the same spot where Budabash used to sleep. We argued for a bit.

"We need a doctor," Gul said.

"Doctors cost money," Zia said.

"I'll get money."

"No, you won't," someone said from behind me.

It was Miriam. She approached our meeting from the middle of a mint patch, wearing her mother's big purple chador. I was the last one to see her. Zia met her first, demanding she return to the den with their sisters, where she might rest up from her illness, but Miriam said she was as healthy as she would ever be.

See, because Miriam was so persistently sick all of the time, the sudden case of seasickness hardly seemed to affect her at all. She wasn't drowsy or nauseated, and she wasn't that dizzy. Her head did hurt a little, but no more than it did every single day of her life.

"I mean, you shouldn't, we shouldn't," Miriam said, and went on to explain how, according to Bibi, who could still speak without speaking, we shouldn't leave the compound until we were sure we wouldn't spread the sickness to the rest of the village, so that meant we couldn't leave until everyone was healed, and everyone would be healed, Bibi claimed, as long as we stayed home and looked after them and didn't run off on another silly adventure. Besides, Abdul-Abdul and Ruhollah Maamaa would be here sometime tonight, and we'd be able to stop them before they got inside, and we'd tell them what happened and they'd be the ones to get the doctor—not us.

"But you have to understand, boys," she continued, "Bibi says that the best thing we can do at this point is to make sure everyone is as comfortable as possible."

She said this all at once, almost in a single breath, making sure Gul and Dawood and Zia and me couldn't interrupt her like we wanted to do about twenty times over during the course of her speech; but by the time she had finished, taking a deep wheeze of a breath, Zia looked at his little sister wearing his mom's chador, as sick as she always was, and he relented. "So what's the plan?"

It went like this:

Me and Gwora would look after Moor and Agha, make sure they were fed and hydrated and that their seasickness wasn't getting any worse.

"You need to check up on them periodically," Miriam said, "so take shifts and make sure that neither of you is being overwhelmed."

"What about Mirwais?" I said.

"Mirwais will be my assistant," she said, taking his hand.

He didn't object.

Miriam assigned herself to Bibi and her sisters, and Zia to his parents. Dawood would care for Abo and Baba, while Gul was to look after Nabeela and her sisters, which Gul had a problem with, since he—as the older son—naturally had the responsibility of taking care of his parents; but Miriam explained to Gul that Abo was still mad at him over the wedding and the motorcycle. And because we needed to keep her as cool and as calm as possible, Gul couldn't get near her. Whereas Dawood, she argued, was actually Abo's favorite.

"He's the youngest," she explained, "and the most hopeless."

Dawood didn't argue. All of the guys were finally in agreement. We would go along with Bibi and Miriam's plan and start up our rounds as soon as we could.

The first time me and Gwora checked up on our parents, we brought them a pitcher of water and fresh veggies from the garden (cucumbers and eggplant and okra), and we found them in their room, cuddled up closer than I'd ever seen. Her head on his shoulder. His hand in her hair.

Moor and Agha were never prone to displays of affection—except on the odd occasion when Agha was in a goofy mood, and he played at kissing Moor, knowing she'd push him away or slap him on the cheek. Sometimes he sang her Pakhto sindaras or old Farsi love poems, but he always did it as a joke, to get her blushing, to embarrass us, or to mock his own silly heart.

They looked dizzy and confused but also content in their dizziness, their confusion. They gave each other soft smiles, soft looks, but nothing about the way they held each other seemed like a joke. In fact, it seemed so urgent that I hardly had the heart to make them stop.

We needed to help them eat and drink, because when they sat up against the wall, they got so dizzy they could hardly hold their cups steady. It was as though by forcing them to be apart, we were torturing them. But after we fed them a little, and they got to lie back down and cuddle up underneath the patu again, they seemed to forget what we did to them. What they did to each other.

"We're going," I told them.

"Yes," Moor said, nuzzling closer to Agha, "you should go now."

We left in a hurry.

Though it was getting dark by then, Abdul-Abdul and Ruhollah still hadn't returned to eat their nightly dinner. In the courtyard, we kids gathered to update one another on the conditions of our patients and we heard many of the same symptoms repeated over again. Dizziness and confusion. A lack of appetite. An excess of affection. And the odd feeling that the sick weren't actually there in the room with you, that they were off someplace else, together, but still lonesome.

"Well, the food is not as important, but no matter what," Miriam said, "you've got to keep them hydrated."

During our second visit, Moor and Agha's mood had changed a great deal. I mean, they were still huddled up together, uncomfortably close, but they seemed to be on the brink of tears now. Their touching was more desperate. They clung to each other. We sat them back up, and we made them each drink two cups of water, which they could hardly seem to swallow, their seasickness was getting so bad. After that, we laid them back down and started to wipe their foreheads and their faces with wet towels.

As I soaked Agha's forehead, I placed my right hand on his chest and he touched it and asked me what happened to my finger. I told him Budabash stole it from me.

"You know," he said, "I once stole a finger too."

And so he began.

The Tale of the Stolen Finger

"Listen, little bird," he whispered to me like when I was a child, "in the autumn of '82 Naw'e Kaleh was dying of hunger.

Our rebellion raged in the mountains and on the roads, but the Soviets took vengeance upon the village. In Wagh Jan, they machine-gunned a bus full of schoolboys because they resembled mujahideen. In the Tangee, they littered the trails with mines shaped like butterflies, and our children picked these up, thinking them toys, only to watch their hands turn into mist. Little bird, even our singers were not spared. Poor Doray Logari, who never touched a rifle in his life, who healed our wounds with his songs, was shot through his heart while singing a ballad.

His final verse.

"We were so afraid to leave our homes, our crops rotted in the fields.

"Fortunately, your nikeh had foreseen the hungers of war. We stored up rice and grain.

"Your Zarmina Khala was not so lucky. She lived over near Wagh Jan with her small children and her husband. He was a lawyer by trade and knew nothing of war, of rationing. They were starving worse than us.

"You have to understand, little bird, Zarmina was your nikeh's firstborn and the child most like him. They were both tall and gangly, with massive hands and a terrible pride. They loved each other fiercely but held on to grudges like tumors. And so it happened that even with the war and the hunger, neither Zarmina nor Nikeh would concede their pride.

"'She will come and ask,' Nikeh would say in his house.

"'He will come and offer,' Zarmina would say in hers.

"And so they waited.

"But I became tired of the waiting.

"You see, Zarmina was a half-sister who always treated me as a whole brother. She fed me mantu and palau, and I danced at her wedding. She'd tell me jokes and stories, and I'd work in her home. When I was a boy, she'd saved me from my half-brother's beatings, and when I became a mujahideen, I planned to protect her from the Soviets.

"So, one night, without asking my father, I stole her a bag of rice and snuck off toward her house.

"When I got to her compound that night, and she answered the door, and saw me standing there with a bag of rice, just a single stolen bag, she almost fell to her knees.

"She kissed my fingers and blessed me a thousand times.

"Listen, little bird, when your half-sister, who loves you as a whole brother, who almost kills herself with pride, who you've never seen so hungry, nor so weak, kisses your fingers and blesses your life for not letting her starve, you will feel the mark of her lips on your fingers forever, and her one thousand blessings will follow you across the earth.

"I begged her to rise. My elder sister.

"She invited me inside to share in the rice with her family, and though I was hungry and planned to spend the night, I could tell by the look of her lips and the trembling in her hands that one bag of rice wasn't going to be enough to get her through the month or even the week.

"So before she could tell me to stop, I slipped away.

"I planned to steal another bag.

"But on the way back to my house, the Soviets bombed our village.

"I heard the first rocket just as I reached the canal near where your Watak Kaakaa would one day be murdered. I jumped down and hid in the mud. While the bombs fell, I trembled and remembered the boys from the tunnel."

The Tale of the Boys in the Tunnel

"Little bird, I recall that the first time my squadron gathered together in a mosque to plan out an ambush for the Soviets, we only had Chinese rifles, a few Kalashnikovs, and a single rocket launcher. Most of us carried these old English rifles captured during the Anglo-Afghan Wars. Our commanders warned us that in the morning the Soviet platoons would be rolling down the main road in Wagh Jan. With tanks and helicopters.

"There were maybe forty of us. Tajiks mostly, but there were quite a few Pakhtuns too. We'd spent two days and two nights in the mosque, waiting for word from the commanders, whose code names we kept mixing up. We prayed often and carried siparahs or tesbihs from fathers or sisters we hoped would protect us in the coming days. We were all boys from the village.

"On the morning of the ambush, we rushed the Soviet tanks in Wagh Jan under the cover of land and bush, firing from the foliage of the Logar River. Two helicopters roared above us, and the machine gunners let loose. Some of our boys were struck with invisible bullets, clutching at wounds that didn't exist and then falling into a death that was actually life.

"As soon as I saw the tanks, I shot six quick bursts without aiming and ran off to hide and reload. My Chinese rifle, stitched together with cloth and tape, bucked in my hands, and I prayed to Allah it would not fall apart as I fired. During the whole length of the battle, I was scared of hiding and being caught. Of running and being hit. Of shooting and becoming a killer. And all my fears warred inside of me, until they massacred one another, so that it wasn't courage that let me fight, but the death of my fear.

"Eventually, my cousin Abdur Rahman, who carried the rocket launcher, managed to set one of the tanks on fire. We smelled the Russians burning. We hoped they would climb out so that we could shoot them dead, but they only escaped, hours later, as smoke.

"By the end of the first firefight, half our squadron was dead or missing. We went to search for them in the waters and found ten mujahideen hiding in a large tunnel beneath a dam in the Logar River. They were dripping wet, lying side by side, clinging to each other like young brothers on a cold morning in the hills. They stank of shit and the rushing water could not cleanse their filth. I was so ashamed for them; I kept fighting.

"I watched Abdur Rahman run out in the middle of a battlefield. Shoot down six tanks with a rocket launcher on his shoulder. Then die at the base of a tree with so many holes shot through him the wind nearly carried his corpse away. I watched my half-cousin Abdul throw down his rifle, shout, 'Fuck war,' and disappear forever. For a long time, I hated him for that, until that moment in the trench with the bombs, when the sky roared so loud I forgot who I was. And where. And which story I was supposed to finish.

"When the bombings stopped, I ran back home and forgot the second bag.

"The jets returned in the night and punished Naw'e Kaleh with fire.

"In the morning, I found out Zarmina's home had been bombed.

"By the time I got to her compound, her neighbors were already sifting through the wreckage. Zarmina and her whole family, save for little Waseem, had been torn to pieces.

"Because it was impossible for us to tell Zarmina apart from her husband and from her children, we could not bring her body home. We buried them all together, the whole family in one large grave, right near where they died.

"That night, Zarmina came to me in my dream.

"She wore a white burqa like a shroud, and I could not see her face, her eyes.

"She begged me to make her whole, but I did not understand.

"The next night, Zarmina returned to me in my sleep and asked me, again, to make her whole, but, again, I did not understand.

"When I awoke, I scoured my room and questioned my brothers, making sure Zarmina was not visiting me by mistake, and I searched every inch of the compound until I found—in the smallest pocket of my waskat—what I stole from Zarmina.

"You see, little bird, as I was collecting the pieces of Zarmina's family, I found, amid the rubble, the tip of a woman's finger still etched in henna, which I knew belonged to Zarmina. In the rush and in the haze of my sorrow, I must have forgotten that I slipped the finger into my waskat, intending to bury a small piece of my sister on our land.

"But when I found Zarmina's finger that morning, a quiet part of me wanted to keep it there, in the pocket of my waskat, and it took a little while, I remember, for that need in my heart to become silent.

"It was only then that I wrapped the finger in a white dusmal and traveled to her home.

"Watak came with me.

"This was days before he would die.

"There, at Zarmina's marker, I buried the finger and prayed that my half-sister would be made whole.

"And there, at Zarmina's marker, Watak confessed that our sister had been visiting his dreams as well.

"I asked him if she spoke.

"He said that she did, that she promised a place for him in the gardens of heaven.

"And so it was."

لوگر

On the Fifty-Eighth Day

It was getting near midnight and Abdul-Abdul and Ruhollah still hadn't shown up. Dawood and Gul held out hope, but the rest of us were less optimistic. We went on with our duties. Miriam made a pot of sarsar, and before we went to feed our patients, everyone gathered in the beranda, where Zia led a Jama'ah Salah but did not recite his surahs aloud. When he said the takbirat, though, his voice seemed to crack.

During our third visit, me and Gwora switched up our caretaking duties. He fed Agha while I fed Moor. It took a long time to feed them even a few spoonfuls, but they actually seemed to enjoy the sarsar. Though it still made them nauseated.

"Who made this soup?" Moor asked.

I told her Miriam did, and I explained to her how Miriam was the one making sure every single person in the house was fed and hydrated and cared for, and I told Moor we probably would've been in a lot of trouble if it wasn't for her.

"She is a smart girl, isn't she?"

I told her she was. Quick and levelheaded.

"And she's good with kids."

"With Mirwais, at least."

"And she prays all her prayers."

"More prayers than me."

"And she's pretty, isn't she?"

This was the longest I'd been able to keep up a conversation with Moor in two days. I didn't want to stop speaking, but I also didn't want to continue.

"Don't you think she might make a nice wife?"

And it was at that point in our conversation that I realized why Zia didn't want me near his sisters. He always picked up on the chatter first. Who knew how long Moor and my khalas had been planning to pair me up with Miriam. Maybe that was why Zia had been acting weird with me all along.

Moor asked me again: "Isn't she pretty, Marwand?"

I didn't say anything just then, but for the rest of the night, out in the courtyard, when I wasn't running an errand or taking care of my parents, I watched Miriam. The thing was, Miriam never stayed still long enough for me to take a good look at her. Even though she was only assigned to take care of her sisters, she broke her own rules by checking in on every other member of the family.

She went from room to room, her lamp floating in front of her, lighting up her path and her dress, but not her face, which, it seemed, she was almost always hiding. Eventually, I was able to catch her for a few moments in the tandoor khana. She was making sheen chai and bread and I offered to help.

"You're going to burn yourself," she said, and made a point of showing me how soft my fingers were.

She kept her lamp in the corner of the tandoor khana. Its flickering light barely reached the black pit of the tandoor. We talked for a bit about what she wanted us to do if Abdul-Abdul and Ruhollah didn't show up or, if they did, how we might go about getting some medicine, but she wasn't too concerned.

"They don't need medicine. They need us," she said.

Just as she did, Dawood came upon the tandoor and said: "We need some medicine."

In the beranda, we all gathered together and Dawood explained that Abo and Baba had gotten more lucid recently and that they had given Dawood contradictory commands on how to cure the family.

"Abo," he explained, "wants us to go out and collect some shrubs and herbs and other ingredients, so that she can direct Miriam on how to mix up a remedy for seasickness, but then Baba called me over and he whispered for me to go ahead and ride out to Wagh Jan, where we should pick up a case of his medications for severe motion sickness."

We got into another argument. Gul and Dawood wanted to go ahead and ride out toward Wagh Jan, but Miriam wanted us to stay put, to make sure we weren't infectious, and to keep looking after the sick. Eventually, our little argument was interrupted by the adhan for Fajr Salah, and we all looked to Zia, waiting for his orders, but he seemed hesitant to say what we expected.

"Shouldn't we pray?" I asked in his place.

"We should," he said, too loudly, as though he'd just remembered.

We prayed the Jama'ah Salah in the beranda again, but this time Zia suggested that Gul should lead the prayer, which was odd, you know, since Zia had never offered up his position as an imam to anyone in his life.

"You're the oldest," Zia argued. "You should lead."

But Gul didn't budge, especially since the Fajr Salah was supposed to be performed aloud, and Gul's tajweed was almost as rough as my own. Zia stood there at the front of our congregation, offering up his spot to Gul, then Dawood, then me. And, one by one, each of us rejected it, until Zia was finally forced to lead the prayer.

I hadn't heard Zia pray since that night on the road when he almost broke my heart with his recitation, but this time he sang so rough and so scared, his voice trembled without grace. Anytime he had to stretch a verse, the pitch kept cracking in his throat. Fell apart in his mouth. I almost wished I had taken his spot from him.

After he finished his prayer, he rushed off into the courtyard without even making dua for the health of the family. I followed his trail and found him in the den, where he read a beginner's Quran, quietly reciting to himself.

"Zia," I said to him before he could stop me, "I understand."

He stopped reciting.

"It took me too long to figure it out, but I did, Zia. I know my moor is making plans, but you don't have to worry about that, Zia. I wouldn't do that. Your sisters are like my sisters."

"What plans?" he said.

"You don't know what they're planning?"

"I don't know anything," he said, and went back to his Quran, the type meant for little kids. He flipped through the pages and started to recite Surah al Fatiha. But only bits and pieces of it. "Alhamdu," he started, but then stopped. "Rabih," he began again, but paused and started at another spot. "Ameen," and then "Rahim" and "Madeen" and "Sta-een" and "Mostakeem," and though the both of us had memorized Surah al Fatiha when we were little kids, neither of us actually knew what those words really meant.

Just then a series of short honks blasted out to the tune of the theme song from *Kuch Kuch Hota Hai*. Gwora barged into the den and told us to hurry up and follow him because Abdul-Abdul and Ruhollah were trying to force themselves into the compound. Zia sat there in his corner with his little Quran and he didn't move. So I followed my brother.

Dawood was on the verge of opening the gate for Abdul-Abdul when we arrived to explain why he couldn't come in.

"So why aren't you all sick?" Ruhollah said.

That was the question Dawood couldn't answer.

"We are sick," I shouted from behind the gate, "but we've been a little sick since we got back, so it hasn't hit us too hard."

"So why isn't Miriam sick?"

"Miriam is always sick," Gul said.

He admitted that was true, and after a few more rounds of arguing, Ruhollah agreed to pick up some medicines for us, and although we explained to him that Baba wanted us to pick up a prescription from Wagh Jan, and that Abo wanted us to make an herbal remedy, he and Abdul-Abdul decided to head back to the base, where they would consult the army doctors and get us American medications.

With that last promise, they drove off.

Almost as soon as they left, there was another knock at the other entrance. Gul went to answer the big green gate, but after he realized the visitor was Hameed, the butcher's son, he asked me to talk to him instead.

Turned out the butcher's son wanted to pay Abo a visit, and when I told him that Abo was sick, he asked to see Baba, and when I told him Baba was sick, he asked to see Rahmutullah, and when I told him Rahmutullah was out, he asked, very politely, if there were any adults in the household at all. I looked back on Gul and Miriam and the rest of the kids and made a face that meant *What the fuck do I do here?*

So Miriam, with her best impersonation of Hawa Khala, told Hameed that she would speak to him in a second. She signaled for me to close the door and then threw a burqa over me. After which, I poked my head out the door and pretended to be Hawa Khala, nodding up and down, while Miriam stood nearby and imitated her soft voice. She told the butcher's son that half the men in the house were out getting meat while the other half was getting medicine. The rest of the ladies were all helping Nabeela try on a dress, and then, to finish him off, Miriam even teased the butcher's son by inviting him to come inside and see his bride. All in a fluster, the butcher's son laughed nervously, denied the invitation, and started back home, wishing good health to our sick.

But, in fact, our sick were not so sick anymore.

When we trudged back into the courtyard, we came to find that Abo and Baba were sitting in the beranda with Zia, drinking cups of chai and chatting about their plans for the wedding. All of us kids approached them in a great rush but slowed down to a trickle just as we got to the entrance of the beranda. Each of us greeted Abo and Baba as if they'd returned from a day trip to Kabul, and when we asked them how they felt, they both claimed that they still felt seasick, but it was so mild by that point they could more or less get along with their day. It seemed that they had just gotten used to the illness.

Shortly after Baba's and Abo's reappearance, Rahmutallah and Hawa Khala stumbled into the courtyard, then Nabeela and her sisters, then Agha and Moor, and, finally, the rest of Zia's sisters returned to the beranda too, dizzy and a little nauseated but still feeling better.

At the end of the day, Abo cooked up a fresh batch of her herbal remedy and Baba sent Gul and Dawood after the medications in Wagh Jan. Two days later, Ruhollah and Abdul-Abdul showed up with enough American medication for about three people (they ended up giving it to Baba and Abo and Nabeela—for the sake of her wedding), while the rest of us took an odd mixture of Abo's potion and Baba's prescriptions, not exactly sure which of the two was the one that was supposed to cure us. Ultimately, just as the work for the wedding racheted up, almost all of the family was feeling—or had at least convinced themselves they were feeling—strong enough to take on all the inevitable troubles that came with the act of binding two people under the laws of Allah. That was, except for me.

I was starting to feel like shit.

لوگر

On the Seventieth Day

The day before I was supposed to swallow the second dose of Abo's potion, Agha decided to take me to a clinic in Kabul. Not for the seasickness, though. For my finger.

See, with the scabbed edges of my open wound refusing to close in on its center of blood and pus, the end of my finger was starting to look like a rotting eyeball. When Agha asked to see it the other night, he got so horrified, he planned our trip to Kabul that very second.

My seasickness, on the other hand, I kept a secret because I thought my family might realize I was the source of the big infection. Abo kept the secret with me (only Allah knows why), and before I left for Kabul that morning, I explained to her that Agha was taking me to see a doctor for my finger. Not my belly.

"It's good you told me," Abo said. "But be certain your baba doesn't find out. His heart has gotten very soft with age. You understand?"

I told her I did.

Just outside the compound, I squished myself into the back seat of our Corolla with Nabeela Khala, Moor, and Sadaf Khala. Agha sat in the front with Rahmutallah.

My khalas and maamaas—along with the butcher's son, who drove in another Corolla right behind us—were coming along to begin the process for the wedding's paperwork. The butcher's family wanted the wedding to be in complete accordance with the new laws of the Kabuli government, so Hameed and Nabeela needed to get themselves a permit or a license, and even though we were still about a month away from the wedding, Rahmutallah Maamaa was determined not to bribe any bureaucrats, which, he claimed, would require patience and time.

"Inshallah," Rahmutallah said when he started the car, "we'll at least get her tazkira approved."

And with that dua, our little caravan was off.

As we drove through the roads of the village, Nabeela Khala warned me not to touch the crank for the window. Turned out there was a trick to it. You had to push the knob in first, twist it a few times, and then pull out completely in order to shift the window. For the whole ride Nabeela Khala lifted and lowered the glass in anticipation of dust clouds, gas fumes, and gentle breezes. When we turned a corner near a kamoot, Nabeela Khala twisted furiously to get the window up, and when we dipped down onto a riverbank, she gently lowered it.

Except for Moor, who sat in the middle, each adult had their own window, and each of them attempted to work in unison.

Agha was always a little too fast and Sadaf too slow, but Rahmutallah and Nabeela were completely in sync. They turned and paused and lifted with the same fluid motions.

Near the bridge to Wagh Jan, we drove upon the work site where me and Zia stole the cement-man's mule. Nabeela and Rahmutallah raised their windows at the same time, and I quickly covered my face with a dusmal, but the workers were so absorbed with the cement, they didn't even glance our way.

The road had grown. Its cement path crawling into Naw'e Kaleh. But even more impressive than the road were the poles. Almost thirty of them now, and while most of the poles were built up on the other side of the bridge, closer to Wagh Jan, two of them had made their way onto our village, looking naked and lonely.

"Subhanallah," Agha said.

"I'd wait until it's finished," Rahmutallah said.

"But still. Power lines in our kaleh. Subhanallah, I still remember the first time I saw a light bulb. They hung from the stalls in Kabul. Red and green and yellow. I dreamt about them for weeks afterward. Thought they were fairies." Agha laughed. Rahmutallah too.

In the back seat, Moor lectured Nabeela about the wedding.

"It's good to cry," Moor said, "but don't overdo it with the sobbing and the shouting. Or you'll just be trading one shame for another. Your mother-in-law won't take kindly to it either, and even if your man is sympathetic to your plight, in the end, he's going to do what needs to be done for his family."

"No worries, my sister," Nabeela said, "I don't plan to cry at all."

Moor forced a laugh. "Wait till the day comes."

"Let it come! I'll laugh the whole time. I'll laugh so much, I won't eat."

"Alhamdulillah," Sadaf said, and failed to muffle her giggle.

Nabeela reached over to pinch her, but Moor got in the way.

"You'll laugh yourself into tears," Moor said. "You'll see."

"Bet me," Nabeela said.

Moor gave her a look like *Are you serious?*

"I'm serious," Nabeela confirmed. "How about if I cry, just one tear, I'll let you name my firstborn daughter, but if my eyes stay dry, I get to name yours."

To my surprise, Moor agreed.

Back in the States she would have smacked me for betting a walnut, but here she was in Logar, gambling away my someday-to-be cousin's name as if it were nothing. Even so, she wasn't done with her lectures. In the middle of Sadaf's explanation of Shireen's dance routine, Moor interrupted her with another word of advice.

"And if we're able to convince the groom to dance—" Moor started.

"Why *if*?" Nabeela said.

"*If* his family agrees," she went on, "it'll be appropriate for you to dance one dance with him, maybe two, but you have to make sure you stay ahjez. Ahjez and classy. Ahjez, classy, and respectable."

"So no ass shaking?" Nabeela asked.

Moor just smiled.

"I'm being serious," Nabeela said. "I've been watching hours and hours of these belly-dancing videos, and now you're telling me that I can't shake it a little for my husband? I smuggled those tapes for no reason?"

"You go ahead and shake your ass," Moor said. "But don't you cry when you fuck up your dress. Those dancers wear spandex and shorts, not Kochi kali."

Nabeela laughed and wrapped her arms around Moor, kissing the tip of her nose and hugging her so tightly, she fell away from me. The extra space couldn't have come at a better time.

As we got closer to Kabul, the scent of the sewers and the smog raced up each of my nostrils and leapt down into my belly, where they joined forces in a terrible tag team of intestinal ass kicking. But, alhamdulillah, when I stepped down onto the concrete streets of Kabul, my bellyaches softened.

We separated near the government districts. Rahmutallah and my khalas went on with the caravan, while me and my parents got a taxi to a clinic in Karte Naw. The doctor there (recommended by Waseem) turned out to be this tiny, bald-headed Tajik guy who had a handlebar mustache and could speak Pakhto, Farsi, and English.

First, he examined my busted finger, real close, to the point where I knew he must have been smelling its stink, but he didn't frown or cough, and I thanked him in my heart for that. Then, just when I thought he was getting ready to press my wound with a witch hazel's cotton ball, he stepped back and asked my parents why they hadn't brought me to a doctor sooner.

Moor told him that her father *was* a doctor.

"He's a pharmacist," Agha interrupted, "who thinks he's a doctor, and so do all his children, but, Wallah, Doctor Sahib, he's usually very good about flesh wounds. I've seen him patch up bullet wounds like they were knee scrapes. Otherwise, I would never have left my son to him for so long. I thought he could handle it, but here we are, almost three months later, and the gash still hasn't healed."

"You should have come to me sooner," the doctor said. "I've dealt with these dog bites a hundred times here in the city. I'll prescribe an ointment that will heal this wound in a few days."

Agha was ecstatic.

Moor seemed doubtful.

And when we reached the pharmacy across the street, Agha's joy turned into a sudden rage, and Moor's doubts were confirmed. The doctor wrote us a prescription for an ointment Baba had already rubbed onto my wound the very first day I got bit. He was right all along.

Agha ended up buying the same ointment anyway, just in case Baba's tube had been expired or contaminated or . . . well, I wasn't exactly sure what Agha's reasoning was there, but he was so mad, it would've been pointless to argue with him. Instead, Moor suggested we get some food, and though I wasn't too hungry, we happened to be close to Ruhollah's favorite kabob shop, which, as it turned out, was also Agha's favorite kabob shop.

Apparently, more than thirty years ago, when he was just a kid and Kabul still had a king, Agha's older cousin Sayed Ahmad brought him to this very shop.

"Poor Sayed," Agha recalled, "he was the first shaheed in our family."

I asked Agha how he died.

"Sayed was a truck driver," Agha said. "He was making a delivery in Wardak, when the local Communists made a pact with the Pakhtun tribesmen in the area. The Communists told the Pakhtun that if they wiped out the Hazara rebels a few towns over, all the land would be given to their tribes. The Pakhtun eagerly agreed, but as soon as the weapons were delivered to them, they turned on the Communists and killed an entire brigade. In retaliation, the Communists bombed the whole village, and even the roads surrounding the village, where Sayed happened to be driving a tanker filled with fuel. He was obliterated by fire a hundred miles from home. When his father found out, he spent weeks looking for his son's remains, just a finger or a bone to bury, but by then the entire district had been turned to ash. Sayed was eaten by the war."

We sat in a small room of red curtains, filled with kabob smoke, and we quietly sipped tor chai until Agha gave us a different memory.

"When Sayed first brought me here," Agha said, "I refused to eat, as my father instructed, but Sayed didn't argue or pressure me. He just ordered two helpings of kabob and told me that if I didn't eat, he would be happy to take both. He knew. He knew that when the kabobs came, I would relent. The idea of paying so much money for two platters of meat seemed wild to me, but then they came, and I understood."

After we ate a whole pile of skewers and drank three pots of tor chai, we left the shop and traveled toward the government offices, but there were so many checkpoints along the way it took us two hours just to get a few miles. At every stop, there was always a whole flock of soldiers, Afghans and Americans both, decked out in layers of armor and gear, the white boys in goggles sitting atop these behemoth Humvees, almost two stories tall, so high I could never see their faces, which made me nervous, because I wasn't sure if they were watching me or not.

Agha—who had a big black beard and the dark face of a desert's nomad—was stopped at every single checkpoint for a pat-down. If it weren't for his magical passport, we would've been stuck all day. "We're Americans," Agha had to keep insisting as the soldier glanced from the photo to Agha and back to the photo again. Wallah, it was like a secret key into the city.

When we finally met up with Rahmutallah and my khalas, we found out that absolutely nothing had been accomplished. Rahmutallah Maamaa explained that after waiting for two hours to get to the front of the line at the Marriage Certificate Department, he was informed by a clerk that Nabeela's tazkira contained a grammatical error. In order to resolve the issue, the clerk told Rahmutallah that either he had to head to the Tazkira Office for an official correction or else he could just pay an extra "fee" and get it fixed right there. Without even seeing how much the clerk wanted, Rahmutallah refused and walked out. But at the Tazkira Office, the clerk claimed that Nabeela's ID card was a forgery since Nabeela looked much older than what her ID card indicated, and he said he'd be able to fix the birth date right there and then for a small "fee." Otherwise, they'd have to get a signed confirmation from the Registry of Births and Deaths to prove that the ID card's birth date was correct. Again, Rahmutallah Maamaa refused to pay the fee and walked out, but, unfortunately, he ended up arriving at the Registry of Births and Deaths ten minutes after it closed one hour early because the manager hadn't been paid in two weeks (poor Rahmutallah got stopped at every checkpoint along the way). To make matters worse, Pretty Hameed got the balls to suggest he would go back and pay the extra "fee" himself, and if it weren't for Nabeela's pleas for raham, Rahmutallah might've torn Hameed's face off right then and there. After arguing for a bit, Hameed proposed that they should come back next week with Ruhollah, since he seemed to have so many connections in Kabul, and in the end, Rahmutallah Maamaa had to admit that was actually a good idea.

"But it's insanity," he vented to Agha later on, once we were back in the car and out of Kabul. "In the days of the Taliban, young boys would get beat for shaving, and now grown men are harassed for having beards."

"There's no regard for the sunna," Agha said.

"For the sunna. For my age. For our lives. None of it," Rahmutallah said, and spat out the window. We drove in a hurry onto the Kabul–Logar highway, which was the smoothest part of the ride. Nabeela lowered her window and my car sickness ebbed.

"How did it go with the doctor?" Nabeela asked Moor.

"The Doctor Sahib prescribed the same ointment that Aba already gave him," she said. "The one we've been rubbing on Marwand's wound since the day that dog—God curse him to hell—first attacked him. I don't know what it is. His finger just won't heal."

Neither, I thought, would my belly.

As we rolled onto the bumpy trails of Naw'e Kaleh, my seasickness rose back up in a way that made me mourn for my lost days of health.

Wallah, I missed being well. I could hardly remember it.

So, for the next four Fridays straight, I drank Abo's potions on time and in front of her. But with each dose of the remedy, I swear to God I felt sicker than before. Abo said this was natural. Explained to me that purging was painful, and though I didn't argue with her, she chastised me for not keeping faith. I tried to see it her way. Wallah, I did. But on the morning of the fifth Friday, which was also the morning of Nabeela's wedding, I woke up to an ache in my belly that left me questioning all her visions.

3

لوگر

On the Ninety-Seventh Morning

The day of the wedding arrived, and I was not ready.

With my belly swirling and aching like never before, I lay back on my toshak, stared up at the ceiling, and whispered the Kalimah under my breath ninety-nine times in a row, until my vision steadied, my belly calmed, and the pulsing of my finger softened. That was when Gul barged in.

Almost dragging my whole toshak, he took my good hand and led me out the room, through the courtyard, into the orchard, past the lines of cauldrons and campfires being prepared for the first feast, and toward the very corner of the orchard where Budabash once ate the tip of my index finger. Dawood was there too. He cradled a big black bag, looking suspicious. I wanted to explain to them how shitty I felt and how I really couldn't handle another scheme, but as soon as I sat down, Dawood pulled three burqas out of his big black bag, and Gul began to explain his proposal. I was too curious to interrupt.

It had been more than sixty days since Gul had last seen his fiancée. In that time, he'd become a little obsessive about her absence: got into the habit of spending more time with the butcher's son just to look in his face for the places that reminded him of his little sister. Dreamed about her too. And in these dreams, she was always saving him from one little calamity or another. A runaway cow. A poisoned Coke. A quick flood.

Nabeela's wedding was going to be the perfect opportunity for him to get near her. His plan went like this: After the butcher and his guests arrived at our house for the first portion of the wedding celebrations, and after we did our part entertaining and feeding them, and while all of the ladies prepared for the march back to the butcher's house, the three of us would slip into burqas, pretend to be girls, and blend in with the ladies just as they headed out on Nabeela's final march. When we reached the butcher's house, we'd sneak onto the ladies' side of the wedding, where Gul might finally get another chance to gaze upon his beloved.

"And you two could pick out your own ladies to love," Gul added.

"But why do you need me?" I asked, and just as I did, Abo shouted that she needed me in the beranda. Before I left, Gul warned me to keep my plan a secret from Zia, who might get too suspicious too quickly and try to stop us. And like he predicted, when I reentered the courtyard, Zia was there to meet me.

The compound was a bustle with ladies dressed, half-dressed, hair up, hair down, wearing old-fashioned dresses of the red-and-green or purple-and-pink ensembles designed by the bride herself. The younger girls rushed to help the older girls get perfumed and powdered. Almost all of my khalas, who were already pretty light skinned to begin with, had caked their faces with layers of this white paste made in China, shipped through Peshawar, sold in Kabul, and snuck into Logar. The butcher's guests were set to arrive within the hour, so while most of the ladies were still rushing to prepare themselves, Zia's mom was in the tandoor khana with Bibi, preparing the cauldrons.

Zia pulled me aside and asked what we were up to in the orchard. I told him we were just planning the attan for the first part of the wedding.

"But you can't attan," he said.

"How do you know that?"

"You told me."

I didn't remember. It must have been in the beginning. Before Budabash got loose, when he wanted to know everything about me.

"You're lying," he said. "Say Wallah."

"Wallah."

"Wallah what?"

"Wallah," I said, peeking back on the beranda, "I got to go see Abo."

Before he let me leave, he recited a hadith about a man who emigrated from Mecca to Medina not for the sake of the Prophet but in order to see a woman he loved. She was called Umm Qays, and because the man's hijra was made for her sake, his true name was forgotten. From that day on, he was known only as "the emigrant of Umm Qays."

"Do you understand?" Zia asked.

I told him I did, three times in a row, and then rushed off

toward the beranda, where Abo sat in her corner as Miriam painted her eyes with kohl. Moor sat beside her, doing her own makeup with a little kit she bought in SF. Abo had her eyes closed and Moor drew mascara. They discussed Abdul-Abdul. Apparently, he was missing.

Earlier that morning, after a bit of interrogation, Abo found out from Ruhollah that Abdul-Abdul's commander had called him in on a very important mission. Ruhollah assured her that it was a matter of national security and that Abdul-Abdul would not miss his sister's wedding for anything less. But Abo admitted she did not believe Ruhollah. "He said it much too quickly. Like he was reciting it."

"Ruhollah doesn't lie," Moor said.

"No, he doesn't. But he did."

"If anything, Abdul told him the story and Ruhollah repeated it to you, just as it was, which is why you don't believe it."

"Maybe," Abo said, and then, without opening her eyes, she placed a little plastic bottle of my antidote before me. "Drink," she said. "This will be the last one."

So I plugged my nose, twisted the cap, and downed the bottle.

For a few minutes afterward, I wandered about the courtyard and the rooms of the compound in a miserable daze as each of the ladies in the household ordered me to do one thing or another, all of which I kept forgetting. Just as soon as I forgot what one khala wanted me to do, another khala told me to do something else, and I went about like this for a while, being ordered and forgetting my orders and setting out to finish tasks that had already been completed hours ago. Eventually, I abandoned my forgotten chores altogether and went off in search of Gul. That was when the butcher's guests finally arrived.

The men came in through the orchard with a legion of donkeys, each of them stacked to the limit with raw meats, veggies, fruits, soups, stews, and bread. Me and Gul and the other guys stripped the donkeys of their supplies and handed them over, conveyor belt style, to the makeshift cooks near the cauldrons. Agha had offered to take charge of the meats, while a few distant cousins, or maybe neighbors, were in charge of preparing the veggies, the rice, and the other platters. Rahmutallah Maamaa led the butcher's men toward the shade of the apple trees, where toshaks and carpets and kettles of chai were already laid out. The butcher's son walked in the front of his parade of guests and sat smack-dab in the middle of all the big-bearded men. He seemed so pale, sitting there among the OGs, he looked almost ugly. I wondered if he even wanted to get married.

The ladies came in through the main gate, and while the men were still drinking their chai and waiting for food, the ladies in the courtyard sang love songs, drummed dhols, and, I imagined, began to dance for the pride of Nabeela. I leaned against the wall of the courtyard, still dizzied in my stupor, and listened for a bit.

Shireen's voice rose above the rest.

Wallah, Moor wasn't lying when she said that Shireen could croon with the best of them: with the sorrow of a young Naghma and the range of an Ustad Mahwash. Had she wanted, Moor claimed, Shireen could've been famous, but she hated crowds and the eyes of men and only ever sang at special occasions and for the ones she loved.

And so, for the sake of Nabeela, she sang the song of Durkhanai.

The Song of Durkhanai

The tale within the song told of this old Pakhtun chieftain named Taus Khan. Early on in his life, Taus Khan suffered the woe of falling deeply in love with the woman he married, and when she died—at eighteen and in childbirth—leaving him just one daughter, he couldn't ever bring himself to marry another woman. With time, this one daughter he had, whose name was Durkhanai, grew up to become a reflection of her once beautiful mother. Taus Khan loved her dearly and denied her nothing, so much so that when Durkhanai, at the age of about ten, asked if she could study the Quran in order to more thoroughly understand the beauty of Allah, Taus Khan, with great hesitation, agreed to hire her a tutor. And though she always maintained her purdah by sitting behind the protection of a large curtain, she learned quickly from her Quranic teacher and was allowed to study other subjects.

Eventually, Durkhanai grew to become a scholar of great intelligence, beauty, piety, and kindness. For that reason, after Durkhanai turned sixteen, a wealthy and well-respected suitor by the name of Payu Khan came calling for her dusmal, and so, by the will of Allah, and with the consent of her father, Durkhanai was engaged to be wed.

Growing up in the same village as Durkhanai was a young man named Adam Khan. A chieftain's son who by all accounts was spoiled and lazy and uninterested in power, but who was also blessed with a singing voice that made beggars throw their coins, ladies throw their scarves, and brought great warriors to tears.

One day, this Adam Khan happened to attend the same wedding as our Durkhanai, and during the celebration, the guests pleaded with Adam Khan to sing them all a few songs for the sake of Allah. At first, Adam Khan gave a humble excuse, claiming he had a cough, but when every single one of the men from the groom's side of the family begged him to sing, he finally gave in and began his performance.

He played the rabab and the flute, sang couplets and ballads, and their melodies floated above the wall of the men's side of the wedding and spilled over onto the women's. When Durkhanai heard the splendor of Adam's voice, she felt herself drown in its rhythm. Falling into a sort of trance, she wandered toward the source of the song, as if possessed, until she came to the edge of the women's side, climbed the bordering wall, and gazed upon Adam Khan for the first time.

Adam Khan—in the midst of his playing, singing, moaning, mourning—happened to glance up toward the sky so as to invoke the beauty of Allah but, instead, met the gaze of Durkhanai.

Promptly, they both fell ill with love.

And just as I was getting into the love story, Gul decided to interrupt my daydream with his announcement of the attan. Rahmutallah Maamaa organized the dance among the men, drew in a few of the boys, respectfully requested the presence of the OGs, and then finally offered the lead spot to Agha, who, of course, denied him exactly three times in a row before taking up his position at the front of the circle.

Some of the butcher's men played the tabla and the bajah in the middle of the circle as the attan started slow: each step and spin still careful, almost timid. Rahmutallah and my other maamaas and a few of the butcher's men lined up behind Agha. Most of them danced too stiff or too loose, but a couple of the younger guys—with their beards trimmed and their long locks oiled—were able to imitate the calm grace of Agha.

After a few orbits of the attan, the musicians picked up the pace and the men spun faster, danced quicker, clapped harder, and while the older men and the lesser dancers left the circle—sweating and weary and about to faint—the young guys kept going: now slapping the earth, kicking up dirt, dancing and leaping and spinning to the rhythm of the dhol.

It made me dizzy to watch, but it was hypnotic too.

Near the end of the first attan, only Agha, Gul, and two of the butcher's boys remained. Agha had at least two decades on all of them, but he still kept pace out of an odd sense of honor. To him, the attan was more than a dance. He used to say that the Pakhtun would perform the attan in the mountains. He said they danced with swords and rifles, that they used machine guns as drumbeats, and that they danced before and after battles. He said that the Pakhtun loves dancing and war more than God. He said that's why our people are cursed. He said it just like that: "our."

In the end, the young guys outlasted Agha. With his shirt

soaked, he gasped for breath and almost toppled over when one of the butcher's cousins raised his hand to stop the drums. Agha pleaded with the drummer to keep going, but none of the boys would join him. The attan was over, and the feast began.

We ate quickly, and while all the ladies in the courtyard prepared to head out toward the butcher's house, me and Gul and Dawood snuck into the den.

There, Gul asked me to put on Nabeela's stolen burqa.

"At least try it," he said.

So I did. At first, I could hardly get the garment past my arms, but when the heavy fabric fell over me, and I adjusted the headpiece and arranged the mesh of the eyeholes, my balance steadied and my belly seemed to calm.

That was until Gul asked me to get my camera.

I told him I didn't know where it was, and he told me to say "Wallah," and I told him he was asking too much.

"If I have a picture, I'll last the next few years without anything else, Wallah, I will. It'll keep me sane while you're gone, and by the time you come back for my wedding, I'll have only you to thank. You understand, Marwand?"

"But it's a sin."

"Where does it say in the Quran that to take a picture of your love so that you do not die of loneliness in the years before your marriage is a sin?"

"Zia said—"

"You think I'm asking this for nothing. But if it was ever the other way around, would I deny you?"

He wouldn't. "The photo will be blurred by the veil," I said.

"Blurry is fine," he said, "I have a good imagination."

So I rushed off to get my camera and barely made it back in time to join the ladies on their march.

Even though many of the ladies warned her against it—on account of the recent uptick in T-related violence—Abo was determined to play her dhol on the road, to sing her songs, and to let the whole village know that Nabeela was going to be married off forever. The butcher's family had marched toward our house pretty much in silence. A quiet song, a thumping of a drum, but Abo was determined to make a ruckus. We all gathered by the gate of the courtyard with base drums, tambourines, burqas, dresses beneath burqas, purses, bags, candies, dusmals, and a solitary old rifle, which Abo hid beneath her chador.

"And when a talib comes to stop us?" Moor asked.

"I have a plan," Abo said.

Everyone, especially the butcher's side of the family, was more than a little bit anxious about her "plan."

"But they might not show," Abo added.

Of course, they did.

The first part of the march went by all right. Abo and Nabeela and Moor and some of the elder ladies led the parade, singing love songs, playing the dhol and the tambourine, while the younger ladies sang quietly in the middle, echoing the elders. Me and the guys trailed in the back, cooing softly, imitating the ladies, and trying not to get noticed. Beneath the blue veil, with only clusters of eyeholes to see through, the roads and the fields and the trees passed me by in glimmers, in little cuts or shards, as though I weren't seeing the country there before me but only remembering it as it happened. I huffed in big gulps of air through the mesh of the cloth. It smelled of mint, cut grain, and new smoke.

As we marched through the first maze, strolled down the main road running through Naw'e Kaleh, and made our way through the center of two intersecting fields, we were met by a trio of Ts. They moved slowly through the wheat, in a uniform pattern and at an equal distance. They wore black kali, black pakols, but the dusmals that covered their faces were white. They carried machine guns, and out of all the would-be Ts I'd met on the road and spotted in the countryside, these guys seemed like the realest deal.

The procession slowed down a bit. Some of the ladies were unsure whether they should stop marching or stop singing or just stop altogether. Abo wouldn't have that, though. She led the procession forward, but instead of singing another love song, she sang the story of Dasht-i-Leili.

It went like this:

Wa Dasht-i-Leili,
Will you return to me my brother?
Wa Dasht-i-Leili,
He is all I have on God's great earth.
Wa Dasht-i-Leili,
Eight years have passed and still I wait.
Wa Dasht-i-Leili,
I sit on the road and watch for his eyes.
Wa Dasht-i-Leili,
I've heard that he has been buried.
Wa Dasht-i-Leili,
That he has been planted alive in the gardens of heaven.
Wa Dasht-i-Leili,
Like the white blossoms of God.

Wa Dasht-i-Leili,
Our mother has gone blind with grief.
Wa Dasht-i-Leili,
His wife will not speak.
Wa Dasht-i-Leili,
His sons do not sleep.
Wa Dasht-i-Leili,
Our father will not walk.
Wa Dasht-i-Leili.
And he only calls me my brother's name,
Wa Dasht-i-Leili.
I work on broken leg.
Wa Dasht-i-Leili,
There is never enough to eat.
Wa Dasht-i-Leili,
Return to me my brother.
Wa Dasht-i-Leili,
And I will never sing again.

Abo crooned by herself in the fields, nearly weeping, and the Ts knelt where they were and listened quietly. They didn't stop us. As Abo led her procession of guests past the Ts, through the field, and onto the road toward the butcher's house, I kept looking back to make sure they weren't following us. When the Ts were out of earshot, Abo wiped her tears, smudged her eyes, and switched to a love song so popular even I knew the lyrics. It was about a missing Kochaay named Laila, who was sick the other night. All the other ladies, including me and Gul and Dawood, joined in too.

لوگر

On the Ninety-Seventh Day

Once we got inside the butcher's courtyard, many of the women took off their burqas, including Nabeela, who wore her purple ensemble with a trailing skirt, puffy sleeves, a violet bouquet, and purple makeup to match. Abo and Moor and a few of the butcher's women led Nabeela to this makeshift throne in the beranda.

The butcher's courtyard was much too small to hold all of the guests at once, so after getting a good look at the bride, smaller portions of the party split up into different rooms in the compound and started their own dances. Most of the guests stayed out in the garden, decorated with flowers and linens and carpets. Toshaks were arranged along every single wall. The bibi hajjis and the anaas sat upon these, playing drums and tambourines, singing of old love, while the péeghla girls gathered in the middle of the courtyard and began to dance for the bride in the beranda.

I sat near the dance floor with Dawood and Gul and a few

other ladies clad in burqas. We watched the girls. I didn't know any of them. Had never seen them and wasn't supposed to have seen them. They wore Nabeela's special dresses etched in flowers or gems or hundreds of little mirrors cut into circles, which when they spun reflected their watchers a thousand times. With only the mesh holes of my burqa, I couldn't really see the girls all at once, especially as quick as they moved. I watched either their hands or the stepping of their feet or their faces. My heart thumped in my belly. My fingers itched, especially the wounded one, and without really thinking, I kept picking at its scab until my blood began to drip. Just a drop or two, but still.

After the first song, I turned to Gul and asked him which of these girls was the butcher's daughter.

"None of them," said the voice of a woman I did not recognize. "They must be in one of the other rooms. How are you related to the bride?"

"My cousin," I squeaked.

"She's a lovely girl," the woman in the burqa said, "but with little purdah."

Disguising my voice as best I could, I thanked her, excused myself, and went off to find Gul or Dawood. I wandered from chamber to chamber, fluttering about in my blue fabric, squeezing past guests who shot me sidelong glances. But under the cover of the veil it was difficult to scope out an entire room or a dance floor, especially with how crowded the compound had become. I had to look at each and every face, one at a time, in order to understand who was where, but it being a party and all, everyone was too mast to stay in one room, to watch one set of dancers, to listen to just one singer, and so all of the guests were flowing about the entire compound. The women sang, danced, chatted, drank chai and soda, ate candies and almonds, some of them laughed and made jokes, some of them argued, and after a few minutes of wandering about in a dizzied rush, I just knelt down near the farthest corner of the courtyard and hoped to Allah that Dawood or Gul might notice me in my solitude.

Instead, Miriam and Bibi were the ones to approach me. They wore Kochi dresses with billowing green skirts etched in threads of golden flowers. Bibi's hair was long and straight and Miriam's was loose and curled, and both of them wore the slightest dabs of blush.

Bibi put her hand on my shoulder. "Mother," she said, "are you all right?"

"I'm a little lost," I said in the creakiest voice I could manage.

"Who are you looking for?" she asked.

But before I had the chance to tell her, we were distracted by an argument between two of the guests. For a second or two I thought it might have been Gul, but it turned out to be a real girl—of no relation to Nabeela or the butcher's son—who was filming the dancers near the corner of the courtyard where me and Miriam knelt. A woman from the butcher's side of the family caught her in the act, called on some of her sisters or cousins, and, after smashing the camera, escorted the girl out of the courtyard. When I asked the girls why they did what they did, Miriam answered me with a story.

The Tale of the Girl in the Blue Dress

I heard of this girl whose name I won't share for the sake of her mother. A pretty Logaray with a respectable family, a pious father, and an unblemished reputation, who one day decided to attend her cousin's wedding, where, after much insistence from the other guests, she began to dance before all the women. Though she couldn't have been much older than fifteen, this girl was already well-known for her talent as a dancer. Her measured grace never intimidated the other guests and only ever drew them in. Like this, she could almost single-handedly revive a dying party. But on that particular day, as she slowly and carefully brought her cousin's wedding back to life, a secret camera hid somewhere amid the guests, recording her every step.

Some way or another, the video of the girl found its way into the hands of a boy from the village, and he, overexcited about the content of the film, shared it with some of his friends, who shared it with some of their cousins, who shared it with a few interested customers, who shared it with a few hustlers, until the short, grainy clip of the girl in her blue dress, her hair unveiled, dancing beautifully in the summer's light, had made it from camera to camera, computer to computer, chip to chip, before it finally reached the bootleggers in Kabul. These lowly men then proceeded to copy the video of the poor girl a hundred times over, selling them in the markets for coins.

With time, the loveliness of her dancing, of her calm, attractive grace, set a sort of spell on a large mass of the perverts in Kabul. Many men were smitten. Brawls were had over her honor. Fiends were stabbed. Jaws shattered. Hearts too. Until a small squadron of her most loyal followers united in the determination to find the pretty village girl, wherever she might be, and to steal her for themselves so that she might be forced to choose a husband among them. Eventually, word of the girl's infamy reached all the way back to her little village in Logar, where all the men in her family prepared themselves for the onslaught of the perverts by acquiring many weapons and staying armed at all times of the day. The fear and the embarrassment of the whole ordeal nearly drove the girl mad.

But, by the will of God, the perverts never came. It was all talk. Maybe they moved on to a different girl. Maybe they couldn't figure out her exact location. Maybe they drank too much and forgot. Whatever it was, though, her brothers stayed armed, and as armed boys are apt to do, they got into unnecessary quarrels with their neighbors and with some soldiers, and two of them ended up dead. Executed in some field or on some road. Their father went mad. Their mother blamed her daughter and fell into a cruel depression. The poor girl never danced again.

"What a sad story," I said, feeling the weight of the camera on my chest.

"People still watch the video," Miriam said. "Even now, it's still famous."

"Have you watched it?"

"My apologies, Bibi Hajji, but I've completely distracted you. Who was it that you were looking for?"

"Oh, it was the butcher's daughter," I said. "The one marrying—"

"Gulbuddin," Bibi said.

"You know him?"

"He's our kaakaa," she said. "Come. We'll show you the girl."

And with that word, Bibi took my hand, the butchered one, and squeezed my wounded finger, which nearly made me scream, and the two of them led me through the party, past the ladies, over the pastries, away from the dancers, until I noticed, sitting at a wall by herself, the old Pakhtana, Khaista, who came to our house that one day and whose story I never got to finish. I told Bibi and Miriam we should go and say our salaams to Khaista Khala and they agreed. I sat on one side of her and the girls sat on the other. We greeted her at the same time. At first, she was a bit suspicious of us, especially me, whose name she didn't recognize, but when I asked about her son, she relaxed.

"My boy," she said, "is doing all he can, so that Allah does not abandon Naw'e Kaleh."

The Tale of Khaista Khala and Mullah Mansour

Apparently, sometime after her husband died and she fled Logar with his extended family, Khaista Khala was able to find work sewing garments in Pakistan. From the meager wages she accumulated and by never sleeping, hardly eating, and remaining patient with the will of Allah, Khaista was able to raise up her son, Mansour, all on her own. When her child wasn't hustling tesbihs at the market, Khaista was able to convince a local mullah to accept him into a madrassa, where he would be fed at least one meal daily.

The poison she drank and the beatings she suffered as a young girl had done nothing to retard her child's mind, and, in fact, her son was exceedingly curious and bright. He took quickly to the Quran, enjoying the lyrical quality of the verses, the philosophical implications of the message, and the emphasis Allah always placed upon reserving justice for the oppressed and the abandoned. The Prophet, too, grew up with no father, he used to tell his mother, and she would say that the Prophet, peace and blessings be upon him, knew many hardships and sorrows and that each one only made him more beloved to his Creator, and this filled her son with a joy, which was her life.

With time, the boy grew from a student into a man, into a qari, into a well-respected scholar, and when the Ts took control of Afghanistan in the mid-nineties, Khaista and Mullah Mansour were able to return to Logar restored and rewarded. Mullah Mansour had made connections with the Ts, and while he never officially joined the political or the armed wings of the organization, he supported them and had made many powerful allies within their spheres. Had he or his mother wished, they could have had all six of Khaista's idiot brothers executed within the day.

But Khaista's heart was more wearied than vengeful. She decided to spare her nephews and nieces the fate her son was forced to suffer. Instead, she took up her own portion of her father's land, built a small compound, an orchard, and a well, and never again spoke with her brothers, who, like all cockroaches, were able to outlive the revolutions, the Russians, the massacres, the civil wars, and the Ts without any sense of gratitude or grace. In fact, when the Americans invaded in 2001, and Khaista's son was forced into hiding, two of her six idiot brothers joined the ANA, and with the backing of newly appointed bureaucrats in the Afghan government, they even tried to oust Khaista from her land.

"I should have had them shot," Khaista concluded.

"But how will you keep your land?" I asked.

"The mujahideen will return," she said, "and my son will return with them, and the laws of Allah will reign over these lands once more. Inshallah."

After we heard Khaista's story, Bibi and Miriam led me toward the bride's chamber near the beranda, where they thought the butcher's twins might be helping their soon-to-be sister-in-law with her dress. Nabeela had changed from her purple piece into the Kochi kali, and she sat on a toshak in the center of the room, surrounded on all sides by her sisters, cousins, and all of the butcher's daughters except, of course, for the twins.

Moor and her sisters were in a rush, applying and reapplying Nabeela's makeup, but every time it seemed they were getting close to a finish, Nabeela would burst into tears and ruin her mascara. It was the first time I had seen her cry. She didn't hold back either. Big green globs swept down her face like burst faucets.

"Oh, Mother," she cried to Abo, "I've fucked my life."

"By the will of Allah," Abo said, on the verge of weeping too, but not just yet, "you've fucked me up too."

"Damn this heart," Nabeela shouted, and struck her chest, stirring a thousand little mirrors.

"If you ruin your dress . . . ," Moor warned, restarting her mascara.

"This is your life," Hawa Khala said, dabbing a glob with a white dusmal. "You mustn't weep for your life."

But this only made Nabeela cry some more as she began to beg Hawa Khala for forgiveness, for the shabby way she'd treated her since the first day she entered their home fourteen years ago, a lonesome young girl from Tangee, her sister by marriage, but never treated as a sister, instead worked, instead cursed, without true love in her heart until she saw Hawa's fate lying before her.

"They'll work me into bones," Nabeela wept, and Sadaf and Shireen kept having to apologize on her behalf to the butcher's daughters, who all watched her, it seemed, without much sympathy.

"I know it because I deserve it," she continued, and looked to Hawa, "but, O Allah, I can't become like a needle or a strand of hair on my husband's head. I want sons and daughters, four or five each, and you need flesh for birth. Not just bone."

Hawa Khala dabbed at another swirling glob and shook her head. "Don't weep, little bride. You're much stronger than I am. More shameless too. If anything, these babies he'll give you will only make you rounder. Boy or girl, fat or thin, dark or light, a bounty nonetheless," she said, and dabbed at one last glob of a tear because there were no more coming.

Nabeela Khala laughed, just one short burst that almost immediately, it seemed, ended her mourning and opened the door for a barrage of jokes. Moor teased her for crying and promised to come up with a terrible name for her first daughter, Abo called her soft and denounced all the rumors regarding her toughness, Shireen sang her a quiet line from a dirty song about her wedding night, and Sadaf chided Nabeela for making her wait so long to get her own man, only to weep for her fortune on the day of the wedding.

Nabeela warned Sadaf to wait until her time, to see what would happen on the day she too had to leave her father's home, a daughter apart, and if she didn't weep big green globs of tears, she would let Sadaf secretly name her second-born daughter, because, as she'd promised, Moor would be naming her first. The room burst with curses and laughter. Rolling with the tempo, Nabeela asked Hawa Khala a question in Farsi, which was actually a dirty joke, which everyone understood except me, and so all the ladies laughed (and me with them), but my fake laugh cut through the rest.

"Who is this?" Abo asked the whole room at once.

"We're looking for Gul's fiancée," Bibi answered for me.

And before Abo could question us further, one of the butcher's daughters (unaware of Abo's temper) interrupted her and pointed us toward a chamber on the farthest end of the compound. I slipped out in a hurry, Bibi and Miriam following after, and the three of us cut across the courtyard, shadowed the walls, climbed a very short flight of stairs, and reached the doorway of a chamber bursting with so many songs and drums, I had to stop and wait and just listen.

Here, I thought, and even before the girls led me inside, I sensed in the tumbling of the waters in my belly that this was the chamber I was meant to find.

The butcher's twins huddled together in a corner of the room, singing and clapping with an older woman that might've been their khala. A few feet away from them sat a pair of burqa-clad guests, one of which was particularly wide and the other of which was very clearly staring at the butcher's twins. I wasn't sure which one exactly. The room was so packed, me and the girls could hardly fit. Eventually, I was able to squeeze into a space offered to me by another woman in a burqa, but Miriam and Bibi had to stay by the doorway. Though they got some nasty glares, the girls waited for me to find a spot before leaving.

I never even thanked them.

With my eyes on the ladies who must've been Gul and Dawood, I sat on the edge of the dance floor, near the doorway, trying to be as inconspicuous as possible, and then, in between each song, I gradually moved from one open spot to another, until I sat next to the impostors.

"Gul?" I whispered, but Dawood was the one to answer me.

"Is that you?" he asked.

"It's me," I said. "Are those the girls?"

"They are."

"So which one is the one he loves?" I asked Dawood, reaching for my camera, but Gul was the one to answer me.

"I'm not sure," he said.

"How can you not be sure?"

And maybe because he could not give me a good response, Gul decided to do the stupidest thing possible. In the middle of the song, as all the ladies were still singing or dancing or enjoying themselves, Gul got up, crossed the dance floor, nearly stumbling, and sat right beside the girl that might have been his love.

The twins gave him a quick glare and scooted aside, and just as they did, Gul slipped his hand from under his burqa and grasped the fingers of the girl sitting closest to him.

At first, the butcher's daughter smiled, maybe thinking the woman beneath the burqa was one of her khalas or amas playing a trick on her. But when she placed her other hand on top of Gul's, she must have felt his hairs, freshly sprouted, or his rough knuckles, blunted in fistfights, or the sweat on his fingers, which trembled uncontrollably, because after touching the top of his naked hand, the butcher's daughter let out a yelp that cut through the singing, that stopped the dancing, that interrupted the party, that got me and Dawood up out of our spots, ready to run, but which, unfortunately, did not do the same for Gul.

He sat there, both hands still locked about the fingers of the girl that might've been his love. The butcher's daughter shouted for the whole room to hear: "This woman is not a woman!" And just as all the ladies were about to jump him, me and Dawood rushed over, pulled Gul away from the girl he wouldn't let go, and flew out the room.

Only a few of the ladies followed after us, but they shouted our misdeeds for all the party to hear. We were already out the door, and almost halfway down the road, when all at once a shot rang out. Gul fell down, Dawood stopped, someone screamed, and I kept on running past the compounds and the fields and the chinar and the canals and the graves and the farmers and the workers and the mules and the flowers and the toot and the flags and the birds and the walls and the doorways until, some way or another, I made it all the way back to the marker by the canal where Watak once died.

لوگر

On the Ninety-Seventh Afternoon

For a long time, I knelt beneath Watak's mulberry tree. Flowers fell from its branches in a rough breeze. Nearby, the canal had flooded, turned into a river whose waters almost touched the stone and the ash at the base of Watak's marker. Through the thousand eyes of my burqa, the dark blue outlines of the linen, I watched the white flowers fall and the floodwaters rise and the mountain winds twist the tatters of Watak's flag, and I knew, at that moment, that I was one hundred years too early to be feeling this old. My stomach bubbled. I wanted to vomit, but I only gagged. There was nothing in me.

I turned toward the maze, and somewhere just outside my vision, I knew, a thief watched it with me. Another bandit in a burqa, not even pretending to be otherwise, knelt beside me. Jawed the Thief spoke to me in an English without hint of an accent, and he told me that what had happened at the party didn't matter, that it was of no consequence whether Gul died or not, whether Dawood held him as he was dying or living, whether his mother was the one to kill him, whether his sister would be abandoned on the day of her wedding, or whether Moor's whole family, almost untouched by the wars, would finally fall apart.

"But Atid is writing," I said, and in response, the Thief recounted for me a hadith recorded in Al-Mu'jam Al-Kabeer, wherein it was reported by Abu Umamah that the Messenger of Allah, peace and blessings be upon him, once said, "The scribe on the right is trustworthy over the scribe on the left because when a person does good, he records it immediately, but when a person sins, he says to the scribe on the left: 'Stay your hand for six hours, and if the believer seeks forgiveness from Allah, then do not write it. Otherwise, it will be recorded.'"

"Six hours?" I asked.

"Six hours," he said, standing beneath the mulberry tree, flowers gathering at his feet.

"How did you find me?"

"You've left a trail," the Thief said, and gestured toward the trickle of blood, which followed me all the way from the wedding. My finger. It pulsed and it dripped and I hardly noticed till I saw its trail. I lifted the skirt of my veil a bit. The folds of my kameez and partug were spotted in blood. Jawed the Thief tore a strip of his burqa and took my finger and wrapped my wound for me.

"If you stay here," he said, "they'll find you."

I could see in my mind all the trails and all the walls of the maze that stood there so close. "They never found Budabash," I said.

"*You* never found Budabash."

"But I might," I said. And then I stood up, flower petals and dust scattering about the skirt of my burqa.

Before we entered the alley, the Thief asked me for the camera I had forgotten was hidden inside the pocket of my kameez and with which I was supposed to have taken a picture of Gul's love. After I handed it to him (stolen, returned, and returned again), he led me into the maze.

The compounds of the maze were built tall and tight and out of a hard, dry mud. The paths were filled with turns and twists, but the Thief was so sure of his way, we nearly sprinted along the trails. The alleys and the surrounding compounds seemed completely empty. That was, until we ran into the interpreter. The same one I met on the road more than two months ago, when me and Zia were waiting for a savior beneath the mulberry tree. His left arm hung limp, and blood leaked out of a wound in his shoulder. His army fatigues were in tatters, and he'd grown a scraggly beard. "Sisters," he almost sobbed after staring at us for about two minutes, "do you know the way out?"

"We do," Jawed replied, and tore off a strip of his burqa, "but first tell us what happened."

"There's no time," the interpreter shouted, "there are gunmen coming."

"These alleys are filled with nothing but time. If they are following you, they'll never find you. Besides, you're leaking." Jawed got the interpreter to sit down, and while he wrapped his wound, the interpreter explained that he'd been lost in this maze for more than two months, that there wasn't a single person in any of these compounds, and that if it weren't for the occasional fruit tree or abandoned well, he and his squadron would've starved weeks ago.

"Where is your squadron?" I asked.

So he told us.

The Tale of the Ambush in the Maze

Apparently, after spending two months raiding each of the compounds in the maze but never finding a single occupant or any other traveler to guide them out of the village, the small squadron of soldiers was on the brink of losing their minds. Then, earlier that day, the interpreter spotted a group of wanderers. Seeing that two of them were armed and that the other two were tied up on a steer, the interpreter wanted to sneak up from behind and get a jump on the gunmen, but the sergeant (who despised his Afghan translator almost as much as he hated the militants) ignored him and told his men to arm themselves. The interpreter himself remained without a weapon. When the sergeant got within shouting distance of the gunmen, he commanded them to halt and to drop their rifles.

The gunmen, of course, replied back with AK fire, quickly cutting down the sergeant. The other soldiers were out in the open. Not a single wall or a tank or a base to hide behind. And because all the doors of all the compounds suddenly seemed to have disappeared, the interpreter had to duck down behind the body of the sergeant just to avoid the next two flurries of machine-gun fire. The gunmen, on the other hand, had their steer and their prisoners to use as shields, and after they tore the other soldiers to bits, the interpreter leapt up, dodged a few hundred bullets, and ran off in a wild fury until he came upon two ladies clad in burqas.

"So all your comrades were killed," I said.

"They were killed and their killers are coming," the interpreter said. "We should go."

"We can't," Jawed said.

"Why not?"

Then Jawed told him a long lie about how we used to live in one of these compounds with a whole flock of other families back in the '70s, but once the Russians invaded and the bombings and the massacres started, many families fled, while the ones who stayed behind tried to figure out ways to outlast the Soviet assault. During a particularly rough period of bombings, the remaining families used an intricate system of tunnels beneath their lands as bomb shelters. They were fairly effective, and if the men could warn the ladies and the children of an incoming air raid beforehand, not too many casualties were had.

"One night," Jawed claimed, "we were informed too late of an incoming air raid and so we got to the tunnels after everyone else. We covered our children with our bodies in anticipation of the bombs. But they didn't fall. That was the first night the Soviets used the gas. All of the women and the children hiding deep in the tunnels, in the safest spots, suffocated immediately, while those of us on the outer edges died much more slowly. Many of the mothers clung to their dead children, but when we heard the coming of a second round of gas, we fled from the tunnels and from our families. They all died and we did not. So now we return to this maze of empty compounds in search of the broken tunnels where our children might be roaming."

The interpreter asked us if we truly meant to find the ghosts of our dead children.

"Even ghosts need company," Jawed said.

The interpreter nodded his head, dug his fingers into the thatch of the wall behind him, and slowly pulled himself up. Then he fled, all the while muttering about the little gunmen and the ghosts he had to outrun. But just before he turned a corner, the Thief snapped three quick pictures of the interpreter fleeing. When I asked him why, he told me it was for the sake of a visual record and nothing else.

Next, we ran into the ugly little T and one of his former prisoners. They held hands, and the both of them came marching down the maze, side by side, old rifles and new machine guns strapped to their chests, carrying hefty rice bags on their shoulders. They both dripped with blood that might not have been their own. When we met them, they set their bags down to rest.

"Sisters," the ugly T said, "have you spotted an Afghan wearing an American costume?"

Jawed told him he had, and then he retold the story the interpreter told us.

The ugly T shook his head. "That's not how it happened at all," he said.

The Second Story of the Tale of the Ambush in the Maze

"First of all," he started, "we were never given any warning to drop our weapons or to halt where we stood. We wouldn't have done it even if they did, but they didn't and that is the truth. In fact, the first thing they did was blow out the brains of one of my prisoners. Afterward, my brother and I ducked behind our steer, pulled down our other prisoner, and returned fire."

He showed us his old bolt-action rifle and continued: "They had machine guns and armor, and we had nothing but these. It was our very first firefight. At least, I thought it was our first. The way my brother shot, how calm and quick he reloaded, how fearlessly he knelt and aimed and fired, it seemed as if he were right at home in battle. While I fumbled with my rifle, he must have wounded two of the Americans by himself. Firing, ducking down, reloading, and firing again, maybe a hundred times in a single minute, which was all he had, one minute, before they pierced him through the throat.

"So there I am, ducking behind my dead steer, trying to drag my brother back toward me, yanking at his pants, which were drenched in blood or urine, and I had my rifle tucked between my legs and I wasn't planning to fire another shot.

"Sisters," he said, "you must understand: my brother was not really my brother, but we grew up in the madrassa, where the one-eyed mullah took us in after he saved us from a rapist warlord's compound of sorrow. The mullah taught us Quran and

Sharia and the atrocity of sodomy, and that we, my pretty brother and I, were bonded by our suffering and by the will of Allah, which was stronger than blood or creed or race, and that when the time came for our martyrdom, we, as brothers, might seek the death that God had written for us, which is very difficult indeed, and so it was, and I could not lift my rifle along with the weight of my shame.

"That was when my other prisoner started yelping for me to free him, claiming he didn't want the Americans to take him. And though I did not trust him, I freed him for the sake of my solitude. In the end, he stayed true to his word and picked up my brother's rifle and fired on the Americans, which gave me back my courage, so I fired too, until we'd killed all of them, save for the spy, who fled into the maze."

"Were you the dealer?" I asked the former prisoner still holding the ugly T's hand. He said that he was but that he had overcome the whispers of Shaytan and planned to join his new ally in his cause for Allah.

After telling his story, the ugly T requested that we guide him out of the maze and help him pursue the fleeing interpreter. Jawed told him we couldn't and that, in fact, we had to go deeper into the compounds.

"But, sisters," the ugly T said, "what could you need to do on such a hopeless path and without an escort?"

So Jawed told them a long lie about how he and I were residents of this neighborhood:

"We traveled here from the north after the Taliban took

control of the country. The warlords had razed these grounds into ash, firing sakr rockets from Kabul. There was nothing here. So those of us who pledged loyalty to the Taliban were given these fertile lands to restart our lives. For a few years, we lived here in relative peace. We built up all these compounds with our bare hands. Our men stacked the bricks and shaped the walls. We women planted the crops and raised our children. We prayed our prayers and read Quran and tried to stay quiet and small.

"We had nothing else.

"But after the Americans invaded and the Taliban were defeated, forces loyal to the Americans and to the Northern Alliance raided our compounds, killed our husbands and our brothers, dishonored our sisters and our mothers, and turned our homes into graveyards. Some of us fled. While our brothers and sisters were killed or dishonored, we fled and hid with our children and listened and did nothing. We hid for so long our scared sons turned into wild men. They sought blood and, one by one, escaped us with vows of vengeance. Now we're after them. We will take back their guns and bring them home alive and without honor. That's why we cannot follow you," he concluded.

And with that word, the ugly T gave us his blessing, the former prisoner mumbled a short prayer, and they went off in pursuit of the interpreter, still holding hands.

Again, the Thief snapped three pictures, and when they were out of sight, he turned to me and said: "He'll kill him in the end."

"Which one?" I asked.

"Either one."

"I thought they were getting along."

"That's why he'll kill him."

Toward dark, we came upon the Kochian. As me and Jawed were approaching one of the gates of the compound I assumed was empty, it suddenly swung open, and there was Zarghoona, the Kochi nomad. She invited us inside. "These trails are devious," she said. "Come in. You'll be safe."

"I know these trails," Jawed said. "I'm from these parts."

"Then for the sake of Allah come inside and advise us on how to get out."

She stood firmly in our path, her gate blocking the entirety of the road. She held a lamp in one hand and I didn't know what else in the other. We went inside.

While the soldiers and the Ts had roamed the trails aimlessly, destined to meet and to die, Zarghoona's small tribe of Kochi cousins had come together, it seemed, to transform the rubble of a compound into a makeshift home. No weeds or overgrown bushes. No trash or clutter. Instead, old lamps hung from the walls and the trees, the pathways of the courtyard were swept clean, and flowers were planted along the edges of the beranda. Sure, there was some peeling paint, a few small craters, and a lingering stink of death, but in spite of the carnage haunting every room and road, the Kochian had managed to cobble together something resembling a life.

When we reached the beranda in the courtyard, Zarghoona asked us to sit down, to take off our veils, and to stay for dinner.

Jawed denied all three requests. "Bring me a parchment," he said. "I'll draw you a map of the maze and we'll be off."

Zarghoona called on her four cousins and they scoured the compound, searching for anything that could be used as a parchment.

Eventually they found a flat slab of dried clay, and all five of the cousins came bearing sharp knives of different sizes for Jawed to use as a chisel; but when they entered the beranda and tossed the slab in front of Jawed, none of them offered up a knife.

Zarghoona knelt before us with a machete in hand.

"Why are you wearing these veils?" she asked.

"For the sake of Allah," Jawed said.

"Not you. The quiet one. What are you doing on these roads, in the cloak of a woman, wandering about in the dark?"

They all put their eyes on me. Even Jawed, whose eyes I couldn't see.

So I told them a long lie about how we lived in these compounds for a long time, outlasting the Russians and the civil wars and then the Ts, and that we were one of the last families not to have fled, but when the Americans invaded and the special forces started their night raids and massacred a few of our neighbors, including my mother's best friend, a young Tajik woman who was eight months pregnant, my mother tried to convince my father it was time to flee. But he refused to leave his father's land. So, about a year into the occupation, two of my brothers were killed by American sniper fire just outside our home. The Americans thought they were Ts and fired without warning. My brothers didn't even have beards. They were too young. We buried them in the orchard, and my father, beset by sorrow, finally decided to let us move toward the outskirts of Logar, where our men still haven't found any work. Were it not for the death of my brothers, they would have become interpreters a long time ago. Occasionally, we return to these empty compounds to find our old home and to pray at our brothers' graves.

For a few seconds, no one said anything. The Kochian knelt with their knives and watched. Finally, Zarghoona asked me if I thought that I had fooled her with my story. "I spotted you as what you were from fifty meters off," she said, and demanded that we unveil ourselves.

"Sister," I said, but could not think up another lie.

I turned my eyes to Jawed and he turned toward me, and just when I thought he was starting to lift up his veil to reveal himself, he fired seven shots from a hidden pistol into the roof, scattering dust and dirt and blinding us all with the flash of a muzzle we couldn't see. Without having to tell me to do what had become, by then, my first nature, I rushed past the ladies, ran out into the courtyard, and fled the compound—leaving my captured Thief to his fate.

لوگر

On the Ninety-Seventh Night

I ran, and just as Gul once said, the deeper I fled into the maze, the darker the walls became: from bronze to brown to the black of the night, to the point where I could hardly see a thing ahead of me, save for the blue of my garment, save for the mesh of my veil; and just as Dawood once said, the deeper I ran into the maze, the tighter the walls closed in, until they nearly hugged my shoulders, until they met in an arc and swallowed the sky and the stars, turning the alleys into boroughs, into caves. I stripped off my burqa, wrapped it about my shoulders, and crawled on hands and knees through a tunnel the size of an inner tube. I was so thirsty by then, I thought of drinking the wet mud from between my fingers, and just then—when the mud seemed most appetizing—I found the first bone.

To be honest, I didn't know if it was a bone. The dark of the tunnels left me supposing that maybe I picked up a branch or a stone or an old tool or anything else but what it was. I dropped it and went on. But a little farther ahead I found another, something like a jaw, and then I found smaller bones that might have been stones or pebbles or teeth or fingers. They were scattered on the floor and in the walls and in the roof of the tunnel above my head. I felt for them in the dark and in the mud, and at first I collected the bones in my arms and in the pockets of my kameez, but there were so many, and I couldn't bring myself to leave any of them behind, so I unwrapped my burqa, and as soon as I did the seasickness struck me. My brain spun and my guts rolled, but even with the aching and spinning, I took up the tatters of my burqa and I tied the garment into a sack.

In this, I collected femurs and legs and toes and jaws and teeth and even horns and hooves and other bones I thought probably belonged to animals, not humans, but I wasn't so sure, and so I gathered it all. In fact, I collected so many different types of bones that my burqa's bag became full, to the point of tearing, to the point where I had to take off my kameez and fashion that into a bag as well. And so, with one sack tied to my shoulder and the other in my hands, I crawled on. And as it went, the second bag also got full. Little bones, big bones. Femurs and fingers and teeth. Eventually, after turning my partug into yet another sack, I collected bones in the mud of the tunnel nearly naked. My skin became filthy, drenched in the earth. I thought about the bones and how much I hoped they actually were bones, and I prayed to Allah that in my sickness I had not turned rocks and sticks into humans.

I prayed for Him to forgive me if I had.

That was when I found the rifle. At first, I thought it was the long bone of a leg or a mujahideen's arm, but as I felt along its barrel, I found the trigger and accidentally fired the weapon in the tunnel, which for just the flash of a second, lit up the darkness, illuminating all of the bones and the weapons and the tatters that lay before me. It took me a while to readjust to the darkness. Afterward, I took up the rifle and its strap, tied it across my back, and went on down the tunnel.

Then the water really began flowing. I mean the mud was wet as it was, but now as I crawled, as I collected bones in my hands and in my clothes and let them fall away when I could carry no more, there were heavy trickles of water flowing past my fingers and knees. Trickles that were almost streams, which I brought to my lips, which I lapped up like a dog or a wolf. Like a lost wolf. Like *the* lost wolf who, as I should have guessed—as Allah had ordained, as the Thief had foreseen, as I had always known in the deepest intestines of my dreams—was waiting for me at the end of the cave.

He didn't seem to recognize me. Maybe the dark or the mud shrouded me and my stink. But he must have heard me. Sloshing through the mud and through the water, I was close enough that I could hear his breathing, his huffing, but I—perhaps like him—could smell nothing but the clay, could see nothing but the dark, and as I inched closer to what I thought was the end of the tunnel I traveled, the mud gave way to bone or rock. The tunnel opened out into what I thought might be the beginning or the ending of a cave. The bones seemed to be stacking up into a pile, a hill, which I climbed, without rush, without fear, without anything, toward the sound of the huffing at the top.

When I felt him there, maybe a few feet or so in front of me, I stopped. The bones were slick with water. Had I tried to collect a few more, they would have just slipped out of my hands. He huffed hard and did not move. I was maybe the same distance away from him as the day he tore my index finger. It was still bleeding. Just a few drops. But still. The rocks or the bones had leveled off. We met each other at the top of the hill in the cave.

"Budabash," I said, not expecting him to speak.

So he didn't.

"Budabash," I said again, crawling on all fours into his circle.

This time, he neither lunged nor bit nor bled me. I crawled closer. I pushed down on my toes and stretched out my arms and pulled forward with my hands. He shook in the dark where he was, maybe thinking, imagining, that I'd come all this way to take back what I'd lost or, at least, to take from him some measure of what had been stolen. He could not know. I got so close that I could finally smell his wet wolf's scent, that I could finally hear his moaning or his purring or maybe the grumbling of his belly, which probably was as empty as the top of the hill where we met. Bone marrow and mud. Nothing else to eat.

Then I touched his dark fur. Water seeped under and around him. It rushed through my fingers, past my arms and my chest. It dripped down through my feet and my toes, and there was such a rush of water that I almost lost my balance. Once or twice, I lifted my bleeding finger and I dragged my hands across the wolf's wet skin. Or what I thought was a wolf. Or what I thought was a dog. Or what I thought was Budabash.

That was when he bit me. With my wounded finger on the small of his back, at the heart of his scar, and my other hand near his throat, he slowly turned his head in the dark and opened his jaw, and there was a moment, I think, when I could have suddenly moved my arm, when I could have saved myself from the bite. But I didn't. And though he dug his teeth softly into the flesh of my forearm, I neither screamed, nor fought, nor bled.

No.

I did bleed.

The torn finger of my right hand kept on dripping as I clung to the fur of his skin, as water flowed past our tired limbs, and as the bones and the mud and the dog were washed in its currents. My finger bled, but from what I could feel, my forearm did not. His fangs couldn't cut through. He was too weak to hurt me, but he wouldn't let go. He trembled and would not release my arm, and my right hand begged to be avenged, twitching toward the old rifle still strapped to my back, which weighed upon my shoulders like a corpse, and as if to remind me of my pain, the ghost of my finger returned to my wound and it wriggled there, curling, and it ached me as it did in its loss. My right hand was free. It continued to beg for the rifle. But the hill of bones beneath us seemed so delicate and the cave so dark. The mouth of the rifle, with its fire and its light and its piercing thunder, I thought, might destroy the whole world. So I took up my right hand, its finger bleeding, its ghost aching, twitching with fury, and I used it to smooth down the wet fur of the wolf. He seemed to shudder. And when I thought there wasn't any time left for anything else, I told him a story.

The First Tale

"Listen," I said, "Allah made Adam from a dark clay for reasons I cannot remember. Then Allah asked all the angels and the djinn to bow to Adam and they all did, except for Iblis, who would not bow before mud since he was made of fire. So Allah, I think, smote Iblis, whose name became Shaytan, and he lived forever after as the enemy of all humanity. Nonetheless, he still loved Allah. As much as he hated Adam, I think, Shaytan still loved Allah.

"May He forgive me if I am wrong.

"For a time Adam lived in the Bagh. There were many plants and fruits and animals and he named them names to pass the days, but he was lonely among the trees, so Allah gave him a companion to share his loneliness. Her name was Hawa. They split paradise fifty-fifty. Like this, it became bearable.

"Things seemed to be going all right for a while. Adam and Hawa ate fruits and slept and talked about nothing because there was nothing to talk about. They went about the Bagh, being very bored, until Shaytan came to them in the form of a snake and told Adam and Hawa to eat a pear from the one pear tree in the whole Bagh he was not supposed to eat.

"Adam took one bite and handed it to Hawa and she took the second.

"That was how Adam fucked up everything ever.

"May He forgive me if I am wrong.

"Adam was expelled from the Bagh and he became the earth's

first refugee. Well, him and Hawa. I always forget Hawa, but she was there too. Them together, living on the earth, which was not their home, which was only ever the in-between, and their lives were very sad and very hard until they had some kids. And for a few years the kids gave them joy, but then, of course, Shaytan, who had nothing better to do, reentered the picture. He convinced the one son of Adam to kill the other son, and after the one son killed the other, the one son fled.

"Hawa and Adam were so beset by the sorrow of death, the first of its kind, the first of many to come, it drove them to the trunk of an olive tree. There they wept for many years. And so Allah, I think, hearing their lamentations, sent them a great flood, and Adam and Hawa were happy to drown in the deserts where they lived, but, unfortunately, they were saved by their murderous son, whose name was also Adam, in a small ark he had built in the mountains after he met another tribe of humans, I think, who took him in and gave him a wife who gave him a child. Upon the ark, his whole family survived. But when Adam and Hawa met the son of their murderous son, seeing that their bloodline would live on forever afterward upon the earth, they died immediately of wonder. The son of Adam went on to blame his own child, whose name was also Adam, for the death of his parents. So after the suns dried the flood and the tops of the mountains were once more clear, the son of Adam brought his child to the edge of a cliff where he intended to sacrifice him for the sake of his father. But Allah replaced the son with a sheep and the son of Adam killed that instead.

"Adam himself fled the mountains out of fear, leapt back into the waters, and surely would have drowned had he not been swallowed by a whale, whose dreams he interpreted for many years as a form of rent. Eventually, though, the whale found a lover, the only other whale on the earth, and the whale's lover demanded solitude in their intimacy, and so the whale—with great apologies—spat Adam back onto the land, which was now filled with many humans and animals and forests and languages, none of which Adam could speak, and so he traveled the dark of the lands, and on his way back to his mother, Hawa, he met his sister, Hawa, whom he came to love, but who never returned that love, understanding it to have become a sin by then; but because he was her brother, from time to time, she still saved him from the many calamities he faced.

"Hawa saved Adam from the Vikings who ate his fingers in the woods and the Crusaders who raped him in a mosque and the French who cut off his toes in a tent and the Spanish who stretched his limbs on a rack and the English who starved him in a dungeon and the Communists who shocked his testicles in an underground bunker and the Americans who experimented on his brains, in a shed, near the Mississippi River. Tiring of the pain of his life, one day Adam stole away into a cave within the same mountain where his father once attempted to sacrifice him for killing his own father, and there, in the dark of the cave, Adam was met by an angel who taught him—at the very end of his life—how to read. The burden of this gift was too heavy for him to bear and so he shared it with Hawa, whom he still loved but who was by then married with many children, and she taught each of these children to read the script of God that the angel had given Adam. Some of them took heed and some of them forgot and some of them were led astray by Shaytan, who, through the many years of his rotten existence still had not forgiven Adam for coming to life."

After I finished, I challenged the wolf to tell a story more miraculous than mine. But when he opened his jaw to speak, he freed my arm and made me stumble backward, just a step or two, and with those little steps, I dislodged a few bones from the top of the hill, and those bones dislodged a few others, so that before the wolf had a chance to tell his wondrous tale, the hill began to collapse beneath us, and we both fell with the bones and the water; and as I stumbled and rolled, and as the great torrents of water poured forth from all the corners of the dark, I realized that the hill of bones wasn't just a hill but a dam, and that Budabash was its builder, its caretaker, and its final stone.

I slipped into black water, and for what seemed like a long time, I tumbled in the darkness of the tunnels with the bones and the weapons and the mud. Eventually, I rose up from its depths shouting a name in the middle of the flood, in the maze, in Logar. I shouted once, breathed deeply, and fell back under the water. I did not know how to float. The flood carried me through the pathways of the maze as I tried to cling to the walls and lift myself up. But it was no good. I clung and slipped and fell back under. Once. Twice. Three times. And it was only after the fourth time I lifted myself and fell that I was able to grab on to the limb of a floating carcass.

It was a soldier. The would-be commander of the white boys on the road. The one who spoke to me in English. The one who threatened me. He was dead. He was dead and still and he floated. So I hooked one arm around his neck and the other about his torso and I tried very hard not to look at his face or to smell his stink or to touch his rotting skin. In this way, we floated along the watery corridors of the maze until the legs of the soldier bumped up against one half of an aluminum gate floating flat upon the water. Using the soldier as leverage, I pulled myself up onto the big green gate, lay back on the wet aluminum surface, and looked up into the sky, which was cloudless and so sunny it was more white than blue.

Afterward, I vomited for so long I passed out.

لوگر

On the Ninety-Eighth Morning

When I woke up, I was flat on the sheet of aluminum without weapon, without kameez or partug, and I stank of vomit. The dead soldier was gone. Eaten, I supposed, by the waters. The flood had calmed as quickly as it came, but the maze and the compounds were still drowning. I floated along for a bit, swaying back and forth, but I didn't feel woozy at all. No nausea. No bubbles in my gut. Then, after I sniffed deep from the mud and the water, my vision became clear. I saw all the roads and the channels of Logar unfurling before me. So I washed my raft and myself, and I set about looking for a way to get back. Back to Moor and Agha and my brothers. Baba and Abo. My khalas and maamaas. My cousins.

In the waters of the flood, there were many bones, and the ones that floated near me, I collected into four equal piles on each side of my raft. Along with the bones floated garbage. Plastic bottles and tin cans and dead flowers and, occasionally, there was even shit. The shit of animals and the shit of men, and it all floated together. Sometimes I had to pick the trash from the bones or I had to wash the shit out of a skull. I collected so many bones, my raft began to sink with the weight, and so I became more selective. I traded. When I saw a skull or a rib, I grabbed it quickly and with abandon, nearly falling a few times. But I almost always tossed back the teeth and the legs. Unless, of course, it seemed like a particularly small bone. Those I kept.

Eventually, I floated past some shreds of cloth, which I hoped did not belong to the dead, though they probably did, but as desperate as I was in my near nakedness, I took them up anyway and wrapped these shreds around my waist and my chest. The cleanest cloth I tied about the small wounds of the bite in my forearm. My finger still bled and I let the drops fall into the water.

Near the middle of the maze, or what I thought might be the middle of the maze, I found a small shovel that I used as an oar. The height of the waters let me peek above the walls of the compounds, which made it easier to navigate all the way back to Watak's mulberry tree. There, the water sloped on toward Moor's house and carried me, I thought, where I needed to go.

Once I got out of the maze, I started to see families sitting up on the roofs of their compounds. I rowed on by, nearly naked, looking to see if anyone anywhere might need some help from me and my makeshift raft, but in general the Logarian wanted to know if they could help me instead. One family offered me food, which I accepted and which they tossed to me in a basket. The next family had an extra pair of dried clothes, which they hurled to me in a ball and which I immediately dropped in the water. I shouted a long series of apologies, but I don't think they could hear me over their own laughter. I laughed a little too.

Luckily, the next family also offered me clothes, but they could sacrifice only a kameez without the partug, and this I caught and wore, and though the kameez was about four sizes too big—so that the leman came down to my calves as if I were wearing a short dress—I was just happy not to be naked in front of all the girls, who hid behind their veils but still seemed to be watching me in my journey. One family offered me tea, another family offered me naswar, another offered me cookies, and another offered me apples, and one particularly observant old woman tossed me a bucket.

"Mother," I shouted, "but this is empty."

"It won't be."

And she was right.

On my raft, in the flood, with all of the world up on their roofs, I was the guest of every villager and not a single family wanted to disappoint. Each of the families had their own piles of bones. The kids fished them out with nets and brooms, and some of the neighbors got into small arguments over who could lay claim to which bone. Of course, it amounted to nothing. The bones belonged to whoever could find them.

I went on with my rowing, wanting to repay the village for its kindness but unable to find a single person to save. In fact, I started spotting other men in makeshift boats, also searching for the wounded or the dead. Some of them rowed by in crates and on aluminum sheets and wheelbarrows or coffins. One group of men—I think they were road builders—drifted by on a long raft made from several wooden poles. The rowers used brooms and pans and drums as paddles. They shouted for their brothers and sisters and they seemed so sad to hear no reply. When I asked another would-be rescuer how many had died in the flood, he informed me that as far as he knew Allah had not taken a single soul.

"Subhanallah," I said.

He sighed and seemed to agree.

Right about the time I was getting pretty close to Moor's house, a few of the families up on the roofs started calling out the adhan. The call traveled from one house to another, so that even with all the mosques drowned in the flood, the entire village was now praying together. I crossed the paths of a hundred prayers and said astaghfirullah a hundred times so that I did not transform into a monkey. Out on the roofs, all of the villagers of Naw'e Kaleh, the ladies and the men, the adults and the kids, prayed above the rising waters.

Well, all of them except for one.

When I finally drifted in toward Moor's compound, the only person to spot me was Zia. The tide of the flood stopped a few feet from the tops of the walls, and the wooden poles were all drowned. While everyone else in Moor's family, including Gul, who looked healthy and strong and without any sign of a wound, prayed the Dhuhr Salah in a congregation, Zia sat by himself on the edge of the wall closest to the big blue gate. His clothes were dripping. He looked so light in the sun, he seemed transparent. Or like he was on the verge of disappearing.

I paddled up to him quietly.

He greeted me with a slow salaam, almost as if he'd been expecting me to arrive just as I was: standing on one half of an aluminum gate, wearing a giant's kameez, with four piles of bones surrounding me on all sides.

He asked me where I'd been, and I told him bits and pieces of the story of my journey, but I didn't mention the tunnel or what I found at the end.

"We thought you died," Zia said.

"Wallah?"

"They still do. Everyone except your parents and your brothers knew you were dead."

"And now you," I said, almost about to smile, but Zia seemed so grim, so tired and lonely, I didn't dare.

"And now me," he said.

After scanning the backs of the worshippers once, twice, four, or five times in a few seconds, I asked Zia for the whereabouts of Agha. But before he told me that, he told me everything else.

The Tale of the Flood and the Missing Musafir

It turned out that Gul and Dawood hadn't been caught, and that Gul hadn't been hit, and that he collapsed on the trail that day only because he thought he was killed and needed to weep for his life. Dawood and him managed to escape thanks to Zia, who secretly snuck in with us just in case we fucked up like we did.

In spite of his efforts, I still ended up ruining poor Nabeela's wedding. As soon as my brothers noted my disappearance and brought it to the attention of Agha, who brought it to the attention of Moor, who brought it to the attention of every single guest in the wedding, the festivities fell apart. They searched for me all day long and then well into the night, but sometime very late during the first night of my disappearance, the usual rumbling from the black mountains was greeted with a series of firebombs in the valley. Quite a few of the dams in Naw'e Kaleh were destroyed. The rivers and the canals filled with water from the mountain springs until they poured forth onto the roads and the fields and the secret tunnels of bones hidden beneath the roads and the compounds. Agha and his people were out searching for me near the butcher's house on the higher plains of the village while my maamaas scoured Naw'e Kaleh. They were almost swept away in the first rush of flood. Rahmutallah Maamaa and Baba nearly drowned. Meanwhile, Abo had gone mad with faith in the omens of the flood, and she would not say or do anything except to pray for the souls of her only husband and her eldest son, who were still breathing, barely breathing, but still. So with the village flooded and with Rahmutallah and Baba knocked out and with no sign of where to search or where to go, Abdul-Abdul took charge of the family. His first order was that no one could leave the roof. Apparently, he had been attempting to call his contacts within the military the whole morning. He promised a helicopter would arrive within the hour, and although Zia didn't think anyone believed him, no one in the family denied him, either. He was now, technically, the eldest son.

. . .

"Your father is still out searching for you," Zia said. "He must be swimming from compound to compound. We haven't seen him in a while, Marwand. I don't know."

Gul said the takbirat in a booming voice. I thought it was odd that Abdul-Abdul didn't lead the prayer. The whole family bowed down into sujud. Zia's six sisters were at the very end of the group. They all wore purple chadors.

"When the family is done praying," I said, "tell them that I'm alive."

"They won't believe me, Marwand. I hardly believe me."

"Tell them that I'm going to find my father."

"Your moor will cut off my hands when she finds out I let you go."

"Tell her you tried to stop me."

"How?"

"Maybe you invoked Allah. Maybe you begged me for the sake of my moor and my brothers and for the family as a whole. Maybe you bargained with me. Maybe you leapt into the waters. Maybe you nearly drowned."

Gul said the takbirat again. Moor's family bowed into ruku. Gwora and Mirwais stood on the edge of the roof closest to the flooded courtyard. I wondered if Gwora's notebooks survived. I wondered where he might have saved them.

"It's the last rakat," Zia said, and at that moment, he looked so scrawny and hungry, so wet and meek, I might have stayed behind just to watch him eat a few apples, which, I realized, were floating in the pool of the orchard just behind him. The chickens and the donkey were walking about on the roof of the cow's pen. But there were no cows.

"My father was not there," Zia said. "We couldn't pull them up without him. Dawood almost broke his arms yanking at the rope. And when I saw that the cows were going to drown, I jumped into the water. They had their snouts raised up for air, and I held one of their necks and looked into its eye. At first, all I could see was its terror. But as I kept peering, I realized that I wasn't really seeing into the eye of the cow at all. It was my own face. My own fear.

"Marwand, ever since that night on the road beneath the mulberry tree, all day and night all I think about is how God will punish me. Or. How He won't. That scares me too. That scares me more. But Marwand, Wallah, the cows weren't scared. They were dying, and they knew they were dying, but they were at peace. There was no hate in them. No doubt. They didn't even cry. They just breathed until they couldn't. The waters rose until it stopped. I was the only one floating."

The family sat in tashuhud. Their prayer was almost finished.

"Zia," I said, "if they see me . . ."

"I know, Marwand. Go and find your father. May Allah return him to you."

"And yours too," I said quietly, and began to drift back the way I came. But before I got too far, I turned around and asked Zia to make a dua for me. He raised his hands up to his face, over his eyes, and all I could see were his lips.

They seemed to be counting.

In my search for Agha, I collected no bones or trash or trinkets, and even when the carcasses of livestock—sheep and donkeys and cows and a dog or two—began to float upon the surface of the waters, I paid them no attention and went on paddling and scanning the rivers and the roofs for any sign of my father. Then, just as I was returning to Watak's flooded marker, I spotted Budabash in one of the highest branches of Watak's mulberry tree. He lay on his belly, slumped across the branch like a sleepy ape or a lizard.

I wasn't going to touch him.

Wallah, I was sick and tired of our war, which I could not win and would not lose.

But when I drifted underneath the mouth of the dog, I saw Watak's red flag hanging from his ugly rotting teeth. And without another thought, I leapt from the raft onto the tree, clinging to one of the lower branches, and like this I climbed up from one branch to the next as my raft floated softly away.

The tree was wet with flood, and so it took me a few minutes to scramble all the way up to the highest branch where Budabash slept. In the light of day, and as close as I was, I finally got to see what Budabash had done to himself. With his fur spotted in many patches, the hundred scars stretching from his long white burn were no longer hidden. All about his body, his back and legs and belly, these lighter scars ran in and around one another, marking out, I thought, the shape of another maze.

I clung to the branch and dragged myself forward on my belly, stopping every few inches to make sure the wolf didn't wake. Then we lay face-to-face. His mouth and snout were covered in toot. His breath was ragged and stank of ash. He did not stir. Occasionally, his shoulders seemed to lift in breath, but he did not smell me or see me or know, I thought, that I was there.

Lifting my right hand, I reached for the flag in his teeth, gripped it tightly, and yanked as hard as I could, so that, of course, as these things tend to go, I yanked us both off the branch and down into the waters.

As we fell and hit the flood, and as we floated amid the bones and the flowers and the dark, dark mud, I never let go of the flag still stuck in his teeth. Even after he woke, even after he struggled against me, thrashing in the water, swinging with his claws, which weren't really claws so much as they were nails, just nails, scratching my skin but not able to bleed me like he would have been able to do when he was young and strong and a great killer.

So there we were, in the heart of the waters, both of us clinging dearly to Watak's flag without either of us knowing (or caring) why the other one wanted it with such a terrible faith. Neither I nor Budabash had the heart to drown, to give up our little beating lives, and so we floated together, him dog-paddling with all four legs and me doing a sort of one-armed sidestroke, sort of being carried (to be honest) but still trying to put in work, so that Budabash couldn't go off one day and tell all the other wolves and the beasts of the country that he'd saved me from the waters.

The current had slowed since the morning, and because neither I nor Budabash wanted to go back to Moor's house, we swam in the opposite direction—toward the black mountains. At least, I tried to swim. I kept up with Budabash for only a minute or two before he began to carry me forward. With one hand I held onto the flag, and with the other I clung to Budabash's throat, and though his strength seemed to wane, he still pushed on against the dying current, this huge mean beast, this wolf or dog or both, this thing that could not be stopped.

In time, he brought me all the way back to the great iron doors of Agha's compound, and it was upon these doors that Agha sat in a manner very similar to Zia. When he saw me, Agha jumped feetfirst into the water, swam forward with tremendous strides, and yanked us both toward the compound. Budabash gave in to Agha's pull almost immediately, and once we got to the top of the roof, Agha wrapped me up in the most terrible bear hug. He pressed me to his rough flesh as if he meant to absorb my skin, which was more calloused and hard and dark than it ever was. But, Wallah, even beaten and fried and burned and cut and sick and dizzy and skinny and toughened and with hair in my pits and arms and the backs of my fingers, still I felt soft in the arms of my Agha.

I let go of the flag.

Eventually, after much sobbing, praying, kissing, laughing, shouting, Agha carried me and Budabash to the corner of the compound closest to the black mountains, just behind Nikeh's mulberry tree, where he set us down, one on each side of him. We sat there together, the three of us soaked and weary, and we looked out onto the flooded fields of trash and bones, drying our skin in the sun, even Budabash, who by then had shed so much of his coat, he was more skin than fur.

Agha had not collected a single bone.

After he examined my torn finger, which, he noted, should've healed by now, Agha asked me for the story of my disappearance.

"There are mountains of bones underneath the Kaleh," I said.

"I've heard the stories."

"When?"

"After we left Logar, when we got to Pakistan, I heard rumors about the tunnels. The massacres. I didn't care. Our compound was destroyed. My cousins, my half-sister, my little nephews and nieces, and all the good mujahideen were dead."

"And Watak?" I asked.

The black mountains huddled quietly at the edges of the valley. They too, I thought, must have been listening.

"And Watak," Agha said.

"He has his flag," I said, pointing to Budabash.

A single corner of the tattered red cloth still hung from the old dog's mouth.

First, Agha attempted to coax Budabash into opening his jaw by rubbing his head, and then he tried to pull the flag out through the gaps in Budabash's fangs. When that failed, he dug his fingers into the dog's mouth and tried to tear open his jaw by force. But Budabash must have been part crocodile. He refused to budge.

After he noticed that I was peering at him in his efforts to retrieve the flag, Agha cradled my sut and covered my eyes and rested my head down onto his lap, and then, while grazing the skin of my forehead with the shattered nail of his thumb, he did something to Budabash I could not see.

Agha's partug was thin and wet, and though the water in the linen sloshed about in my ear, I could still hear the beat of his heart through a vein in his thigh, and I felt his muscles tense, and I heard him or Budabash grunt and strain, and the whole time my eyes were open. Red light shone through the dark of his small hands.

A few moments later, his muscles relaxed and he lifted his fingers from my eyes.

I sat up and looked away from Agha and Budabash.

Down the road or the stream from which I came, I could see, or thought I could see, a woman in her burqa, floating on a raft. Behind her were many more women in burqas, on rafts, paddling forward. At that moment, Agha wiped at his eyes and his cheeks with the torn cloth of his dead brother's marker. He could not see that the ladies were coming, and that they would be here soon, and that they might (if Allah willed it) save us from this country, which was drowning. It was only then—with Budabash asleep or dead, with Watak's flag dripping in his fingers, with my moor and khalas floating toward us, with Abdul-Abdul waiting for the soldiers, with Zia afraid, Gul confused, and Dawood hungry for the scent of white poppies, with Rahmutallah and Baba knocked out, with Nabeela still péeghla, with Abo weakened and weary, with my brothers together someplace far away, with the ghost of my finger still wailing, with my dark skin drying in the face of the sun—that Agha finally decided to tell me the story of Watak.

It went like this:

د ژوند یادونه

زه او زما کشر ورور چې دولت خان نومیده او مشهور په هوتکي وو په ګډه سره مو په یو کور کې ژوند تیراوه. زمونږ پلار سپین ږیری او د قوم مشر وو. زمونږ میرني ورونه له مونږ څخه مشران وو او کله، کله به ئې مونږ وهلو. زمونږ پلار له دې کبله چې د قوم مشر وو زیات وخت به له کور څخه بهر وو. کله چې به کور ته راغی نو مونږ به د میرني ورونو له شر او ظلم څخه خلاصیدلو. مونږ چې کشران وو نو د پلار لپار مو د امسا مثال درلوده او د کروندې په کارونو کې به مو مرسته ورسره کوله. پلار مو د ښوونځي سره علاقه نه درلوده او اجازه ئې نه راکوله چې ښوونځي ته لاړ شو. زه د خپلې له مخې چې د زده کړې سره مې درلودله ښوونځي ته په خپل سر لاړم او داخله مې تر لاسه کړه. خو زما ورور هوتک د پلار د خبرې سره سم ښوونځي ته لاړ نه شو او ورڅخه محروم پاتې شو. په دې ډول هوتک د پلار سره کرونده کوله او مالونه به ئې پټې او ډاګونو ته د څرولو لپاره بیول.

هوتک غلی، عاجز او غریبکار انسان وو. د بې کارۍ وخت به ئې د همزولو سره په اولسي او کليوالي لوبو تېراوه. کله چې رالوی شو نو ژوند مو ورځ په ورځ ښه او نېکمرغه کېده. يو عادي ژوند مو درلود خو د خپل غیرت او عزت سره برابر وو او په کې خوښحاله او له خدای څخه راضي وو.

شخړه او جګړه مو کله هم ليدلې نه وه. همدارنګه مو د کليوالو ترمنځ مرګ او وژل هېڅکله ليدلي نه وو. کله چې زه اتلس کلنۍ ته ورسېدم زمونږ په ولايت کې دوه تنه په قتل ورسېدل. دواړه د محمد آغې د اولسوالۍ اوسېدونکي وو. د يوه نوم ګل احمد د ده نو د کلي او د بل د کتب خېلو د کلي مشهور په موټړوان و. د وخت په تېرېدو سره د ظاهر شاه د پاچاهي دوره تېره شوه او په بدليدو سره ئې د داوودخان د جمهوريت دوره اعلان شوه. زيات شمېر خلک په سياست نه پوهيدل او په خپل عادي کار او روزګار بوخت وو. بدبختانه چې د قرارۍ او ارامۍ ډېر وخت دوام و نه کړ. کوم وخت چې کمونستانو کودتاه وکړه د کابل راډيو د څو ساعتو لپاره خاموشه پاتې شوه. له کابل څخه د توپونو ډزې او بد اوازونه اورېدل کېده. خلکو ويل چې په کابل کې جنګ دی. خو څو ساعته وروسته له کابل راډيو څخه يو کس د قادر په نامه اعلان وکړ چې فيوډاليزم مو نسکور کړ او اوس د غريبانو حکومت راغلی دی او نېکه عقيده لري. وروسته خلکو ته معلومه شوه چې د فيوډالۍ قصه هسې يوه بهانه او چل وو. خلک به سره ټولی ټولی کېدل او دا به ئې ويل چې حکومت کمونستانو د خدای ج منکرو خلکو ونيوه. کوم وخت چې دغو وحشي ځناورو قدرت تر لاسه کړبشر ته ئې داسې يو تاريخ پرېښود چې د دوی په شان ظلم هرګز په بله کومه پاچاهي کې شوی نه وو. هره شپه د مسلمانانو په کورونو چاپې اچول کېدلې. مسلمانان بې عزته کېدل. سپين ګيري، ځوانان، ښځې، حتی ماشومان ئې په زانګو کې شهيدانول. علما، مشايخ او پوهه خلک د ورځې خپلو کورونو ته تللی نه شول. دوې به ئې په همدې دسيسو نيول او يا به شهيدانول او حتي ژوندي به ئې د خاورو لاندې ښخول. ډېر خلک تر اوسه پورې ورک او معلوم نه دي چې

په زندانونو کې پراته دي او که په وحشیانه ډول شهیدان شوي دي. په دې جمله کې یو ستر شخصیت مولوي عبدالستار او ورور ئې قاضي وو شامل وو چې د هغه وخت د والي صلاح الدین په دې موضوع کې لاس درلوده. مولوي صاحب او د هغه کشر ورور ئې دواړه له کور څخه وویستل. د هغوی شهادتنامې ئې خیرې کړې او په لاره کې ئې وغورځولې او دواړه مبارک اشخاص ئې په موټر پسې تړلي تر واغه جان پورې په خاورو کې کش کړي وو. دوی ئې شهیدان کړل. د فاسد حکومت د دې وحشیانه ظلمونو سره سم خلکو د کمونستي نظام په مقابل کې پاڅون وکړ او د جهاد اعلان ئې وکړ. ته هغه وخته پورې چې د جهاد صفونه مقدس او پاک وو ځو ولایتونه د فاسد حکومت نه د الله (ج) په مرسته فتح شول. د کونړ ولایت اسمار اولسوالي، پکتیا، د وردګو د چک اولسوالي، د وردګو د شجاع او قوي ایمان په لرلو سره د مجاهدینو په لاس کې د الله ج په نصرت فتح شول. زما د تره ځوی چې سیداحمد نومېده د شهادت درجې ته ورسیده. د هغه شفاعت دې خدای ج مونږ ته نصیب کړي. څه موده وروسته ببرک لالا د خپل چره یي ټوپک سره لوګر- کابل عمومي سرک ته ووتلو او د جهاد په اسلامي شوق چې په خدای ج او رسول ص مینه ورسره وه د روسانو سره په جګړه کې د الله اکبر د نارې په ویلو سره د روسانو له خوا په شهادت ورسید. روح دې ښاده وي. د ده د غیرت اوازه په ټول وطن کې خپره شوه. کمونستانو او د هغوی غلامانو شرمندګي ومنله او خپل شکست ئې قبول کړ. کله چې روسان په دې پوه شول چې د حکومت او کمونستان د شکست سره مخامخ شوي دي نو هغه وو چې خپل ۱۵۰۰۰۰ عسکر ئې افغانستان ته راواستول. دغو وحشیانو د انسانانو د ناموس، عزت، غیرت کوم قدر او پروا نه درلودله. هرې خوا ته ئې د وینو سیلابونه وبیول، هر چا او هر کور ته ئې غم ورواړاوه. ټول افغانان ئې سره تیت او پرک کړل. روسانو به د شپې چاپې اچولې او خلک به د ورځې د خپلو کورونو څخه ورک او ناخبره وو. د شپې او ورځې به د الوتکو په وسیله بمبارۍ کیدله او خلک بې ئې شهیدانول. یوازې زمونږ کور ۷ ځله د ورځې له خوا بمبار شوی وو. د افغانستان خلک سره له دومره زیات تکلیفه تسلیم نه شول او د روسانو

غلامي ئې و نه منله. افغانان په تشو لاسونو د الله ج په مرسته د روسانو د لښکرو سره وجنګېدل او هغوي ته په هر ځای کې ماته ورکړه. زما کشر ورور دولت له مجاهدینو سره مرسته کوله. د روسانو د شتون او د شومو دسیسو به ئې خبرول. کله چې به نابلده ترکمن، هزاره او نور مجاهدین له نورو ولایتونو څخه زمونږ کلي ته راتلل د هغوی سره به مو تر دوبند حتی تر پېښور د لارو پورې رهنمایي کوله. د روسانو راتګ زمونږ ایمانداره اولس راویښ کړ او یو له بل سره به مو د جهاد په برخه کې مرستې کولې. همدغه عامل شو چې مونږ د خان شېرین د زامنو سره د غنمو لوون کول او کله چې به د هغوی کار ختم شو نو بیا به هغوی له مونږ سره مرسته کوله. میرزاګل د خان شیرین زوی زمونږ قوماندان او د کلي مشر وو. خوله به ئې همیشه له خندا ډکه وهاو مونږ ته به ئې نیکې لارښوونې کولې. زما ورور دولت خان وربانديې ډېر ګران وو.

یوه له غمه ډکه شپه وه چې ناڅاپه د روسانو له خوا محاصره شو. له هرې خوا ډزې کیدې او کوښښ مو کولو چې له کور څخه خپله وسله راواخلو. کله چې کور ته رانژدې شو روسانو قلابند کړو. په میرزاګل ئې مخامخ ډزې وکړې او کور ته مخامخ شهید شو. کله چې ما او هوتک ډزې واورېدې مونږ د قلا شاته د هغو ځایونو نه چې روسانو په بمبار او ډزو وران کړي وو ځانونه و غورځول. ډېره لږه مسافه مو مزل کړی وو چې د روسانو د ډېر شمېر عسکرو سره مخامخ شو او په مونږ ئې یرغل وکړ. ما په خپل لس ډزي ټوپک روسان تر برید لاندې ونیول. دوی ځانونه د باغ خوا ته وغورځول. ما غوښتل چې ځان د غونډۍ شا ته کړم . له بده مرغه زما وړوکي ورور چې کله ئې جګړه لیدلې نه وه ځان له ما څخه جلا کړ او د دښتې خوا ته لاړ. روسان او د هغوی مزدوارانو اوازونه کول چې منډې مه وهۍ. زما سره مرمۍ پاتې نه وې. زه ورته له دې کبله حصار نه شوم چې ژوندی مې نه پرېږدي او د دوی له وحشیانه وژلو نه د یوې مرمۍ وژل اسان تماميږي. له هغه وخته مې تر اوسه د کلاکوف، راکټ او کلاشنیکوف ترخه اوازونه په غوږونو کې پاتې دي.

کله چې پوه شوم چې ژوندی پاتې یم نو په خپل ورور پسې مې وکتل او په دې پوه شوم چې هغه ئې ژوندی بیولی وو. ما ویل چې ورور مې وړوکی ماشوم دی ژوندی به ئې پرېږدي. خو وحشیانو روسانو هغه په برچو باندې د مور په مخ کې په هغه ځای کې چېرته چې مولوي عبدالستار تدریس کاوه سوری سوری کړی وو. الله ج دې زمونږ د مورکۍ او زمونږ او زمونږ د نورې کورنۍ په زړونو د صبر پټۍ کېږدي. اوس ئې هم د شهادت په ځای د شهادت بیرغ رپیږي. روح دې ښاده وي. کله چې کور ته راستون شوم مورکۍ او خویندو مې د هوتک، هوتک او میرزاګل چیغې وهلې او فریادونه ئې کول. پوه شوم چې دواړه شهیدان شوي دي. په دې پیښه کې زمونږ د تره ځوی میرزاګل د شهادت سره یو ځای په خواني باندې هم د راکټ ډزې شوې وې او هغه هم زخمي شوی وو. کله چې مو د ورور جنازه کور ته راوړه ټوله کورنۍ مو د وحشت له ډاره نادرکه او پټه شوې وه. زه تنها د جنازې سره ناست وم. د ورور له بدنه مې وینې څاڅکې، څاڅکي بهیدلې. د مورکۍ او خویندو د ژړاګانو او فریادونو فضا ډکه کړې وه. زما میرنی ورور محمد ظاهر هم زخمي شوی و.

د آغاجان اکا میرمن هم زخمي شوې وه. د قیامت ورځ جوړه شوې وه. کله به میرزا ګل ته ورتلم او کله به له خپل ورور سره اوسیدم. د مازدیګر وخت وو چې جنازې مو خاورو ته وسپارلې. له صبر سره هم له ژوند څخه بیزاره وو. په دې فکر چې سبا به روسان مرداروم یا به ما شهیدوي. په همدې شپه مو کور پرېښود او د ظفرخان کور ته مو پناه یووړله. خوب مو په سترګو کې نه وو او زړه مې نری، نری خوږېده. د شپې په نهو بجو چې د ګلنار بیګم اواز تر غوږه شو. ځان سره مې وویل چې په دې کلي کې خو قیامت تیر شوی دی. دا بې رحمه او د کلک زړه خاوند څوک دی چې زړه د مسلمانانو په حال نه سوزوي. له ځایه پاڅیدم چې وګورم دا څوان څوک دی. ګورم چې ولي جان د بړستنې لاندې رادېو اوري. میرمت یې ورته وویل چې شیرین دې مړ شه نن وړوکی وروکی

شهید شوی دی. هغه ورته وویل چې هغه شهید شو خو زه ورسره ځان یو ځای شهید کولی نه شم. سبا چې له خوبه راویښ شو ګورم چې مشرې خور مې کشره خور په غیږ کې نیولې د سوفې خوا ته پناه وړې. نو زه د ځان په فکر کې شوم چې که چیرې زه شهید شم نو د دوی سرپرستي به څوک کوي.

پلار مې ډېر زیات زهیر او سپین ږیری وو نو د پلار د پریکړې سره سم د الله ج د رضا لپاره او د محمد ص د لاربښوونې سره سم مو خپل اصلي وطن ترک او د مهاجرت لار مو ونیوله.

لوگر

On the Ninety-Ninth Day

After Allah dried the flood, and after the village came together to bury the bones and repave the roads and rebuild the melted walls, and after I begged every single member in my family for forgiveness, and after they all forgave me because the news of my life reversed all their bad omens (Rahmutallah and Baba woke up and the butcher's family visited and Nabeela's wedding was replanned and nothing was suspected of Gul and the Americans never arrived and not a single shepherd died anywhere in Naw'e Kaleh), and after we searched for, but never found, Budabash's body, my little brothers led me to the secret location of Gwora's hidden journals.

They had buried them in the spot where Budabash once slept.

Early in the morning of our last day in Logar, the three of us got up before everyone else (even Rahmutallah) and we dug up the remnants of the pages, which had more or less disintegrated, so that we were mostly digging up the mud the pages had been lost in. We gathered some of this mud into little plastic bags and hid them in our luggage. Because the roads were still pretty wet, no taxis could get into Naw'e Kaleh, and so me and pretty much all of my relatives in Logar made one last march through the village. We marched past the fields and the laborers still at work in the fields. We marched through the mazes still dripping of mud, and we marched past the orchards and the floating apples and the broke-down electric poles and the remnants of the cement road the government was still trying to build, and at the outskirts of Wagh Jan, we—that is, me and Moor and Agha and my brothers—tried very hard not to cry.

Then we cried.

Saying our final salaams, the men wiped their eyes with shame, while Abo and the ladies wept proudly. Dawood saluted me the way Abdul-Abdul had taught him. Gul held my good hand, and Zia recited a final dua for my family.

He prayed that Allah would lighten the hardships of our journey, and that we would travel safely on the road, and that one day, Inshallah, we would all return home.

"For surely," he concluded, "unto Allah we are returning."

Ameen.

On our way out of the country, near the borders of Logar, our taxi was stopped at a checkpoint by a squadron of American soldiers very similar to the ones who died in the maze. They might have been clones. The soldiers searched Agha and the driver and found them clean. Then, somehow spotting me through the dust of the back seat's window, the soldiers asked me to step out of the vehicle. Moor and Agha shouted about us being citizens, about me being a child—being harmless—but I wasn't so sure.

Three of the soldiers surrounded our taxi, just in front of these concrete slabs, and while one soldier opened my door and helped me down from my seat, guiding me to the edge of the road, another soldier—their translator—tried to calm Agha. Facing out toward the dry lands and the faraway mountains, I raised my arms and the soldier ran his hands up and down my waist and legs and crotch. Then he turned me around. I still wore my kameez, and it had many pockets. He searched them all but found only hair and fur and dirt and blue strands of cloth. Near the end of the pat-down, the soldier asked about my bandaged finger.

"If your father hurt you," he whispered in English, "you can tell me."

Like all the other soldiers, he wore a helmet and shades, and in the reflection of his glasses I could see me standing against the backdrop of the dry lands.

"Na," I said in Pakhto, "it was me."

And almost immediately afterward, I made the mistake of looking toward my brothers. First Gwora. Then Mirwais. Once they saw me seeing them, my brothers snuck out the other side of the taxi, came around the back, and with their hands in the air, they demanded to be searched as well.

The soldiers wouldn't obey. Instead, they let us leave.

Near Maghrib, just as we got to the Khyber Pass within the White Mountains, our taxi ran into a mass of traffic. Buses and trucks and Humvees and donkeys and shepherds and flocks of sheep and rickshaws and packs of dogs and hustlers selling candies out of wheelbarrows and broke-wing robins and Kabuli commandos and pockmarked addicts and Uzbeki goat drivers and cartloads of djinn and Tajik butchers and Kochi tribeswomen and howling roosters and American robots and armless Sufis praying for the grace of their legs and weeping virgins and carsick kiddies and militiamen drunk on gasoline and big-bearded imams and the oldest of OGs and maybe even the shadow of a wolf or two, and it was in the middle of this commotion, this jumble of a migration, that my brothers asked me for the true story of how I lost Budabash.

We sat in the back of the van, and even though we bobbed up and down with the cuts on the road, I didn't feel sick. Just very tired. The driver slept and Agha drove. Moor sat up front with him. They whispered to each other, maybe arguing, maybe telling secrets.

"Look here," I said to my brothers, and bringing my right hand up into the shine of a truck's headlight, I unwrapped the gauze from my torn finger, which had yet to heal, and just as I did, its ghost woke up and started to writhe and howl at the end of my wound.

"Do you see it?" I asked. "Do you see?"

They did.

They swore on the name of Allah—the ever merciful, the all-knowing, the timeless—that they saw.

Acknowledgments

Alhamdulillah, many generous and talented individuals played a crucial role in the formation of this novel, so I have a lot of people to thank.

First off, Yiyun Li. Without her, this novel as a novel would not exist. She was absolutely instrumental to its foundation, its development, and its publication. Doug Rice, my first mentor, for being a constant source of support and wisdom. Hellen Lee and David Toise for your early collegiate guidance. Thank you to Lucy Corin, Pam Houston, Joe Wenderoth, Parama Roy, and my entire cohort at UC Davis, but especially Ryan Horner and Zach Kennedy-Lopez, who helped me to figure out the timeline of this story. Lan Samantha Chang and Justin Torres for your sage advice and generosity. Amy Goldman for persuading me to take my first creative writing class in high school. The Truman Capote Literary Trust, the Iowa Writers' Workshop, the Writing By Writers Workshop, the UC Davis Creative Writing Program, and the Napa Valley Writers' Conference for providing me with time and space to write. Jin Auh, my agent, and Laura Tisdel, my editor, for promoting this novel as valiantly and tirelessly as you have. Thank you to both teams at Wylie and Viking. Alexa von Hirschberg, Faiza Khan, and Nicole Winstanley for making my novel an international project. Brigid Hughes, Megan Cummins, and the entire staff at *A Public Space* for publishing my first short story when I was just a starving grad student. Brandon Taylor and Pam Zhang for helping me fix those first few chapters. A huge manana and a tashakor to Almas Farooqi Lodin, Weeda Azim, Homaira Faquiryan, Haroun Dada, and Sarah Rahimi for being my resident Afghan advisors. Your encouragement and critique were deeply needed and deeply appreciated. Tanzeen Doha and Mohammed Harun Arsalai for their efforts in promoting the novel. A special, special thanks to Muneeza Rizvi, whose seal of approval was absolutely essential to the conclusion of this project.

Now, to thank the people who I really shouldn't need to thank because they're family and this is their job, but I'll thank them anyway just so there's no beef. Asila Nassem for your translations and Salim Nassem for your enthusiasm. Thank you to Namra Kochai for being an early reader/supporter. Rana and Breshna for your secretarial support. Marwand Kochai for letting me use your name and not making a big deal about it ever. No, but really, your thoughts and critiques have been both unexpected and very precious to me. Jalil Kochai, my first editor, promoter, publicist, manager, and reader. This book belongs to you too.

Nazifa, zma shireena khazi, deera manana. Your support has brought a newfound joy to my life. Thank you, Athai, for your stories. Finally, to Moor o Agha, you have been such a great mercy upon my life. Though I don't deserve all your sabr and your love, I pray that I will never cower in the face of it.

Ultimately, all praise be to Allah (subḥānahu wa-ta'ālā).